Praise for Mary Morris's

THE JAZZ PALACE

"A bittersweet, deeply lyrical but eyes-wide-open look at Chicago before and during Prohibition." —*Chicago Tribune*

"In this incandescent tour de force, Mary Morris takes us on a riveting journey that soars and tugs on our heartstrings just as if it were music itself." —Dani Shapiro, author of *Family History* and *Still Writing*

"*The Jazz Palace* is a sweeping tribute, a jazz ode, by a wonderful writer to her native city." —Valerie Martin, author of *Property* and *The Ghost of the* Mary Celeste

"Haunting and dreamlike. There is no other word for this novel but 'masterpiece.'" —Caroline Leavitt, author of *Is This Tomorrow* and *Pictures of You*

"Packed with so much love, heartbreak, endurance. . . . In *The Jazz Palace*, Mary Morris has written an exquisite love letter to her hometown, Chicago. And yet the book transcends time and place." —Peter Orner, author of *Love and Shame and Love*

"A graceful and involving affirmation of the transcendent power of art." —*Booklist* (starred review)

"As fluid and nuanced as the music it celebrates, Morris's narrative brings physical details, the power of music, and the sweeping history of Chicago . . . to memorable life." —*Publishers Weekly* (starred review)

Mary Morris

THE JAZZ PALACE

Mary Morris is the author of numerous works of fiction and nonfiction, including the novels *A Mother's Love* and *House Arrest*, as well as the travel memoir classic *Nothing to Declare: Memoirs of a Woman Traveling Alone*. The recipient of the Rome Prize in literature and a grant from the John Simon Guggenheim Memorial Foundation, she was raised in Chicago and now lives with her family in Brooklyn, New York.

www.marymorris.net

THE JAZZ PALACE

THE JAZZ PALACE

A Novel

Mary Morris

ANCHOR BOOKS
A Division of Penguin Random House LLC
New York

This book is for the Piano Man
and for Larry, of course

FIRST ANCHOR BOOKS EDITION, MARCH 2016

Copyright © 2015 by Mary Morris

This is a work of fiction. Names, characters, places, and incidents either are the
product of the author's imagination or are used fictitiously. Any resemblance to
actual persons, living or dead, events, or locales is entirely coincidental.

The Library of Congress has cataloged the Nan A. Talese / Doubleday edition
as follows:
Morris, Mary.
The Jazz Palace : a novel / Mary Morris. — First edition.
pages ; cm
I. Title.
PS3563.O87445 J39 2015
813'.54—dc23   2014043501

Anchor Books Trade Paperback ISBN: 978-1-101-87286-4
eBook ISBN: 978-0-385-53974-6

Book design by Maria Carella

www.anchorbooks.com

Printed in the United States of America
10 9 8 7 6 5

For, while the tale of how we suffer, and how we are delighted, and how we may triumph is never new, it always must be heard. There isn't any other tale to tell, it's the only light we've got in all this darkness.

—*James Baldwin, "Sonny's Blues"*

One

≡

It was a hot July morning and the green river stank. The Onion River, the French called it. The Potawatomi named this place Chicagoua after the garlic that grew along its banks. As Benny walked to the bridge, he had to hold his nose. A light rain fell, but he didn't care. He heard the music before he saw the big ships, and it made him pick up his pace. Pausing on the Clark Street Bridge, Benny took his time. A parcel, wrapped in brown paper, dangled from his hands. Though he was short for his age, he had a sturdy chest and arms that seemed to reach the ground. His hands were big as catcher's mitts, and he swung his parcel to the beat.

He was late, but it was Saturday. Time to be in the vacant lot, playing ball. "Time to make deliveries," was what his father said. Benny stared into the churning waters, which flowed west toward the Mississippi, not into Lake Michigan as nature had intended. In 1900, the year he was born, engineers reversed the current to make Chicago's drinking water safe. It was the feat of the century, sending the city's polluted waters downriver to St. Louis. Cholera and typhoid would follow.

Thousands milled on the docks. Western Electric had invited its employees on this mandatory picnic across the lake to Michigan City. They made the receivers, amplifiers, and vacuum tubes for Bell Telephone. In the twine room they sat on benches, wrapping wires.

That winter Alexander Graham Bell dialed from his phone in New York, and his assistant, Thomas Watson, answered in San Francisco. These workers had woven the cables.

They came in droves. Wives in creamy linen paraded with their husbands in Panama hats. Rows of siblings in matching dresses and suits walked hand in hand. Little girls in pigtails wore satin ribbons in their hair, and budding young women who worked on the assembly lines hung on the arms of their beaus. Grandmothers chased after toddlers, and a Hungarian man had brought all of his friends. Whiskey flasks were tucked into pockets. A sea of parasols floated by. It would require five ships to take them, and the *Eastland* was boarding first.

Benny marveled at the state-of-the-art steamship with its white-and-gray hull and sparkling deck. The crew in navy jackets and sailor caps dazzled him. The *Eastland* was outfitted with the latest in life-saving equipment. Three years before, the *Titanic* went down with lifeboats for fewer than half on board. Afterward Woodrow Wilson signed the Seamen's Act. Lifeboats had to accommodate every man, woman, and child. Earlier that summer, extra rafts, weighing four-teen tons, were added to the *Eastland*'s upper deck. The crew knew she was top heavy. The first officer just shook his head.

Because of the rain many had gone below. Others stayed on top and danced. On the bridge above, Benny swayed to the rhythm of Bradfield's Orchestra. The piano player was pounding out a tune on a shiny Kimball upright. Couples glided along the promenade deck. They leaped to a polka, then to a daring fox-trot, their smiles bright under broad-rimmed hats. The hats made Benny remember his errand. He glanced at the parcel in his hand. His father manufac-tured crisp white or heavy blue uniform caps that his sons distributed throughout the city. Every butcher and motorman in Chicago wore one of these. When he delivered to the stockyards, Benny heard the shrieks from the Bridge of Sighs. Guts and animal hair coated his shoes.

Today he had only one delivery on the North Side, then he could play ball. He'd meet up with his pal Moe. In the afternoon they'd sneak into Comiskey Park to see the White Sox wallop the Yanks.

Faber was pitching and Benny wanted to be there. Now he lingered as young Bohemian and Polish men and women boarded. He shuffled his feet to the tune of "Alexander's Ragtime Band." When the orchestra switched to "The Girl I Left Behind," Benny rocked in the morning rain. He thought about the girl who sat in front of him in history class. She had a long black braid and a Polish name. Perhaps he'd see her on one of these boats. In class he pictured himself caught up in the strands of her hair. He'd climbed into its darkness until all of history was lost to him. He envisioned her in his arms, black braid swishing across his face, her hips pressing into his.

Off the bridge a street vendor was selling sausage smothered in sauerkraut. If he had a nickel, Benny would buy one, even though it was *trafe*, but he didn't. He was mad at his father for not giving him more than one-way carfare when he set out on his errands. "You'll do a better job," his father reasoned, "if you're working for tips." Benny had walked home many times from the South Side or hitched a ride on the back of a trolley, cursing his father all the way.

His mouth watered as Bohemian women passed with baskets, tucked under their arms, filled with creamy potato salad, deviled eggs, chickens that had been slow roasting for days, pickled beets, sweet-smelling breads. He was tempted to tag along so he could sample what they had. Instead he tipped his cap as the women sauntered by and men in gray jackets and starched shirts tipped their straw hats back. Benny's hands clasped the railing, and his package swung by the string. He tapped out the music his fingers heard as he went along—not the Chopin and Beethoven his mother wanted him to play, but the tunes that were caught in his head.

He heard his own music everywhere. It was in the movement of his feet on wooden sidewalks, in the clomp of horses' hooves, in the clatter of the "el." He banged it out on garbage can lids and on his desk at school. In the morning he hummed in the tub. At dinner he held the beat with a knife and fork until his father ordered him to stop. Then he played on his sheets at night as he drifted to sleep. The music that came from his hands was different from the ragtime he listened to now. He heard his music on the deliveries he made to the neighborhoods where the black people lived. It came from behind closed doors or out lonely windows where men in white undershirts played the horn on summer evenings.

Before he began running deliveries for Lehrman's Caps, Benny didn't know much of the world beyond the neighborhood where he lived, the White Sox for whom he rooted, and the piano he played. He had seen the first cars rumble down Chicago streets and heard that airplanes could fly. He knew the Great War had begun in Europe and that Wilson was president. That spring the *Lusitania* sank in eighteen minutes, killing most of the passengers aboard. Anti-German sentiment spread throughout Chicago. In western suburbs dachshunds were poisoned. But his deliveries took him in a different direction, down an old fur trader's trail called State Street by some, Satan's Mile by most. People claimed the devil lived downtown, but Benny wanted to go to the South Side where the rail workers and meat-packers lived.

In the back alleys the city was starting to roar. Hot music, he heard it called. In February Joe "King" Oliver and his New Orleans band had caused an uproar on the South Side. They had all those horns, going at once. Joe Oliver was a big man with a wandering eye. Behind his back the musicians called him Cockeye. But he had a sixth sense. Everything was about to change. Blacks and their music were moving north. They were building shacks along the tracks where the trains let them off.

After school Benny raced through his deliveries. Then he lingered on the smoky streets. A few nights before he'd stood at a door where a cornet played beside an out-of-tune piano. It wasn't off by much, but it grated on his nerves. Still Benny stayed. There was something in that alleyway music he'd never heard. He couldn't see where it was taking him. It was as if it had no rules, except for the ones it was making up. It had no beginning, no end. No one to scold him or tell him what to do. No one to be mad if he was late or his homework was due. This music just went on, the piano talking and the cornet listening, then the cornet talking back, the piano laughing as if two strangers, bent over drinks, were having a conversation into the night. Eavesdropping, Benny caught what he could.

As the ballast tanks were emptied, he was tapping out a tune. He hummed, trying to remember a refrain he'd heard. Water poured from the hull of the ship. Soon the gangplank was level with the river. Now the crowds climbed more easily aboard. The boat's horn gave a deep, harsh honk. He dallied as any child would, waving from the bridge as if he were about to leave. The passengers rushed to starboard, raising up their children and flicking their kerchiefs in the wind. A nearby tug sounded its horn and they ran to port. Benny heard the laughter as the ship pitched beneath their weight, then back again. Shouts of good-bye rose from the crowd. They would only be gone for the day, but they acted as if this were a journey across the sea.

It was 1915. The city was safe. Except for the accidents that happened in the streets because children had nowhere else to play, there was little to fear. Doors were never locked. There were no thieves. Big Bill Thompson would soon be mayor, and George Wellington Streeter was selling home brew from a sandbar he claimed to rule as the District of Lake Michigan. Except for Sundays, liquor was legal. Gangsters, bootleggers, and pimps hadn't begun their rule. On hot summer nights people slept on the beaches and in the parks.

Benny's eyes caught those of a woman, standing beside him. Her hair was the color of burning leaves and her body round as a plum. She had come up on the Clark Street Bridge as he had for a better view. The woman held a girl by each hand. The youngest was pale and fragile as a porcelain doll, and at first Benny mistook her for one. The older girl was dark with olive skin and looked grown-up for her years. They were dressed in creamy linen with matching hats. "It's a beautiful sight, isn't it?" the woman said, turning to him.

"Yes, ma'am, it is," Benny replied, resting his arms on the railing.

"I bet you wish you were going with."

He nodded. "Yes, I do."

"My boys are." She pointed to three young men who were scampering up the gangplank as a crew member motioned for them to hurry. It was ten minutes after seven, and the gangplank was raised. The crew began turning others away and sending them over to the

Theodore Roosevelt, which was ready to receive them. The young men raised their fists in victory as their mother waved back. They were the last to board.

The older girl looked up, and her brown eyes caught his. "Jonah was supposed to come, too, but he wouldn't get up," the girl said. She spoke as if he knew about whom she was speaking. "That's why we're late."

Benny smiled, not quite listening as his fingers kept time. "Who's Jonah?"

"He's my deaf brother's twin. His name is Wren." Her eyes scanned the water as she pointed to the boat. "Four of my brothers work for the company, but only Robin, Wren and Jay are going. Not Jonah. He overslept."

"You have a lot of brothers," Benny replied. She looked warm in her high-collar dress with the cinched waist. She kept tugging at the neck. Beads of sweat formed on her forehead and on the forehead of the little blond girl as well as they clasped the railing, looking down.

"They're named after birds," the girl said, waving to her brothers on the deck. "We're named after gems." She pointed to the blond child who held her mother's hand.

"Pearl, leave the young man alone. Is she bothering you?" the mother asked.

"Oh, no," Benny said. "Not at all." He was just talking, not really paying her much heed.

The dark-haired girl spoke rapidly as if she could never get a word in. "Jonah wouldn't get out of bed. I tried to wake him, but he wouldn't budge."

"Well, he must have been very tired," Benny said, amused by her chatter. "I wouldn't get up if I didn't have to. Why don't you join them?" He pointed to the boats, five of them now, ready to sail.

"Oh, I can't. It's my birthday," the girl went on, her voice filled with anticipation. She gestured to her mother and her golden-haired sister. "We're going to Buffalo's for ice cream."

Raising his face to the wind, Benny kept his eyes ahead. He was worried that the Sox game would be called off because of the rain. The wetness glazed his cheeks. He was glad to be standing there with the ship before him and the music pouring from its deck. He decided to humor the girl. "I bet you'll have strawberry," he said.

Her eyes widened. "How did you know?"

He smiled, shaking his head, not looking her way. "Oh, you seem like a strawberry kind of girl." The horn sounded three long honks as the ship's lines were released.

The girl blew kisses to her brothers as they vanished below. She kept waving long after they were gone. She turned to Benny once more. "They'll have a wonderful time."

"I'm sure they will," he replied.

Suddenly the mother pointed. "Look," she said, "there's Wren." They followed her finger to the promenade deck where the deaf boy, dressed in a snappy blue jacket and beige pants, signaled with the flapping motions of his arms. He fanned his face at the wet, warm air. He walked in circles, doing an imitation of Charlie Chaplin, who was in Chicago that summer making a movie about a vagabond who falls in love with a farmer's daughter.

In the midst of the dancing passengers Wren performed a jig. He waltzed with an invisible partner, twirling her with one hand. Dipping toward the floor, he put his hands on the deck to feel the beat. He teetered back and forth like a balance, and his mother and the girls laughed. He made a clown face and they laughed some more. Then he stopped and frowned. He sniffed the air like a hunting dog. Looking up at his mother, the boy shook his head. He held his empty palms up to the sky. Then raced toward the stairwell to warn his brothers. "Something is wrong," his mother said as he disappeared below.

The ship was unmoored. It listed to starboard, then over to port. Dancers glided from side to side. Passengers braced themselves, clasping their hats to their heads. On the wharves a watchman shouted to a crew member, "You're leaning." A deep, harsh horn sounded again as the boat pitched. Nervous laughter rose. Deckhands noticed the sway beneath their feet, the little skips they had to do to keep from falling.

The chief engineer ordered the refilling of the ballast tanks. In the hull salt and pepper shakers rolled off tables. A cabinet toppled over, and beer bottles crashed to the floor. A player piano in the dance hall smashed into the wall. Two crew members looked at each other, then scrambled topside. The music stopped. Dancers paused in mid-step, waiting for it to begin again. On deck laughter ceased. A strange silence hung in the air. All Benny could hear was water slapping the hull.

He was still waving when the *Eastland,* just feet from the wharf, tilted ever so slightly, and then more, until the ship pitched under the weight of its lifeboats. It made a gurgling sound as if someone had pulled an enormous plug. Benny's hand froze in midair as the ship turned on her side and sank in twenty feet of water onto the river's bottom. Sheet music flew like aquatic birds. Musicians clung to the railing. A bass fiddle careened into the river, taking an infant in its wake. Mothers clutched children as they toppled over the side. Men were hurtled off the deck like torpedoes. Below passengers were tossed right, then left, from one end of the hull to the other. They raced for stairwells, men shoving women and children aside as the water rushed down upon them.

The screams did not resemble any Benny had ever heard. His mouth was open, his arms raised as if he could somehow stop this behemoth as it settled into the silty bottom. His package of uniform caps slipped from his hands and fell into the river, bobbing for an instant before sinking out of sight. He barely noticed it go. People were caught in the cloudy waters. Others had been hurled from the deck. One woman seemed to reach toward him, then vanished, and only her hat with its straw brim, its green and blue feathers, remained. Picnic hampers, derbies, thermos bottles drifted by.

As Benny raced to the dock, his eyes met those of the woman who'd stood on the bridge beside him. Her mouth was opened wide as a continuous shriek came from somewhere deeper inside of her than the water in which the *Eastland* sank. The younger, blond girl wailed as the dark child pressed her hands over her ears, pleading with her mother to stop. But the woman seemed to be drowning as if one could drown not only from water but from air as well. The woman uttered one endless cry that ceased only when she saw Benny on the dock. She stared into his gray eyes as if there was something she needed to tell him. Instead she clutched her two girls. "Go," she shouted at him. "Dive." And Benny ripped off his shirt, his shoes, and his trousers.

As he hit the water, he was startled by how cold the river was and how quiet. He could see nothing in the darkness, only a silhouette of limbs. He swam in the direction of arms and legs, but they eluded him. Surfacing, he grasped a piece of wood. Egg crates, chicken coops, ropes from other vessels, were hurled from the wharves. Benny shoved a crate at a flailing boy, then dove again. He reached his hands around the hips of a little girl who fluttered like a fish as she slipped away.

Gasping, he pulled himself onto the hull. He coughed up water as he tried to catch his breath. Then he heard the muffled cries. Beneath his feet he felt the pounding of fists. People were trapped inside. The hull was slick, and twice he almost fell. Ironworkers, welding on a nearby bridge, rushed to help as a tugboat coated the slick hull in ash. With his hands and feet Benny helped spread the ash, and his skin turned black. Then the ironworkers set to work. The flames of their torches seared the hull. Captain Pederson tried to stop them. "You're ruining her hull," he shouted as passengers wrestled him away. As a hole was carved, a welder took Benny by the arm.

Benny, who was small but strong for his age, bent and reached into the dark pit. Arms groped up for his. Like a midwife he pulled out a boy, howling a newborn's cry. He reached in once more and this time took a girl from her father's clasp. He raised her easily into his. She wore a linen dress, covered in soot, and he caught her by her narrow waist. She was lithe and moved as if she was waltzing.

He had never held a girl before. He had only imagined what desire would be. To have a girl in his arms, her body close to his. He had envisioned the softness of skin, the smell of freshly washed hair. Now her breasts, which were round and full, pressed into his chest, and he grew aroused. He was stunned by the pulsing in his loins. He longed to see her grateful eyes. Perhaps she would tell him her name. But as Benny dragged her onto the hull, her legs dangled against his thighs. There was no warmth in her breath. Her arms hung limp around his neck.

Easing her down, Benny saw the fixed stare in her eyes, her blue lips. As he handed her to the next man, he began to weep. Standing on the hull, tears poured down his face. He could not bear the fact that his first embrace was in the arms of a dead girl. He found himself growing afraid of things he could not name. Somewhere above him Benny still heard that woman screaming on the bridge, and he dove back into the water to escape her.

As her eyes scanned the river, Anna Chimbrova wasn't sure where her screaming came from. Her bird children were on board—the boys she'd named Robin, Jay, Wren. She had broken the Sabbath by letting them go. She carried money to buy ice cream for Pearl. She hadn't heeded the warning signs when her deaf son, Wren, pointed to the sky and on their way to the river said he heard crows. Now she watched as bodies were pulled from the hull and placed in a neat row on the dock.

It wasn't long before a boy in the blue jacket and beige pants was laid out beside them. Wren had been the last to go down. It made sense he'd be one of the first to leave. Her sons were dead. She despised herself for even thinking this, but how, without them, would they survive? It was as if she'd looked into one of those mirrors her first husband, Samuel Malkov, used to bring in from the street and found herself face-to-face with what she'd always feared—a person she didn't know.

As she dragged her girls from the bridge, she thought that she hadn't always been afraid of mirrors. At one time she'd even admired herself in them. But as she made her way through the Shadows, a desolate place of brothels and saloons, that seemed like long ago. Anna staggered by the noisy bars of Clark Street, ignoring the women, their faces painted like clowns, who called out from the window above. She passed the grim iron gates of the county jail. Turning east, she crossed against traffic. Horse-drawn carriages came to a halt. A newly minted Model T sputtered and honked while a trolley slammed on its brakes. At Pine Street a policeman shouted, "Lady, watch where you're going!"

Pearl chased after her mother, clutching Opal by the hand. Her mother kept moving. The ocher sky threatened a worsening storm, but Anna had to tell Samuel that his sons had drowned. He had circumcised those boys himself with a sharp razor and his own careful hands. Though he'd been gone for years, she'd look for him in the waters that had frightened her when she was a child.

They boarded a trolley. Soon the soap factories and tenements of the Shadows slipped away. There were no shops, no Hebrew letters written above the stores. No women stood on corners haggling over fish. No pushcarts lined the streets. The houses got bigger. They were made of granite and redbrick. They were more like castles with turrets and walls. Black cars were parked in circular driveways. Anna didn't notice. It was Samuel she was looking for as the bus carried them north. She missed him on summer evenings when the sound of cicadas filled the air. Before they were married, he took her for walks to the park where a calliope played. In a dense grove he pulled her to him, and for the first time she felt the heat and hardness of a man. Anna rubbed the spot where tree roots had pressed into her spine and stones had left their mark.

The trolley stopped near the lake, and Anna led the girls off. "Where are we going?" Pearl cried, but her mother ignored her pleas. Pedestrians looked at Anna and shook their heads. News of the *Eastland* hasn't spread across town. Some asked if she was all right. Others assumed she was drunk. Or old and dotty—perhaps even the grandmother of those children. In fact she had just turned thirty-eight and she was their mother, widowed for the third time with nine children left in her care. She'd struggled to keep her family intact. A Bohemian neighbor had taken pity on them and gotten the oldest boys their jobs at Western Electric. "Don't tell anyone you are Jews," the neighbor had warned. "We'll all get fired." They said they were Czechs. They had been desperate for work. It was a sin and Anna knew it—to pretend you were something you were not.

The lake was a steely gray, the color of humid days and stormy skies. The shades of pavement and impoverished walls. Its surface imitated the sky and it was difficult to tell where one ended and the other began. But Anna wasn't frightened. As she led her girls to the shore, the water beckoned.

Two

In 1673 an explorer, armed with astrolabe and compass, and a priest, carrying the Word of God, followed the advice of an Indian boy. They took a detour from the Mississippi on to the Illinois River, where they sailed through billowy waves of grass. They traversed a portage until they came upon an inland sea. To the priest, this was a miserable marsh, but Joliet got out of his canoe. He was also a geographer. Walking along the plateau, he envisioned water spilling off of it, heading south to the Gulf of Mexico and east to the ocean. He reported back to the governor of New France that he had found a place of "great and important advantage" where the lake would meet the sea. On his way back Joliet lost his all maps and journals in a shipwreck, and he died in obscurity.

Benny stood on the rise where Joliet had imagined a great city. He gazed across the river toward the sullen lake. It took a long time for him to realize he was naked. He felt no chill; only a numbness between his thighs. The greasy river clung to his flesh, but he didn't notice. He didn't feel the breeze on his skin. He stared into space as robbers stole jewelry and wallets from the dead and photographers snapped pictures. These pictures became postcards that were mailed around the world or collectors' items sold at auctions.

He fumbled in the pile where other trousers and shirts and shoes had been tossed, but it seemed like such a foolish thing to do; to search for your clothes with so many dead. Around him people wept. A breathless man, his face streaked with tears, held up a sign, KRISTEN, AGE 4, IN A RED DRESS. A grandmother wailed over the bodies of twins. But at least the screaming woman was gone. There was only the slow tedium of tragedy before him now. The *Eastland* lay resting on her side like a dead whale, and Captain Pederson was being led away in handcuffs.

Benny saw no shame at his nakedness. He was a boy of fifteen, but he could be dead tomorrow. He had learned this two years ago when his youngest brother, Harold, disappeared in the snow. Benny had been responsible for his brothers that day as they trudged to school. His mother had tied them together with a sturdy rope through their belt loops. But Harold was not with them when they arrived, and Benny had raced through the snowbound streets, shouting his brother's name. He had thought that nothing could be worse than his parents' anguished search, but now he knew this wasn't so.

He found his clothes, lying in the heap. As he pulled on his trousers and was buttoning his shirt, he began looking for his order. After a few moments he recalled that he had dropped it into the river. Crossing Wacker Drive, he wondered how he would explain this to his father. Since Harold's death, his father blamed him for everything. If orders were slow, if a light was left on. It could all be traced back to Benny.

State Street seemed eerily dull. Shoppers moved in slow motion. Some stood frozen like statues, staring toward the river. Others raced to the water, but most went about their business with grim faces. An impatient woman tugged on a child's arm. The air smelled of caramel corn and horses. From the distance came the sound of sirens.

Looking up, Benny saw the dusty opaque windows of his father's workroom. He tried to remember where his order was going. And he wondered if the women would be paid for their work. As he crossed State Street, Benny began rehearsing what he'd say to his father.

———

Lehrman's Caps was located near the corner of Wabash and South Water, not far from the river, in a dilapidated building. The stairwells were dingy, with holes in the walls. In the large open room a dozen Bohemians sewed elastic around a cloth circle or finished buttonholes by hand. It was a hot Saturday morning. For years Leo Lehrman had ignored the Sabbath, and the sewing machines hummed. The humid air was thick with dust and the sweat of women with unshaved armpits, hunched for hours over machines. The Bohemians were hard workers, and Leo Lehrman, a burly, bald man with a temper he reserved for his family, was good to his employees as long as they stayed bent, hands guiding cloth through the foot-pedaled machines or stitching swiftly by hand the needle-work required for the buttonholes.

Lehrman's Caps was only a small company. But it earned Leo enough to feed his wife and boys and had enabled them to move out of the tenements of Maxwell Street and the cold-water flat where Benny was born. Now Leo rented a three-bedroom apartment for seventy-five dollars a month in Albany Park. He paid his workers and covered the expenses on his factory. Still he wasn't a man to think small.

Wasn't Chicago a place where you could package beef, ship wheat, and make a fortune the way Armour, Pullman, Swift, and McCormick had? Where you could flex some muscle? So why not Lehrman? Many deliverymen and soda jerks throughout the city already wore a Lehrman's cap, so why not every meat-packer and grain-elevator operator? Why not every railroad worker, not just in Chicago, but across America?

Leo was proud of his designs, which were displayed on the heads of faceless mannequins around his office. When you bought from Lehrman's, you got two for the price of one. The rim was lined in buttons. The crown had buttonholes. With each cap you purchased, two crowns were provided. "Wear one, wash one" was Lehrman's motto. His biggest idea had come just a week ago. He had taken his boys down to the South Side to the new steel-and-concrete Comiskey Park to see the White Sox play. It had been a dull game on a hot afternoon. Collins couldn't seem to get a hit and Red Faber was pitching lackluster innings. Even Leo's boys slumped in their seats, waiting for Faber to wake up or for a batter to connect.

Nervous, Faber adjusted his cap two or three times, and Leo stared. His chief competitor, Kaplan Brothers, made the gray-and-white caps the Sox wore. Leo had cornered the market on meat-packers and rail workers, but Kaplan had most of the bigger hotels, the ball clubs, and factory workers like Western Electric. Leo looked as Faber pushed his cap back, then pulled it forward again, just before the windup, and the idea came to Leo. "They should have the name of their team on those caps. Or better yet some trademark. Not those plain white-and-gray things they're wearing."

As Benny walked through his father's workshop, denim and thread sticking to his shoes, Leo Lehrman sat at his desk, fiddling with a design for the White Sox. He drew a white sock with an *S* down its side, then scratched it out. He drew a *W* and an *S* inter-weaving, then he scribbled an *S* with an *X* through it. He liked this last one. Leo was imagining every major team in America, wearing a Lehrman's cap with a trademark embroidered on the rim when he looked up and saw Benny, his face and hands blackened with ash, a glazed-over look, scraps of cloth stuck to his shoes. "What happened to you?" his father said. "Were you in a fight?" Glancing at his watch, Leo pursed his lips. Benny shouldn't be here now. He should be done with his delivery and heading home.

Head down, Benny trembled, "No, I wasn't in a fight . . ."

A constricted feeling rose in Leo's chest the way it did whenever he was about to yell at someone. He saw the river water dripping from his son's hair, the muck on his skin, his coal-streaked cheeks. Leo put down his pencil. "Benny, what's wrong?" his father blurted. Benny stammered as he did only in front of his father. The words were tied in his throat. Leo looked at him, then down at the Sox design on his desk. "What is it?" He wanted to tell his father about the ship and the woman screaming on the bridge. And what it was like to be in a dead girl's embrace. But words were not his medium. Instead he said, "I dropped the deliveries in the river."

"You did what?" Leo jumped up, all five feet six inches of him, his hand pounding on the desk. "What are you talking about? What were you doing? Fooling around? That was four dozen." Just moments before Leo had been thinking about the big plans he had for his caps factory. Now Benny, his intended heir—a dreamy boy who preferred to sit at the piano, running his hands up and down the keys, not even practicing really, but just banging out tunes—stood before him, bringing him more bad news.

What reverie was Benny lost in when he let the order fall? But it was just like him, wasn't it? The son he had loved first and most, the one he'd placed his hopes in. The litany of blame rose easily. He comes back late. He forgets to get a signature on delivery. He drops his orders in the river. It was Benny, wasn't it, who'd been in charge when Harold wandered off? Why would Benny get anything right?

Benny stood before his father, examining a scrap of denim that clung to his shoe. With his other foot he tried to tug it off, but it was stuck. There must have been some glue. Perhaps it was a scrap that belonged to one of the caps he'd dropped.

Leo stared, waiting for an answer, but Benny had none. "We spent a week on that order," his father boomed. Leo did the calculations in his head. Twelve needle workers who could not speak English depended on him for their livelihoods. How would he meet their payroll if his son was dropping orders into the river? Even as it dawned on Leo Lehrman that his son's eyes were a rheumy red, and sirens howled outside, Benny tugged at the denim stuck to his shoe.

"What happened?" his father asked, his voice softer.

"Nothing," Benny said. "I have to go." He tossed the scrap into a wastebasket, then raced through the workroom as his father called after him. He heard his father yell as he dashed down the stairs. He caught the "el" north, and it took him as far as Belmont. At a drinking fountain, he rinsed the ash from his hands and face. Then he ran the rest of the way home.

Three

Hannah didn't hear Benny's footsteps coming up the stairs. She didn't hear him outside, hurling stones against the fence in the empty lot. If she had, she'd have known right away that something was wrong. Hannah had learned to read the signs in her boys. If they didn't look her in the eye, if they shoved food around on their plate. If they hesitated coming home. Boys should eat hearty meals. They shouldn't drag their feet. But Hannah was in her bedroom, dusting her glass figurines.

Hannah cleaned the ferocious bear she had carried in her rucksack from the old country, the doe with fragile legs that stood, ears perked, in a grove of trees, the rosebud with its hundred carved petals her husband had given her for their marriage. The rosebud reminded her that once she and Leo had danced at their wedding. They had reveled when Benny, their first son, was born. Hannah returned to the task of folding her husband's clothes. She had just pressed and ironed his undershirts, and she held the warm cotton against her cheek. His drawer was messy as she reached into the back to straighten up the wayward socks. Leo could hardly complain about his clothes not being neat, but still he did. As far as Hannah was concerned, he had nothing to complain about. But, since Harold died, he complained all the time. He complained that the soup was too cold or the coffee too hot, the meat overcooked or underdone. Nothing would ever be right.

She looked about the dreary room. It was dark, and the walls were stained. There was a smell of shoes and cigars she couldn't get rid of. Hannah had tried to let light in, but their bedroom overlooked an alley, and what little light seeped in was a dirty gray. She kept the room clean. She had made colorful bedspreads and airy curtains, but, no matter what she did, the apartment never felt cheery. She had not managed to make it into a home.

Hannah was sitting motionless on the bed when she heard someone staggering up the stairs. No one should be coming home at this hour. Quickly she rose and straightened the spread. Then she rushed to open the door. As Benny walked in, Hannah took one look at him and placed a hand to his brow. "Benny, what is it?" She saw the sooty skin, the greasy hair. "Are you all right?"

Though Benny had perfected the art of keeping things from his father, he was less successful with his mother. Perhaps because he didn't want to. As her warm hand touched his cheek, words poured from him like a sieve. He blurted out that there had been a terrible accident. Hundreds, he told her, had drowned. At first Hannah did not believe him. She could not see how such a thing could happen. But as Benny told her what he had seen, tears streamed down her face. Hannah listened, a quivering hand cupped over her mouth. Her mind ricocheted from the poor people who had drowned to this latest disaster that had befallen her oldest son. "How is this possible?" She shook her head. She made him a hot bath of baking soda and salts.

She got on her knees and, despite his protests, scrubbed the river from him. She scrubbed until his skin turned red and raw. When she was done, she dressed him in flannel, though it was a hot July day, and made him drink a bowl of scalding chicken soup. She'd sweat the river out of him. While Benny sipped the soup, perspiration dripping from his forehead, his mother sank into an armchair and wept. She cried because it seemed as if wherever her son went, disaster followed. Benny could think of nothing to say to comfort her. He couldn't tell her about the child who'd slipped out of his grasp. About the dead girl he'd danced with on the hull. He hadn't been able to save his own brother either. So on these matters he was silent.

When he was finished with his soup, Hannah took the bowl, rinsed it in the sink, then her hand went to her head. Benny saw the look as if an ax had struck her skull. She went to her room and closed her door. She had come down with one of her headaches—the kind that sent her to bed for days at a time. Hannah could not bear light or almost any noise. She had to lie with a towel across her face in the darkened silence of her sewing room. She had gone to bed for weeks with the curtains drawn when Harold died. The only sound she could bear was music. Chopin preludes, Beethoven sonatas, soft, lilting pieces that she asked Benny to play.

Benny sat down at the oak piano with its rich, clear tones. He ran his hands across the golden wood surface. Its brightness shone against the dullness of the apartment. The sheet music from his lesson was open on the stand. Since they'd purchased it secondhand five years ago, his mother's goal was to make Benny into a great pianist. She herself had studied music at a conservatory as a girl, and, if she hadn't married, she often told the boys, she would have continued with her musical studies. Hannah had aspirations for all her sons, but none so great as those she harbored for Benny. She had found Dimitri Marcopolis, a Greek Jew, through a former teacher of hers who told her that Mr. Marcopolis had once had a concert career until circumstances forced him to leave Europe. He was a teacher she could afford.

Hannah would see to it that Benny had that career. He would elevate himself above the world of caps and crowded apartments. She envisioned him in tails, a soloist onstage with the Chicago Symphony. He was better, she thought, different from her other boys with his brooding gray eyes, those long, strong arms. It wasn't because he was her first but because he was the one who felt the most. Even as a baby, when he cried, he curled into himself. He wept as if whatever upset him came from somewhere deep inside. But when he sat down to play, something happened to him. He opened up, unfolded. His mother watched him bloom.

Now, with his hair still wet and the terrible day etched in his mind, he wanted to try out the rhythms he listened to in the alleyways on the South Side. He could lose himself there. But his mother wouldn't approve, and it wouldn't draw her out of her darkness. In his lessons Benny was working on a Beethoven sonata, and he was having trouble with the second movement. Mr. Marcopolis insisted that he stick to the piece, but Benny didn't want to. He couldn't hear the music in his head, and he could barely make out the notes. Benny had never really learned to read music. He hadn't needed to because he was good at faking it. If his teacher played a piece for him two or three times, Benny could pick it up. But he had to hear it in his head and he wasn't hearing it now.

He played best by ear. Anything he heard he could repeat. Anything he was told, he could remember. That was how he'd gotten through his bar mitzvah. He'd memorized his Torah portion, never bothering to learn to read the Hebrew. It was the same with music. First he heard it in his head, then in his heart. And finally in his fingers. He had been able to do this since he was young enough to talk, and he thought of this as a strange, useless talent, like someone who can memorize all the numbers in the phone directory or say words backward.

He could name notes the way a painter could name colors. In fact he saw them in colors. C major came in yellow and A major in orange. G was green and F a shade of blue. The minor notes were the muted shades of sunsets—mauve, rose, tangerine. Benny knew in what key the wind howled or crystal when it chimed.

Now he struggled with the first few bars of the Beethoven sonata, but quickly switched to Bach. He played fast and too hard. He didn't have that light, elegant touch. Then he stopped and listened. When he was sure his mother was resting, he switched tunes. He roughed out the rhythms he'd been humming just before the *Eastland* sank. He switched it to a minor key. The music was filled with forgetting. The colors swirled. Splashes, a kaleidoscope, raced through his head.

It was earlier than usual when Leo Lehrman got home. He'd heard about the sinking of the *Eastland*, as had the rest of Chicago. He walked home from the "el" thinking of what he'd say to his son. It was only after he'd yelled at him and the boy had run off that Leo understood what Benny had seen. Leo stood in the doorway to his son's bedroom, where Benny was stretched out on the bed.

Leaning into the doorjamb, Leo stared at his short, compact body. He was startled by the black fringe on his boy's upper lip. His son's fingers were flitting across the page of his book. Leo wondered why Benny couldn't sit still. For an instant he felt the urge to ease his way down on the bed and stroke his son's hair. But Leo couldn't look at his son and not think about the blizzard two years before. He couldn't look at Benny and not remember that Hannah had begged him to let the boys stay home. "I never stayed home," Leo had shouted. "I never missed a day of school." This wasn't actually true. Leo had missed many days of school. He had frittered away his afternoons in pool halls or shadowboxing on street corners. It was one of the dozens of lies he'd made up about his life, lies even he had come to believe.

But on that day when Hannah saw her husband was insisting, she'd tied the boys together with a rope. "Be careful," she'd told Benny as she pulled the rope taut through their belt loops. She'd gazed out at the sheer whiteness beyond her window. "You're in charge of your brothers." Hannah watched her four sons, vanishing into the snow, their footprints trailing off until they disappeared.

Even now, as Benny lay stretched on his bed, Leo could see him, racing up the stairs, breathless, crying. As he stood in the doorway, he wished he could gather him into his arms. Instead what he saw was his oldest son telling him that six-year-old Harold, the boy with the dimpled grin, had not been on the other end of the rope when the brothers reached the school—a school they'd found closed due to snow. And they would not find Harold—who had curled against a fence to fend off the wind—until the spring. It was difficult for Leo to look at his son and not think of that day and the days that followed. "Benny," his father said, louder than he intended.

Benny leaped up. Though a book lay open on his bed, he hadn't been reading. He had been somewhere else altogether—a place where he'd left behind the events of that morning. He had been trying to figure out a tune he'd heard in an alleyway on the South Side the week before. It was a lilting melody with too many notes, and whoever was playing seemed to take up the whole keyboard. His head was full of musical notes, and he wished he could write them down. Though he'd never cared before, it bothered him now. He'd been tapping out a tune on his sheets when his father opened the door. Benny clasped his hand to his heart. "I didn't hear you." Already he'd lost the refrain.

"I'm sorry I yelled at you today," his father said. "I didn't know what happened." Leo took a step closer into the room. Benny looked up at his father with the same glazed look he'd worn that morning that made Leo pause.

His body stiffened at the sound of his father's voice.

Leo clung to the doorjamb. "It's a terrible thing, and I am sorry you had to see it."

Benny nodded. "I'm all right."

"Well, good. That's good then." His father struck the wall as he turned to go. "Dinner's ready."

His brothers were already at the table. They too had heard about the *Eastland* and wanted to know what Benny had seen. "Tell us," Ira, who was closest to Benny in age, said. He had a reddish complexion, and his skin looked especially red that evening. "Tell us what you saw."

Benny's mind was a blank. He remembered that festive moment. A ragtime tune was playing, and he smelled chicken and fresh-baked breads. He'd chatted with a woman and her two little girls. Then the woman's mouth opened into a scream. "I saw a feathered hat," Benny said.

Ira bent closer to his brother. "I don't understand."

"Leave him alone." Hannah slapped Ira with a serving spoon. "Pass this."

Hannah rubbed her head with her hands. "Be quiet," Leo told the boys. "Your mother has a headache." Ira, whose face was now very red, passed the casserole dish to his father. Leo Lehrman sat hunched over his food. When Arthur, who was younger than Benny by five years, reached across for a piece of bread, Leo said, "And break your bread before you butter it."

Arthur broke his bread into four pieces, buttering each one separately, cowering before his father, but his gaze was fixed on his older brother, who seemed more like a hero, back from the wars, than a boy with a propensity for disaster and a musical ear.

The Regency Theater was four blocks away, and after dinner Benny wandered over. He'd been going to the Regency since he was small. The dank theater consisted of eight rows with six folding chairs in each, a small balcony with a dozen more chairs, a tattered sheet that served as the screen, and a projector. The piano player wore her hair piled on her head and held up with two chopsticks. She never took her eyes off the screen, and the light from the picture illumined her face. Benny kept his eyes on her. He never cared much for the stories that were on the screen. He came for the music.

As the tension mounted, the piano player worked up from the bass with a rising crescendo. With each rescue she struck a heart-wrenching set of right-handed trills. She hit the keys in ways that imitated slaps, claps, knocks, and falls. She played romantic melodies to introduce the love interest, bold chords for the hero, and minor chords in the bass brought on the villain. She played ragtime between reels or to announce the happy ending. And it was always happy.

In the dark theater with the notes rising, all the stories blended into one. Women tied to a chair, tied to a railroad track and freed, women released just before they tumbled down Niagara Falls, as they bounced through white water, rescued at the edge of a precipice, delivered from poverty, from grief, from having to sell their bodies, from having to sell their souls. In ten finger crescendos women swooned in the hands of an evil man. The boy next door rescued them. Every man wanted to save a beautiful woman. Everybody wanted to save someone.

Four

The gem sisters slept in the order in which they were born. Pearl lay in the middle, with Opal and Ruby on either side. Ruby slept against the wall while Opal teetered on the edge. Though this should have been reversed, Ruby, who was almost ten when their youngest sister was born, refused to give up her place against the wall and, as a toddler, Opal seemed to prefer the outside. It was Pearl's task to keep her from falling.

Anna wanted her children named after tangible things. In the old country she had spoken only *mamaloshen*, the mother tongue. In the Yiddish of the shtetl there were only two words for flowers—violet and rose. No words existed for the varieties of wild birds or trees. But in English, Anna learned, everything had a name. Before, all trees were simply "tree." Now there was oak, maple, elm. She found hawk, peacock, cockatoo. Lily of the valley, Rose of Sharon, jack-in-the-pulpit. In the end she named her oldest boys Robin, Wren, and Jay after birds—except for Jonah, her firstborn, because she liked the story of the whale. She called her middle children, Moss and Fern, after woodland plants. And the final three became her precious stones.

While the others came from air or the soil, the gem sisters emerged from the depths. Anna told Pearl that she came from water, from the grain of sand that disturbs the oyster, and that her gem sisters came from the deepest of mines. In Burma and Australia, dark men dug into the earth to find them. "But you, Pearly, you're lucky. You come from the sea." And Pearl trembled, thinking how her mother had tried to return her there.

Of all the children Opal and Pearl looked the most alike. They bore no resemblance to Ruby, with her fire-engine-red hair and tiny pinched features, who looked like an Irish girl. Opal and Pearl shared the round Slavic cheeks and broad smiles. They were identical, except that Opal had piercing blue eyes and hair the color and texture of corn silk, and Pearl was opaque, a chocolate brown. When they stood together, it seemed as if Pearl was her sister's shadow.

Since Opal was born, Pearl had taken care of her little sister. In winter she made sure she ate hot broths. In summer she bathed her every evening. As an infant Opal had wheezy breath. She shivered when it wasn't cold and burrowed deep into her sister's arms. On the hottest nights Pearl swaddled her in an extra blanket. At times, confused about whom her mother was, Opal tried to nurse on Pearl's tiny breasts, which made Pearl laugh even as she pushed the baby away.

But now, as Opal slept, Pearl tasted the sand between her teeth and felt a hunger she could not name. As she tried to sleep, she saw a darkening sky and felt as if she could not breathe. The night sounds came together like water, rising over her head.

Though it was a warm, breezeless night, Pearl lay awake. There was a chill, locked in her bones. She listened to the noises of the house as an animal does for danger. She could hear a creak on the stairs, the clang of trash cans in the alley. A sob reached her ears. No one else could have heard it except Pearl. Downstairs in the saloon someone wept. Since the *Eastland* went down, Pearl had been afraid to close her eyes. She was wedged as always between Ruby's bony hip and Opal's warm breath.

She nudged Ruby. "Ruby," she whispered, "wake up. Someone's crying." But her sister just groaned and pressed herself closer to the wall. Pearl turned and wrapped her arms around Opal's waist, and even Opal pushed her away.

Her mind raced as she remembered Wren and his solitary dance.

She missed her brothers who'd drowned. Robin, the oldest, used to pick her up at school and carry her home on his shoulders. Jay played tunes on the harmonica before she went to bed while Wren mimed stories that made her laugh. Opal was too young to remember such things, and Ruby had begun drawing in a notebook every spare moment when she wasn't at school or busy with chores. Besides, Ruby hadn't been there that day, but Pearl would never forget. Even when she wasn't thinking of her brothers, she saw the boy on the bridge and the package he swung by a thread. In her half sleep Pearl watched as the parcel slipped from his fingers into the water below. It left a hole on the surface of the river as it sank. His tapping fingers and sad, dark eyes stuck in her head like a song that wouldn't leave.

Then she arrived at blank space. It came to her as if in a dream, only she'd been awake. It felt as if it had happened to someone else. Like a story you tell and think is your own. At the water's edge Anna had pressed her hand against the small of Pearl's back. Cold water soaked Pearl's skirts and seeped into her shoes. Her feet disappeared on the sandy bottom. Children born inside their cauls never drown, Anna told Pearl when Opal was born encircled in blue slime like a baby chick. But since the day when the *Eastland* settled into the river's mud, Pearl wasn't sure.

Clasping Opal's tiny fist, Pearl had persuaded her mother to get away from the shore. There was somewhere they had to be. It took three streetcars to bring them home. *Our mother tried to drown us, too,* Pearl wanted to tell her siblings when they asked what was wrong. But who would believe her? "You just want all the attention," Ruby would say.

Instead Pearl grew hard and silent as a stone.

By day she roamed, looking for a secluded place. Sometimes her oldest sister, Fern, found her dozing in the back of the cedar closet, the fresh scent of woods in her hair, and she'd carry the girl to her proper bed. In the house she walked around with her hands pressed over her ears. She complained that she couldn't stand the jammering, the footsteps and sighs, the bathroom noises, the farts and belches, the guffaws and laughter, the bronchial coughs and fog horn sneezes, the whisperings that came through thin walls, the shouts from room to room. But her father was dead and her brothers drowned. Her mother had tried to return her to the water from where she'd come, and Pearl did not know that the sound she could not stop hearing was the scream inside her head.

But the crying seemed to be coming from below. Pearl eased her way out of bed and to the top of the stairs, then made her way down. The wood was rough under her feet. Often she got splinters, but tonight she didn't care. At the landing she gazed into the bar. In the dim light she saw her mother slumped across a chair. Anna, draped in black, heaved like a despondent beast. Pearl wanted to go to her, but she didn't dare. The impression of her mother's fingers was etched on her wrist.

Anna had always kept her from harm. She left a honey pot open in the kitchen to trap bad spirits floating by. If someone told Pearl she was pretty, her mother retorted, "Like a pig," then spit in the air to drive the evil eye away. When Anna sewed Pearl's dresses right on her back, she made her hold a thread between her teeth for good luck.

Now Pearl's skin burned from the sun. Small blisters covered her nose, and the freckles emblazoned on her cheeks would remain. Her birthday was a sad memory of a July day that she'd never celebrate again. She'd never taste strawberry ice cream and not feel her throat constrict. Pearl had pulled her mother from the water's edge on to a streetcar, going the wrong direction. For hours they'd been lost in the city. When they got home, they found Jonah, sobbing, certain that they were all dead.

Turning away, Pearl tiptoed back up the stairs. Her heart beat as if someone had jumped out of a dark corner to frighten her. She thought she would die if she went back to bed. She could not bear to lie awake, entombed between her sisters. In the hallway she paused before the photograph of her mother, trim and smiling, standing in front of the first Ferris wheel. In 1893 Anna had strolled the Chicago World's Fair on her father's arm and thought that this was what her life would be. All white with gondolas sailing in man-made lakes, women in elegant gowns walking by. Music coming from wooden boxes. The classical white buildings, the pillars. Everything before Anna was white, shimmering.

No wonder they'd called it the White City. Chicago had risen from its ashes. A carpenter who worked on the Court of Honor named Elias Disney would tell of its wonders to his son, Walt. A Chicago writer, L. Frank Baum, reinvented it as Oz. Through the pavilions Anna had caught glimpses of herself in windows and mirrors. Her russet hair piled on her head, and her body trim in its green dress as they shopped for Turkish delight on a Cairo Street, viewed a Bavarian castle, and paused before a Hindu snake charmer.

Anna had ogled Little Egypt, the belly dancer, and laughed at what scandalized the fair most—the first zipper. Already newspaper editorials bemoaned how easy carnal knowledge would be. She ate handfuls of a nutty snack called Cracker Jack. In the Palace of Electricity she shrieked as sparks flew from the fingertips of a man named Tesla and swayed at the Haitian Pavilion as a young piano player played his "Maple Leaf Rag."

Two years before, her family had come to this city where pigs could not walk on Michigan Avenue on a Sunday. They had crossed a roiling sea where Anna had lain across her father's lap, the sea having entered her as well. Her father stroked her hair and promised her dresses of silk, indoor plumbing, and a pony in the New World. He had made good on most of these.

On the Midway, men turned their heads. A photographer snapped her picture, and her father took it home. It would be the only image of Anna as girl. She was aware of her small waist and plump breasts, her fleshy thighs. There was a sweetness in the air like spun sugar.

Anna did not know then—nor would she have cared—that the fair buildings she passed were sheds of tin and lumber, coated in a mix of plaster, jute fibers, and cement. That they would burn in the fire which, along with the assassination of the mayor, would bring about the end of the fair. Or that even as Scott Joplin played his "Maple Leaf Rag," Frederick O. Douglass was complaining that the White City was just that. White.

She had been oblivious to all. Anna was sixteen years old and secretly in love. She had no idea that this was the last time she and her father would enjoy a stroll. That everything was about to change. She begged him for a ride on the first Ferris wheel. As they rose in the glass cage, she clung to her father's arm. People were small as ants; carriages and buildings looked like toys. Individual lives seemed insignificant from her vantage point. She wondered not how but when she would tell her father that she intended to marry for love.

As Pearl listened to her mother's sobs, it was hard for her to believe that the girl in the picture had become the woman crying downstairs. Anna's father had disowned her when she married Samuel. Even after Samuel's death her father refused to forgive her. And now their sons were gone, and it seemed to Pearl that her mother was no longer right in her head. Pearl snuck into the kitchen and opened the door that led to the back porch. She did this often when she couldn't sleep. She stepped outside and knelt down. The wooden slats pressed against her flesh.

Tucking her nightgown under her thighs, Pearl gazed into the smoky sky. There were no stars, no moon. Just the humid, still air. She leaned against the brick wall and listened to the sound of distant waves, pounding the shore.

Five

The crack of a bat worked its way into Benny's dreams. He heard the shouting and, gazing out, saw Moe Javitts with a group of their pals, playing in the lot below. Moe, like Benny, was dark skinned and small, with curly hair. He was pitching and threw an impressive fast ball. Some of the boys from the nearby neighborhoods were good, and because it was summer and there was no school the boys played whenever they could.

The vacant lot was a dry patch with a few tufts of grass and weeds, tucked between two buildings, and Benny had lived most of his life across from it. He hung out here with his brothers and the neighborhood boys. It was covered in broken bottles and trash. Albany Park was only a few blocks away, but this was where the boys preferred to be. They'd played mumblety-peg, hurling pocket knives at their feet. They'd made pushmobiles out of orange crates and old roller-skating wheels. As they grew older, they played ball. In the winter they brought girls here and roasted potatoes over open fires. They slipped their hands into the warmth of soft skin and wool coats.

Benny gave a holler across the dusty expanse, and Moe waved up to him. "Come on down," Moe shouted from the pitcher's mound. If he hurried, Benny could get in an inning or two before his music lesson. He wished he could skip it. He was tired of Mr. Marcopolis and the Beethoven sonatas that he didn't want to learn. Though he

went through the motions of practicing, he'd never play them right.
Now he didn't bother bathing or brushing his teeth. He just threw
on a shirt and trousers, his shirt hanging out, and gulped down a
bowl of cold cereal and juice. Despite Hannah's efforts to run a comb
through his hair, Benny dashed out the door.

It was the bottom of the third, and the Tuley High School boys
were ahead. He stuck his sheet music under a makeshift bench and
took the field at shortstop. He fielded a few grounders and made a
good play at second. At bat he doubled, and then scrambled to third
on a line drive. On a bungled catch he stole home. In the next inning
he ran down the line hard to get a single and caught a scorcher
barehanded. His palm ached and his fingers burned. For a moment
he wondered if his wrist was broken. When he heard the church
bells chime nine o'clock, he walked off the field. "Come on, Benny,"
Moe shouted, "forget about it." Moe, who played the French horn,
thought nothing about missing his lessons.

"Can't." He shook his head. "I gotta go."

"Mama's boy," somebody called.

Benny shot a glance and scowled as he walked to the corner
where he hopped a streetcar heading west. As the tram moved up
Lawrence, Benny brushed the dust from his knees. He rubbed his
sore fingers, which still smarted from his catch. His hand stung as
he got off at his stop. On the street a pushcart peddler was selling
rags. Benny walked past the tumbledown buildings whose corridors
reeked of herring, pickles, and faulty plumbing. Climbing the stairs,
he stood in front of his teacher's apartment. As he raised his fist to
knock, he froze in midair. He wasn't going in. He didn't think he
could bear to be inside that apartment with its odor of stale tea and
unlived lives.

He turned and snuck down the stairs, then dashed back into the
street much faster than he had come. He caught a tram heading east
and then south. The houses got bigger. There were trees and street-
lights. He got off at the river near the Shadows where the dockwork-
ers and prostitutes dwelled. Red-lipped women called to him, but
he ignored them. He wandered along the wharves as a crew toted
bushels of corn and potatoes, lugging boxes of cargo off the ships.

The *Eastland* still lay on her side while a pitch-black tug with the strange name of *Favorite* was trying to right her. Benny sat on the dock as the sailors on the hull struggled to secure more lines. He thought about how many people in his neighborhood were gone. A man across the way had lost his wife and his daughter. At night Benny heard his sobs. One woman had lost all six of her children. How could a person go on after something like that?

His mother had only lost Harold. But he was the youngest and the sweetest of her boys. Benny couldn't help but chuckle as he looked again at the tugboat's name. *Favorite*. That's what Harold was. Her favorite. It had been a knife in Benny's heart. How Hannah doted on him. She saved for him the juicy chicken thighs, the marrow bones in the soup. The tenderest cut of brisket was never for her husband, always for Harold. And then she'd lost him, and though she'd never say it, Benny really was to blame. She had entrusted him with the boys. She cried for a year, then one day she stopped. But the head-aches began, and they'd never gone away. Somehow the three boys who were left didn't count. It made no difference when Benny said to her, "You still have me."

"How's it coming?" he shouted to the pilot of the tug.

"Good as can be expected," the pilot called back with a wave. Benny lingered on the docks, then hopped the "el" that they called the Alley, which would take him downtown. He was happiest in motion. He didn't want to sit still. If he could, he'd just keep going. He had thoughts of getting away, heading to some of the river towns. Davenport or St. Louis. Maybe even to New Orleans. He rocked with the rhythm of the "el" as it took him down Satan's Mile past the saloons where Mickey Finn rolled customers for their wallets and left them naked on the streets. Benny didn't care if the South Side was dirty or dangerous. He got off at Thirty-First Street and walked the rest of the way.

The alleyway smelled of grease and dog shit, of piss and smol-dering trash. The stink of a Chicago summer got into his clothes and his hair. He put his ear up to the tavern door and soon the music seeped out as he knew it would. Even at this early hour someone was playing the keyboard. At first he thought it was two people. It didn't seem possible that it was only one. Whoever was playing seemed to be hitting all the notes at once, but the right hand ran wild while the left kept a steady bass. The notes swirled in murky colors, and the key kept changing. He couldn't make sense of the chords.

He didn't know what this new music was called or if it even had a name. He just knew he heard it when he went to those places where his mother said he didn't belong. Often Hannah chastised his father. "You shouldn't be sending that boy on deliveries down to the South Side. He's too young to go there." She had read *Chicago and Its Cess-Pools of Sin*. Evils awaited her son in that part of town. "Lost souls" was what she called those who went there. But Leo protested, "He's the only one who wants to go."

Not many of the boys would venture down to the South Side because it was rough. Sometimes they had their tips stolen, but Benny begged his father for those jobs. It didn't matter to Leo who did the South Side as long as it got done. He didn't want any competition in the area of rail and stockyard workers, so he gave Benny that part of town whenever he asked.

When the music stopped, the silence was slow to reach him. He stood motionless as a huge caramel-skinned man in a soaked white shirt flung open the door. His hair, the color of molasses, was cut short, making his big head look like a balloon. His eyes were molasses, too. Bees must flock to him, Benny thought. The man glared at the boy who stood gaping. "What're you doing here, son?"

"Just listening." Benny shook as he said it. The man gave him a smile, and a diamond stud glittered in his front tooth. "Was that you playing?" The man nodded, staring down at Benny so he thought he'd better say something more. "I was wondering, that music, what's it called?"

"Why do you wanta know?"

Benny shrugged. "I haven't heard anything like it before."

"What's it worth to you?"

Benny dug into his pockets. All he had was his carfare home. "I've got this."

"Ah, forget about it." The man gave him a grin. "It's called jass."

Benny stood, not moving, repeating the word. "Jass."

"You know, son, this is the devil's music. The demon dwells here. It's Negro music, boy. Whorehouse stomping. Coon shouting." The man was taunting him now. "It's what your mama told you to stay away from. So you better do that. Now you get outta here." And the man planted a kick in the air.

In August the White Sox bought Shoeless Joe Jackson from Cleveland for twenty-five thousand dollars. In sandlots boys were slamming line drives into left field, hoping that one day Shoeless Joe would miss one of theirs. On a hot Saturday afternoon Benny hit a grounder onto Leland Avenue. He had a good stance and a strong swing, and he whacked it out of the lot. He rounded the bases with his mother hollering from the window that he'd be late for his piano lesson. As he touched home plate, he gave her a wave and waited until she went back inside. Pocketing the money she gave him to pay his teacher, he hopped a trolley, heading south.

Once more Benny got off at the Shadows and walked along the docks. Now the black tug was gone, and so was the *Eastland*. The river was devoid of the tragedy as if it had never occurred. Nothing marked the spot where 844 people drowned in the hull of a ship. The river flowed, greasy and dark, and Benny shuddered as he walked along Clark Street. The sounds of Tom Brown's Ragtime Band, coming from the Lamb's Café, made him pause.

Inside a piano man was warming up. Benny stared at the poster of Joe Frisco, the "American Apache," as he danced "the frisco" bug-eyed with derby and cigar. At the bottom of the poster Benny saw the word written for the first time. JASS BAND. He stuck his head in as the band was setting up. "Hey, when's the show?" he called to a waiter in a white tie and tuxedo, but the waiter shooed him away.

"Scram, kid," the waiter chimed, slamming the door in his face. Benny waited outside, hoping the band would warm up again. When it didn't, he took a school pencil from his pocket and crossed the *J* out of "Jass." ASS BAND, it read. Then he caught the Alley to Satan's Mile until he stood again in the alleyway near the trash cans where a dog chewed a bone. The stink of rancid meat made him swoon. He put his ear to the door and recognized the sound.

That caramel man was pounding out a tune, and those buttery hands never missed a note. Pigeons roosted overhead. The shadows grew longer as Benny tried to see the music in his head. But the colors weren't coming out clear. They were kind of gray, fuzzy around the edges. Everything that was jumbled up inside him was flowing through that door. He tried taking the notes apart, but nothing was making sense. This was no written-down, planned-out thing. Nobody had played like this before. Benny listened the way a sleeper listens to his own dream. He wanted more "jass."

As he was leaning against the door, it opened, and he tumbled against the trash cans. Startled at first, the big man laughed. "You back again?" He was rolling a cigarette, licking the paper with his long pink tongue as Benny nodded. "You must be stealing," the man said nonchalantly.

Benny looked around the alleyway. What was there to take? "Stealing? I never stole anything in my life."

The man laughed. "Music. That's what white kids steal."

Benny shook his head. "I don't understand."

The man lit his cigarette. "So what d'you want here, boy?"

Benny tried to find the words for what he wanted, but they eluded him. "Nothing," he replied, though he knew this wasn't true. He did want something.

"Then why you keep showing up?" The man stared at him, but Benny held his ground.

A few minutes ago he hadn't known what he wanted, but now he did. "I want to come inside."

The man let out a gruff laugh, thick with smoke. "Well, be my guest." He flashed a smile with his diamond stud and poppy-seed kernels between his teeth. Making a deep bow, he let the boy pass through a haze of perfume and smoke. Billiard balls clacked in a corner while two girls with red nails and creamy red lipstick leaned against the bar. Their breasts were pushed up almost to their chins, and they wore black lace stockings hooked onto a garter belt and red bows in their hair. Benny had never seen girls dressed like this before, and he looked at them more with curiosity than desire.

Honey Boy Bailey crossed the room, his buttocks shaking like Jell-O. "Hey, Honey," one of the girls called. "You gonna let that doughboy sit in with you?"

"He's not white." Honey Boy held up Benny's tanned arm. "Look at him. He's almost black as us. Besides this boy likes our rhythms. And you can see he's got the heebie-jeebies, so why don't you go outside and get us some business, Velvet?"

The man pulled up a chair beside the piano. "Okay, you just sit here and watch." He stretched out his long black fingers that moved like termites in a house on fire. He took up the whole keyboard as his pink nails flitted up and down. His hands went in different directions while his feet danced on the floor. His elbows jabbed the air as he kept the melody moving with his right hand. Benny kept his eye on the left hand as he tried to figure out the chords.

Honey Boy played his rags and the blues, but then the tunes took off on their own, and Benny had no way of following. His right hand crossed over his left and Benny couldn't keep up. Honey Boy seemed to be using the instrument more like a drum than a piano.

His hands glided for an hour, a day; Benny had no idea how long. All he knew was that he couldn't follow the tune by just sitting there. And that this man wasn't called Honey Boy because of the golden brown color of his skin. He was Honey Boy because when he played, what came out of him was sweet and smooth.

When Honey Boy was finished, he looked at Benny, who was concentrating very hard. "What are you thinking?"

Benny shook his head. "I'm thinking about how you do that."

Honey Boy laughed. "Well, when you solve it, you come back and show me." Reaching into a jar, he swallowed a handful of poppy seeds. "Jelly Roll Morton, he thinks he invented jazz. But let me tell you, I taught him a thing or two before you were born. Now you go work on that, then come back for your next lesson." Honey Boy laughed, giving Benny a pat on the back. "And eat poppy seeds," he said, holding up the jar. "It's good luck. It'll make a success out of you."

As Benny stepped into the warm air, he was surprised at how dark it was. He tried to ignore the laughter trailing after him. They were making fun of him, but he was too busy, trying to figure out what he'd just heard. He ran the music over in his head. There were two or three chords he could make sense of. The rest was a cloudy river with no bottom in sight. As he walked, his fingers worked, laying out a melody on top. He didn't even notice that he was heading the wrong way home.

It was called the Stroll, that part of South State Street where the music lived. The Dahomey Stroll to some. A strip of flashing bulbs, all blue, red, and yellow, where midnight was like noon. The music was coming from there twenty-four hours a day. From the Elite and the Vendome. From the Grand and the Deluxe. It was said that if you held a trumpet in the air, it would play all by itself. They called it the Bohemia of the Colored Folks. Rome, Athens, Jerusalem, and South State Street, those were the epicenters of the world.

Postal workers and delivery boys, hotel maids who cleaned toilets, and men who hosed down the stockyard floor, they went home, took a shower, dressed to the nines, then headed out again. They put on their fur coats and sharkskin suits, their felt fedoras, their boas and flapper dresses, and moved to the music, dancing until dawn. They paused at the dance halls and the cabarets, the thousand bars that filled one square mile, dining on hot chili, chop suey, and ice cream. Then at five in the morning they went to the public baths, took a long steam, went home, slept for an hour, put on their uniforms, and went back to work.

Benny ambled on. Blacks in their shiny green and purple suits, women in long white gloves and cigarette holders, sauntered by. He paused at the Dreamland Ballroom. Beneath the flashing lights bouncers in red capes swung open doors. From inside the sounds of horns and laughter rose. At the Firefly Senator Sam's Rhythm Band from New Orleans was featured. Even from the street the fast dance tempo made him move his feet, but it was almost too fast. He wanted something slower that suited his mood. He walked around the corner at Thirty-Fifth until he stood beneath the flickering red light of a cock's comb.

The Rooster wasn't much of a spot. Nothing fancy like Dreamland or the Firefly. It was more of a sawdust joint that served ribs, but the music caught Benny's ear as he gazed down the corridor into a smoky room with a few bare bulbs. On the door a scribbled note read "Napoleon Hill on Trumpet," and from the street he heard the melody the piano set, the rhythm of the drums, and the soft smooth rise of the trumpet, quiet as a secret, and Benny had to lean in to listen. He went around into the urine-soaked alleyway where a window was ajar, and he rested his back against the brick wall. There were no barroom distractions. No drinks being poured or voices shouting. No scraping of chairs, toilets flushing. No din he had to strain to hear above.

There was something sad in that trumpet he'd only heard in the winter wind. It was lonely as a boy who comes home to an empty house. A boy who's lost his rabbit's foot or a China-blue marble. Maybe he dropped it on the street, and someone picked it up and didn't know it was his. Or maybe they just wanted to keep it for themselves. Sad as an orphan boy, searching for his true father. But that sound wasn't only sad. It was something else he couldn't name. It went through him so that he didn't know where the music stopped and his body began. As the tune picked up and grew warmer, it radiated through his bones.

Someone tapped him on the arm. "Past your bedtime, isn't it, son?"

Benny shook his head as if awakening and stared at the policeman. Why did everyone treat him as if he were a boy? He was almost sixteen, old enough to be out on his own. "What time is it, officer?"

"Time for a fellow like you to be tucked in, don't you think?" The officer tapped his billy club against the side of the building, then pointed toward the street.

"Yes, sir." Without bothering to ask again, because he couldn't bear to have his father come and fish him out, Benny caught the "el" north. It was an almost-empty train with two or three other people on it—night workers heading back, sleepy people who had to be at their jobs in a few hours. He collapsed into a seat as the train rumbled along. He hoped his parents were asleep and that they hadn't noticed he was gone. If he had to, he'd come up with a good lie.

The "el" clanged as it moved on its tracks. The stifling air smelled of leather and tired bodies. Benny rocked back and forth. He shut his eyes. He went to that place by the window where he'd stood listening to the lilt of a trumpet he couldn't see. "Let me play," Benny said, making his pact with no one in particular. "I'll do anything if you'll let me play."

Six

The French brought perfume to New Orleans and, with it, the scent known as oil of jasmine. In the brothels the whores dabbed oil of jasmine behind their ears, on the backs of their knees and wrists. "Hey, baby," their customers chanted, "give me some of that jass." In Storyville where Napoleon Hill once went to look for his mother, he'd heard the music they were starting to call jass. Once he heard it, he was done with ragtime. With jass he could make it up, and he didn't have to write it down. Nothing with jass was set in stone. One change led to the next. And change was what Napoleon Hill was good at, like a chameleon, he thought as he stood admiring himself in front of the mirror.

His trumpet lay polished and shiny in its case. He was getting ready to go where he'd never been, and he wanted to be sure he looked right. A large man, he was squeezed between the narrow bed and the dresser, straightening his tie and talking to himself. He shared this room with Maddy Winslow, though he never actually slept with her. It had been their arrangement for years that he was crawling into bed as she was getting out.

He wished Maddy was home so he could ask her if he was doing the right thing. She was good for that. Telling him if something was right or not. She'd weigh it carefully, then shake her head or nod, and over all the years they'd lived together he'd listened to whatever she said. But today was her double shift and she wouldn't get home until late. Napoleon played trumpet at the Red Rooster six nights a week, but he could do whatever he wanted on the seventh, and that was Monday night.

So Napoleon was going to cross the river and play his horn at a white establishment on the North Side. He'd take Jonah up on his offer and stop by Chimbrova's saloon. All summer, until that ship toppled over in the river, the boy with the black eyes and hair like coal had been coming by the Shoestring Diner for his morning coffee, which he drank just as black. Jonah didn't sleep well and he was often late for work at Western Electric where he assembled telephones.

To make ends meet Napoleon did an early morning shift at the Shoestring, busing tables and pouring coffee, a few days a week. Those mornings he didn't even bother going back to Maddy's to sleep. He just went straight from his gig. By nine he was done. One morning as he was pouring steaming cups of coffee, Napoleon noticed the dark circles under the boy's eyes. When he asked if he had trouble sleeping, Jonah told him about his drowning dreams. "I keep seeing water, coming over my head."

"Maybe it's your name," Napoleon said.

Napoleon also had dreams of water. "I won't go near the stuff," he told the boy. And he believed in them. In his dreams he wasn't in the water, he was on it. He was in a big boat, and around him the sea was roaring and waves rising. As he struggled in his sleep, ropes burned his wrists, and irons cut into his ankles. He was hungry deep in his gut and missing what he had to leave behind.

Napoleon recognized it as an ancestor dream, and it had happened to someone he didn't know but who knew him and knew where he was. Someone who wanted to warn him, he told Maddy when she held his trembling body against hers, only for the warmth, never for more. That was the way he was with everything. He had to be free, no matter what. No one—nothing, not even his horn—could hold him down.

Napoleon wasn't his real name. It was Edgar James, but he'd been Napoleon since he could remember. Even as a boy he'd had a wrinkled brow and looked older than his years. He had small eyes and puffy cheeks like a fish, skin the color of cocoa beans, and stubby fingers with pink crescent nails. Until his first growth spurt, he was a small boy with a stubborn streak. A neighbor dubbed him Napoleon. The nickname suited him and it stuck.

Napoleon liked to hum as he poured coffee on his morning shift, and one day Jonah asked him, "What are those tunes?"

"Oh, it's just little numbers I make up."

"You make them up?" Jonah asked, and Napoleon said he did.

"All the time," he replied.

"You write them down?"

"Never write them down. Don't know how." Napoleon pointed to his head. "I keep them right up here." It came out that Napoleon played the trumpet. He had a regular gig at the Red Rooster, but Napoleon's playing didn't earn enough to keep him in his double-breasted box suits, his straitlaced shoes and gold watch bands, the brown and gray fedoras with the black bands, and what he called his roast beefs—the tuxedos he wore when he played special gigs. To keep up his expensive clothes habit, Napoleon worked days as a busboy and waiter at the Shoestring Diner where he'd met Jonah, then played all night at the Rooster downtown. "Most of the boys I jam with don't even know ten o'clock happens twice in the same day," Napoleon told Jonah, "but I've got these expensive tastes I have to support."

Jonah said that his family ran a small saloon where people came on the North Side and played ragtime and the blues, and Napoleon said if he was welcome, he'd come by sometime. Jonah hesitated for only a moment, trying to recall if a black man had ever walked into Chimbrova's before. But Jonah could not recall, nor did he care much about such things. "You'd be welcome anytime." For weeks Napoleon had tried to bring himself to go. Now he felt he had to. He kept thinking about that boy with the dark circles and his fear of water who hadn't come back to the Shoestring since the *Eastland* went down. He should have gone sooner, if only to see if Jonah was all right.

It was just past eight on a cool fall evening as he straightened the lapel of his gray silk suit, his rosy pink bow tie. Taking a deep breath, he adjusted his gray fedora and patted the gris-gris bags he wore around his neck. The first bag his pale-skinned mother—high yellow, they called her—had tied around his neck when he was six years old and left him on his grandmother's porch. In it was a mandrake root for protection and the skin of a turtle to attract a lover when he grew older. His mother knew what he'd need in this world. She tied it solidly at his throat, kissed him on the head, and, without a glance back, drove off in a borrowed cart and mule.

Napoleon had listened to the crunch of her wheels on that dirt road as the cart churned up gravel and dust. After that, his grandmother said, he always seemed to be listening. He listened to the wind blowing through the chinaberry trees, to the chickens clucking in the barnyard. He listened to the track callers joreeing as gandy dancers drove in railroad spikes. He listened to his grandmother, singing as she did the housework. Or he stood on the porch, eyes closed, listening for that cart to come back down the road.

When he wasn't listening, he was banging on pots and pans, whistling through blades of grass. He'd take his grandmother's washboard and thimbles and grind out a tune. He clanged on anything he could find. A neighbor who couldn't stand the banging anymore showed him how to make a diddley-bow out of broom wire. It was quieter than the washboard. He plucked at this all day, little tunes that grew out of the sadness in his head.

His grandmother decided he needed all the help he could get. When she taught him about the bag his mother had tied around his neck, she added one of her own. This bag contained John the Conqueror. John was a trickster who crossed the ocean with the slaves. He was always playing jokes on the masters. He made cuff links go astray and ham hocks disappear. He brought rain on days when nobody wanted to work. And sometimes a whip broke in two or a starving shackled man slipped out of his chains. When slavery ended, John thought he'd stick around in case the Africans needed him, so he found a hiding place in the roots of the tormentil plant, which grew throughout the South.

From an early age Napoleon knew that there were forces the eye could not see, things beyond his control. Every morning his grandmother swept the house, the steps, the yard, and down the walk—not to keep it clean, but to sweep away whatever spells may have been cast against them in the night. She warned him against eating eggs from strangers because a root worker might serve snake eggs. Baby snakes would hatch in your stomach, slither through your veins, and drive you mad.

Just before she died, when she gave him the gris-gris bag with John in it, she told him, "You keep him with you; he'll make you laugh. Everyone needs a trickster in this world." Though he begged her not to go, he was nine when she left him. No wind shook the leaves of the chinaberry that day. There was no sound of tires and gravel. The cotton fields shimmered like a silver lake.

Napoleon wandered out of Rolling Fork, heading south. That was the way he'd seen his mother go. A few miles down the road they were laying track. Four black men stood on each end of a six-foot railroad tie as the track caller sang. At each beat the men took the nuts out of the old rail, uncoupled it, put in a new one, took the bars, and coupled it back together. One rail, one minute, twenty rails, twenty minutes. They moved in perfect rhythm to the track caller's song. They were done before the train came through.

Napoleon caught the rhythm and clapped along. The foreman saw him, skinny and forlorn by the side of the tracks, and made him a water boy. All through the hot, summer months, he raced to the levee where he hauled a bucket back for the thirsty men as they toiled, lining the rails, bracing them. Driving spikes. Four to a tie, twenty-five hundred ties to a mile. It meant raising a maul sixteen hours a day.

At night they went back to the levee camp where the track caller, named Chance, played the fiddle. He played all kinds of songs—about a runaway boy whose dog showed him the way, about a man who convinced his wife he was blind, but he could see. Napoleon found that he liked to blow. He blew on water jugs as he carried them empty for a refill. As Chance joreed, taunting the men with his calls, telling them to line the bar, now raise it, now swing, Napoleon blew on the jugs in time. He blew on the grass reeds that swayed in the wind during a break when he rested by the side of the road. One night as Chance fiddled, he handed Napoleon his harmonica. He showed Napoleon how to purse his lips and cup his hands.

One of the men on the line had a bugle, and he let Napoleon blow into that. Napoleon tightened his lips and made a high screech. He widened them and produced a moan. He pressed down hard and deepened the sound. As soon as he heard those blasts, there was no turning back. The owner of the instrument said, "You've been playing that all your life, right?"

"Nope," Napoleon replied, "that was my first time."

Napoleon tried to give the instrument back, but the man wouldn't take it. He believed Napoleon was a devourer of antelope horns and elephant tusks. "You keep it, son," the man said, covering his face with his hands. "You'll be the devil's own bugle boy—of that I feel sure."

It was the bugle that got him to New Orleans, where the music came at him from every direction. It came from the brothels and bars. He raced to find it on the docks where stevedores sang Negro songs. He chased after it in the cemeteries where he slept, but whenever he got close, it eluded him and came from somewhere else. He stood on street corners, dressed in rags. He blew so well that people dropped coins into his cup. When his cup was full, he pawned the bugle and bought a trumpet. He practiced using the valves, and then went back to the street corners where people kept giving him their change. One man gave him a toilet plunger and told him to try it as a mute. Napoleon gorged on what he found in the trash, ate what he was given. If he ever made money, he told himself, he'd wear silk shirts and gold rings and eat steak all day long.

He took a job in Storyville, thinking he might find his mother there. He accompanied a piano player behind a Japanese screen so they could not see the creamy-skinned women press their nipples into the faces of white men, the girls kneeling at their feet. Though he knew the whores were white, Napoleon couldn't help wondering if there weren't any high yellows passing for white. Or maybe not even bothering to pass. In every woman's face, in her voice, he searched for the smooth-skinned woman who'd tied a bag around his neck and left him on a delta porch.

———

Napoleon had never been to the North Side. He'd never been much above Twelfth Street before. He stayed close to that straight line of cottages along the railroad tracks that people were starting to call the black belt. He even stayed clear of the Loop. He'd been to that five-and-dime where he drank Coca-Cola from the red-bottom cups so that whites wouldn't have to touch their lips to the same glass. He confined his travels to the Shoestring on the West Side and the clubs he played on the Stroll. Since coming to the city and moving in with Maddy, Napoleon had never crossed the river. He'd had no reason to until now.

As the streetcar clanged, the coloreds got off, and white people got on. Soon he was the only black person on the tram. He stared out the window, surprised when he came to the river. It was a dirty, green trickle. Napoleon laughed to himself. He wasn't sure what he'd expected, but this river was not like the one on whose banks he'd grown up. His big muddy river thought nothing of bursting its levees and drowning the cotton fields and its inhabitants for miles.

The ride across was brief, but once he was on the other side, everything looked bigger, brighter. Whiter. The cars, the buildings, the people. He thought about turning back, but he was enjoying the movement of the tram as he rode, humming along, his horn resting in his lap. Then he got off at Broadway and walked until he stood in front of the sign for Chimbrova's Saloon and Sweets.

The corner tavern was a long two-story brick building, painted a rusty red. In the front were canisters filled with lemon drops and sassafras balls. Napoleon could see through into the back where the bar was. He looked for the side entrance. There was a family door where wives snuck into the taverns, but not a black man. He walked into the alleyway where the stables were, but he could not find a service entrance. In the fancy establishments he had to go in the delivery entrance or the kitchen. He never just walked in the front as if he owned the place.

And he was troubled by the tattered black ribbon that hung across the lintel. They had lost someone recently and he was worried for the boy named Jonah who had nightmares of water. He was worried for himself, too. For half an hour he stood, watching men coming and going, hoping he'd see a black man. But there were none. Still he'd come this far, he reasoned, not that it was really that far, though it seemed like as long a journey as he'd ever been on, and he stepped inside.

A dozen or so men leaned across the bar. They wore dark jackets and hats and were drinking mugs of foamy beer with their backs to the door. The regulars had been coming in a steady stream for weeks now. With a somber face, Jonah poured Lev Walenski, the butcher, a double whiskey as he slumped at the bar. Bert Winkler still wore a black armband, and Bud Hansen's bouquet of baby's breath and roses lay withering across the bar. Mrs. Baum's dead husband was there as well. Though Mrs. Baum had him declared dead a decade ago so she could collect her annual death benefit of seventy-nine dollars, he still lived nearby. When he came to see his children, he stopped in to sip a few at Chimbrova's.

Balaban and Katz sat at a table in the corner. When they were bedraggled boys, they came to Anna's candy shop after school where she sold two hot dogs with a soda for a nickel. They never had more than a penny apiece, but Anna couldn't stand their hungry eyes. She always gave them a hot dog and a soda, adding a gumdrop or a root-beer ball, and told them to save their pennies, which they did. "That's why you don't make any money," Chimbrova had scolded her. Now they were in their twenties, plumper but still inseparable, scraggily boys who could pass for brothers. They had saved their pennies—a lot of them. Soon they'd be opening a theater they'd bought on the North Side. Every night since the *Eastland* they'd come to pay their respects. "Tanta Chimbrova," they said when they arrived, "is there anything we can do?"

Anna shook her head. "Please remember my children."

Each night before they left, they put a two-dollar tip on the bar. They were starting to refurbish their theater, where they planned to show movies and have vaudeville acts. They were looking to find colored entertainers, and their eyes settled on a black man as he hesitated at the saloon door. In his silk suit, horn in his hand, Napoleon stood in the entrance of the smoky-blue dive with the sawdust on the floor, not so different from the Rooster, except that here the clientele was white. Lev Walenski, with his bloody hands and distended belly, leaned over and whispered something to Mr. Scheffield. Mrs. Baum's dead husband turned as well. Outside of the voices it was quiet at the bar. There was no music at all.

Napoleon's eyes scanned the room. He was terrified of letting his gaze lock with a white man's. Long ago his grandmother taught him that they can cast a spell with their blue eyes. He looked sideways, but not straight on. He thought he should get on the streetcar and go back the way he'd come. He was about to turn around and walk away when Jonah spotted him from the bar. "You made it," Jonah said, waving him in.

"Yes," Napoleon replied, patting his gris-gris bags, "I did." He breathed a big sigh. "I guess you did, too. I haven't seen you at the Shoestring in a while so I was worried . . ."

"I'm not working there anymore . . ." Jonah shrugged. After the *Eastland* Jonah refused to return to Western Electric. He could not bear to think of his brothers who were gone. He and Moss promised Anna they'd run the saloon and make it work. "I couldn't go back," Jonah said.

"But you're all right."

"Yes," Jonah said, "I am." He pointed to the black cloth that covered the mirror. "But my brothers weren't so lucky."

"I am sorry for your loss . . ." Napoleon nodded, dropping his gaze. He did this not only out of respect but because he saw the impenetrable sadness in the boy's eyes, which he was able to recognize because it mimicked his own. He knew that Jonah would grow into a solitary man, rarely leaving these four walls.

"I slept through. I was so tired I missed the boat." Jonah paused, shaking his head. "Now I'm tired all the time."

"Missed the boat . . . Well, there must be a reason," Napoleon said.

"What reason could there be for my brothers to drown?" Jonah shook his head, and there was nothing Napoleon could say. "What'll you have?" Jonah asked.

Napoleon slid his horn at his feet. "I'll take a whiskey." He barely spoke in a whisper, then leaned against the bar, nursing his drink, wondering what he was doing in a North Side dive that was in mourning and had probably never seen a black man inside its four walls. He was unsure of where to put his hands, where to look as his eyes scanned the room. They came to rest on the piano.

It was sitting neglected in a corner, an old Vose & Sons upright, shiny as ebony. He'd hardly ever seen a piano naked like that with no one at the keys. It was lonely, Napoleon decided, as lonely as the people in this place, and he felt badly for it. Putting his drink down, he strolled over and struck a few chords. It was in perfect tune and the keys were smooth and loose. Most joints don't keep a piano this nicely. "Does that piano just sit there all night?" he asked Jonah. "Or does somebody come and play it?"

"Mostly it just sits," Jonah replied. He didn't want to explain that Vlado Slovik, the piano tuner, kept it tuned in exchange for shots of gin. "Sometimes people pound on it, but not very well." In truth, no one played much more than patriotic war tunes like "Keep the Home Fires Burning" which were sung fervently by tearful drunks, remembering the boys overseas. Or romantic ballads like "Gypsy Love Song," which brought another set of tears.

"Well, that's a shame," Napoleon said, fondling the white and shiny keys. He played a few bars and was aware of people shuffling behind him, turning to listen. "It's a good instrument."

"Yes," Jonah said with a pensive nod.

Napoleon could see that someone took the time to take care of that piano, even if nobody played it. He thought about this for a while. He tucked his horn under his arm. He wasn't going to play tonight in this tired saloon. He needed a rhythm section for that. "Mind if I come back sometime?"

"No." Jonah shook his head. "I wouldn't mind at all."

A few weeks later on a warm fall evening Napoleon Hill returned with his horn and a piano player with onyx skin and watery eyes named Earl "the Judge" Winston, who could play the blues all night. "I brought my friend along. Is that all right?"

"That's fine with me," Jonah said.

The Judge roughed out a few chords while Napoleon checked his mouthpiece, thrust a bore-brush through his bell. The Judge looked up at him with a nod. "It's good," he said, a smile on his face. At the Rooster where the piano was out of tune, the Judge played in a different key than Napoleon in order for them to stay in tune. Here they'd play in the same key.

"This is a little thing I wrote," Napoleon said. "It's called 'Rags 'n' Bones.'" He drummed his valves and noodled with a warm-up. The Judge riffed on a melody, playing the opening run until Napoleon picked up his horn and was blasting away. He held the brass hard against his wide, red lips. He wanted them puffy, just the way they were. He never took any time off from playing because they would go down. He kept them oiled with a salve made from ground eucalyptus and pig fat. He knew horn players whose lips had split during a performance, blood flowing down their shirts. Some never played again.

Halfway through the first chorus, Napoleon was dripping. His shiny suit was mottled with sweat, but he never saw the spots. They dried before he was done. He dabbed his face with a small towel he kept draped across his shoulder. He began with a haunting refrain that grew from his early mornings on the New Orleans streets when he collected old clothes and bottles. Even when his tunes were loose and funky, they were always a little sad. His rags and bones.

Using a tiny pillow as a mute, he let that quiet sound start deep, then grow. He switched to the open horn, then reached for the different objects he'd placed on the piano lid—a drinking glass, a child's sand pail. The audience laughed when he put a plumber's plunger to his horn. "Hey," Napoleon said to the crowd, seeing they were with him, "you shoulda seen the look on the guy's face in the hardware store when I told him I didn't need the stick." But they grew still when he produced a deep sound that was almost an echo as if he were blowing at one end of a tunnel.

He puffed up his jowls and found notes no one had ever heard on the North Side before. Or almost anywhere else for that matter. For his low notes he bent down as if he were going to pray, and for the high ones he raised his trumpet toward the ceiling as if he could make the walls tumble down. The music seeped up through the floorboards. The sound of a high-pitched trumpet and a stride piano made its way up the stairs, down a corridor. It moved like a fog, filling a room, taking up all the crevices and corners. It enveloped sleeping children as it drowned out the night sounds that made them restless and afraid. Its melody drifted until it came upon a dark-eyed girl who was sitting up in bed.

Pearl was wide-awake, listening. The music had a rhythm to it that made her think of that boy, the one who was drumming his fingers on the railing just before the *Eastland* sank. Pearl could still see his hands, moving, and the sound that rose from below coaxed her out of bed. She tiptoed to the landing, pausing there.

A trumpeter had a horn to his mouth. His thick lips were pressed against the mouthpiece as rivulets of sweat poured down his face. He was blasting out a tune until his eyes floated upward and all she could see were the whites. When he brought his trumpet down, he glanced at the girl in her pink nightgown. She froze on the landing. "Well, what have we got here?" he said, a smile breaking across his face. "Looks like a little night owl, don't she?" Hearing the deep rumble of his laughter, Pearl scurried back up the stairs.

Seven

≡

The Potawatomi, before they were driven west of the Mississippi, had a saying. The first white person to settle in Chicago was a Negro. Pearl learned this in Illinois history class. Jean Baptiste Point DuSable was a handsome well-educated Negro who settled in Chicagoua. Some say he'd come from Santo Domingo and planned a settlement for free Negroes on the shores of Lake Michigan. Others said he was the descendant of a slave and a French fur trader. For sixteen years he lived with his Potawatomi wife and two children at the site of the evil smell.

Outside of the picture of DuSable in her history book, Pearl had never seen many black men. The ones who came north settled near Twelfth Street Station where the train let them off. Few ventured to the North Side. Pearl imagined they would speak French, be tall and lean, with onyx skin. She hadn't envisioned the stout trumpeter with the coffee-colored skin, thick lips, and an accent that came from the depths of the delta. But week after week, as the music found her upstairs, awake in her bed, she made her way more boldly down to the saloon.

There was a space under the stairs and she tucked herself inside, thinking that if she curled into a ball, small enough, no one would know she was there. Of course everyone knew, but they pretended not to. It was dusty and cobwebbed, but Pearl was more comfortable in that space than she was in her own bed. Many nights after the bar closed Jonah carried her back upstairs, asleep, gently laying her in the middle, between her sisters, and pulling the covers up to her chin.

Napoleon took a liking to the girl with the dark eyes and hair to match who looked mysterious, shadowy, to him. She was plain, it was true, not like the fiery sisters she was sandwiched between, but there was something about her Napoleon couldn't quite put his finger on. He'd see her crouched under the bar, her legs tucked beneath her nightie, gazing out as if she couldn't be seen. She had something the others seemed to be lacking. If he had to give it a word, he'd say that she was curious. She seemed to take everything around her in. Each night he waited for her to answer when he called, "Hey, girl, what's your name?"

Pearl crouched down, as if she could make herself into her namesake, a smooth rounded gem. But he could still see her. He called out and taunted her until finally, after seeing him week after week for months, in a whisper she told him. "I'm Pearl."

Napoleon was struck by her deep, throaty voice. "Pearl." He rolled her name around on his tongue like a marble. At any moment he knew she'd dart up the stairs. "I'm going to write a lullaby for you. The next time I see you, we'll have . . ." He hesitated, and then chuckled, "We'll have an oyster for Pearl." Then he picked up his trumpet as she stayed hidden under the stairs.

Pearl was growing used to the black man who laughed so loudly, but she feared he was saying these things to tease her. When Napoleon came to play on Monday nights, she remained in her bed, pretending to read or sew. Even Anna noticed that her insomniac daughter was no longer slipping downstairs when the music was playing. Her siblings were concerned that she was unwell, but after a visit to Dr. Rosen proved her to be sound, the family ignored her stubborn refusal to slip back down to the bar. But she was listening for what she hoped would be a song written for just her. All through the long winter and into the next spring she didn't hear it and thought he'd forgotten, but Napoleon wanted to make it right. When he played the first version for Maddy, she said, "Why are you writing a song for a white girl?"

Napoleon shrugged, "Because I want to." And then he added as an afterthought, "Because I think she's afraid."

"What's she got to be afraid of?" Maddy asked, hands planted on her wide hips.

"I don't know," Napoleon replied. "She just is."

Then Maddy softened, "Well, you don't want to make her cry, do you? Write a happy tune." She was right about that, the way she was right about most things. Napoleon changed the tempo until it was light and airy as angel-food cake. He put in a little laughing sound with a few barnyard animals, including a neighing horse, thrown in. But still he wasn't satisfied. He worked with the Judge who moved the melody to the upper registers, lightened the tone, and played the chords an octave higher as well.

When it was ready, Napoleon went back to Chimbrova's to play for Pearl. It had been weeks since he'd seen her, sneaking down to the landing, and he wondered if she was all right. He said to the crowd, "We're going to play a song for the little girl. It's a blues lullaby I wrote to help her go to sleep. It's called 'An Oyster for Pearl.'"

Pearl was lying in bed, her eyes open, with Ruby and Opal slumped against her, when the simple chords rose through the floorboards. She heard a pig oink and a car honk, the sharp awakening of the trumpet before it settled in to a lullaby. When she heard the sweet melody, she knew this song was for her. It lured her out of bed and down the stairs, first to the landing, and then under the steps where she hid with her knees to her chin. The tune was soft and lilting, a hush, but with a little swing laid under the melody. She listened as he played it through.

When he saw her, Napoleon shifted his melody and improvised on his tune. She listened as if she'd waited her whole life for someone to play this song for her. This was no hand-me-down. Nobody else had this first. It was all hers and she wrapped herself in it like a blanket where she'd find her rest.

Eight

In the fall of 1917 Leo Lehrman took out a loan to hire six Slovakian women who could make the smallest stitches in the world. In the old country these women made lace, sewed the most diminutive of flowers onto lapels, embroidered monograms on the handkerchiefs of gentlemen. They made wedding gowns and tablecloths that would be considered priceless in fifty years. That year, America entered the Great War. Recruiting parades were marching up and down Michigan Boulevard, blasting away on John Philip Sousa, and Leo hired women to sew trademarks onto baseball caps.

They sat, hunched together on one bench, dressed in plain cloth dresses with bright-colored babushkas on their heads. If Benny was early and his order wasn't ready yet, he plunked himself down and watched the Slovakian women pulling thread through the thick denim cloth. He was amazed at the precision of their stitches, the tiny strokes they made so swiftly that the human eye could barely see.

Benny peered at their pursed lips, the concentrated stares at the fabric before them. Leaning forward, he watched the rise and fall of their breasts. Feigning interest in their stitches, he could look down their blouses. If he leaned forward a little more, he saw the dark circle where their nipples began. While he barely noticed the ruby-mouthed women at the tavern where Honey Boy played, Benny couldn't keep his eyes off of these.

One afternoon at the caps workroom the most buxom of the women patted the bench beside her and invited Benny to sit down. She kept sugar candy, the flavor of cherries and oranges, wrapped in paper, in a pocket of her apron. She offered him a piece as if he were a child. When she laughed, her front teeth flashed gold. She was not beautiful, but there was a pungent odor to her that seemed to come from deep inside. Marta had pendulous breasts that swayed with each stroke of the needle. As the thread came through, her breasts rocked forward and, as she pulled the thread out, they fell back.

As he waited for his next round of deliveries, he watched. Like a dog he sniffed her. He wanted to run his tongue along her thick arm and taste her. As he felt the throbbing in his groin, Benny couldn't help but wonder if at last he'd fallen in love. He didn't notice his father, emerging from his office to survey the floor. "Don't just sit around," his father yelled, causing Benny to leap into the air, which brought tears of laughter down the Slovakian women's faces. "Make yourself useful. Sweep up if you've got nothing better to do." It angered Benny that his younger brothers had their paper routes and could play ball after school. His father didn't make them sweep the factory floor. Even as he dragged the broom, Benny's eyes lingered over Marta's breasts.

When his father at last told him to go, he gathered up his schoolbooks and left. He climbed the stairs to their apartment and, when he saw no one was home, slipped into his mother's sewing room. The sewing room was the only place in the dark dingy apartment that was not impeccably clean. On the floor Hannah kept a basket filled with bits of cloth. Colored spools hung from hooks, nailed into the wall. Thread was strewn across the floor. Benny never went willingly into this small, cramped space. He only entered if Hannah needed to fit him for a new pair of trousers or to fetch something; otherwise he stayed out.

He couldn't bear seeing the picture of the four of them—the only picture that existed that his mother kept on the dresser. It was in winter and they were all lined up around a sled. In the center was Harold with his crooked smile. There were no other family pictures on display. Leo didn't believe in pictures or keepsakes.

He didn't believe that the past should be commemorated or even remembered.

Benny couldn't bring himself to look at the picture any more than he could bring himself to look at the pencil marks on the wall—the ones Hannah made to show them how much they'd grown. Above each line a name was scrawled. Harold's stopped abruptly a few years ago while the others had gone on, inch by inch, over the years. At the funeral Benny had vowed to name his firstborn after him. Like his mother he had preferred Harold to the others. His brother Arthur never got his jokes, and Ira was the opposite, almost too fast, ambitious for all the wrong reasons. Even as a small boy he tried to sell Benny things he didn't want like a broken toy or a tattered shirt. Ira had get-rich schemes. He wanted to own retail stores. But Harold had that big smile. He'd grinned from the moment he was born. He laughed at shoes, at wooden spoons, at silly faces. He'd laughed at Benny's jokes even though he was too young to understand them. When they crossed the street, he took Benny's hand.

Benny couldn't forget the slackness of the rope that should have been taut. The swirls of thick snow as he staggered, calling Harold's name. What haunted Benny most was an image of his little brother, the smile waning, as he searched for a way back, a doorway to huddle in, a place to escape the cold. Benny did not want to think that Harold had called out for him. That he'd cried as he fumbled like a blind person, shouting his brother's name. Why didn't their names meet somewhere in the center of that storm? Why wasn't there a place where they found each other? Sometimes at night Benny woke up, trembling, thinking he'd heard someone calling him.

The sewing room was the place where Hannah lost herself. Here she allowed cloth to drop to the floor. She could make a mistake and rip it out. Not like the other mistakes she'd made like letting Leo send her boys out in the snow. Then letting him blame it on Benny. It was here that Hannah allowed herself to cry, and when she was done crying, she sewed a hem or fixed a sleeve. She gazed at herself in the mirror and resigned herself to the fact that she was not a pretty woman. She was too dark and small to be pretty, but she was sturdy and trustworthy, and even if her husband had never really loved her, he respected her. And that, Hannah understood, was something, too.

Though Benny had rarely gone into that room since Harold's death, unless he had to fetch something, now he did. It seemed as if he became lost inside his mother's inner life, the same way as she. She floated here, in a maze of pin cushions and needles, patterns and thread. Once he found the pattern for a small winter jacket and he knew it was intended for Harold. Though years had passed, this still made Benny weep.

But since the Slovakian women had come to work at Lehrman's Caps, Benny found himself drawn to the sewing room. He lived in a household of men and grief. Now it was as if Marta inhabited this room. After school, if no one was home, Benny opened the door and went in. Though the pattern for Harold's winter jacket had been folded away, he was careful not to look at the picture of the four boys in the sled or at the pencil marks of their heights on the wall.

He vanished as his mother did among the scraps of cloth and thread. He touched the spools with his fingers, let his hands wander in the basket of cloth, and thought of Marta with her earthy smells and her golden teeth. As he grew hard, he took a scrap he knew his mother would never miss. Some scraps felt better than others. Wool and denim rubbed him raw. He dug deep into the basket for cotton and flannel and when he found a piece that suited him, Benny sat on the small cot that was usually a clutter of patterns and cloth and envisioned Marta in this room, perhaps at the sewing machine, her pendulous breasts swaying back and forth with each stroke as he leaned forward until he could see the dark crescent where her nipple began.

When he came in the scrap of cloth, Benny tossed it out the window—for the sewing room looked over the open garbage cans in the alleyway. He looked to make sure no one was coming, then took careful aim. Once or twice he had to dash down to the alleyway to retrieve the wad of cloth that missed the can. Then he rearranged the scraps in the basket and tiptoed out of the room.

On days when he had no deliveries, Benny raced home. He was in his last year of school and he paid little attention to his studies. Hannah did her shopping in the late afternoon and often, if he hurried, he could get an hour or so alone before anyone arrived. He'd sit at the piano, roughing out whatever ideas he had in his head. Sometimes he just fiddled, trying to remember a tune he'd heard the last time he listened to Honey Boy. He found he could stand in the alleyway and figure out some of the chords. Then he rushed home and tried to remember them.

He lost interest in everything else. Even when Hannah cooked his favorite dishes of chicken with prunes and kasha, he ate with distraction. She would lay ironed shirts on his bed or try to run a comb through his hair. Though she complained that he couldn't leave the house like that, he'd throw on his wrinkled clothes from the day before, grab the dirty cap he wore from his father's factory, and head out the door.

He'd begun wearing the cap a few weeks before when he found it on the cutting room floor. It was a reject with a mismatched seam. He dusted it off, then slipped it on his head. The simple brown cap fit his head as if it had been made for him. It had no trademark or even "Lehrman's Caps" written inside. But Benny liked its blankness. He wore it all the time, even inside the house and during meals, until his father yelled at him to take it off.

One Monday afternoon shortly after he began wearing the cap, Benny got on a streetcar that took him a few miles west. It was a route he knew well, though he had not gone for some time. Once again Benny found himself climbing the dingy stairs. He knocked and at first thought no one was home. He wasn't even sure if his old piano teacher still lived there. He realized how foolish this was—to return after being away so long.

Then he heard the shuffling and soon Mr. Marcopolis opened the door. The odor of tinned fish and stale socks was not so different from what Benny found in his own apartment, and he shuddered with the thought that this was what his life could be. In his wrinkled shirt and uncombed hair, Benny thought he'd end up just like this.

Mr. Marcopolis stared at Benny as he opened the door. "Benjamin, this is a surprise," he said. "To what do I owe the pleasure?"

As he heard the door close behind him, Benny took a deep breath. The apartment hadn't changed since he'd last come for a lesson when he was fifteen. The shelves were still cluttered with ancient books, stacks of yellowed and tattered sheet music, small sculptures of Mozart and Beethoven, an immortal cat named Schubert whose fur was everywhere, teacups and pipes, and a picture of his teacher when he was young and handsome, his hands perched over the keys as he gave a concert in Budapest. "I'm sorry I didn't do better," Benny muttered.

His teacher nodded. "So am I. You had great promise."

Benny hesitated. "I never really learned to read music very well, but I want to learn now. I can pay you." He also wanted to thank him for never telling his mother that he'd stopped coming to his lessons, but he thought better of it.

"And why now, when you haven't bothered before?"

For a moment Benny thought of giving his old teacher an answer he wanted to hear. Instead he admitted, "So I can write down what's in my head."

"And what is in your head?"

Benny shrugged. "The music I hear."

His teacher looked at him askance. "What music, Benny?"

"Jass," he said in a whisper. "I want to write it down."

Mr. Marcopolis dragged his feet toward the piano. "You've always been playing by ear, haven't you?" Benny nodded, staring down at his shoes. "Yes, of course you have. Would you like some tea?" Benny was surprised since Mr. Marcopolis had never offered him anything before. Without waiting for a reply his teacher shuffled into the kitchen, fumbled around, and returned with a tray of tea, honey, and biscuits. In silence they sipped the tea, and Benny munched on a biscuit that was stale. Then Mr. Marcopolis said, "When I was your age, I already had a concert career. I showed great promise, even from an early age."

Benny swallowed the dry cookie with a gulp of the tepid tea. "I don't want a concert career."

"I know that." Mr. Marcopolis took a last sip, then put his cup down. "Why don't you play for me what is inside your head?" Benny sighed, then shrugged. "As I'm sure you know by now, I won't tell your mother."

Benny sat down at the keyboard. He roughed out the refrains he'd learned at Honey Boy's door and improvised a few bars before he took off, jumping into the tune. Soon he forgot where he was. He forgot that he was in an apartment in a building and that an old man with aging bowels and unlived dreams was seated beside him with his eyes closed. Benny may as well have been a bird, circling in the sky, or a waking child, opening its eyes. As he played for no one in particular, he lost himself. He didn't notice the deepening shadows of the day or the clang of the trolleys in the street. When he ran out of steam, Benny stopped, and his teacher was silent for a while. When Mr. Marcopolis spoke, Benny was startled, for he'd forgotten that he wasn't alone in that room. "We'll begin with middle C," Dimitri Marcopolis said. "Do you know why it's called that?"

Benny struck the note. "Because it's in the middle of the keyboard."

"No," Mr. Marcopolis said, drawing lines on a sheet of paper. "Because it's in the center of the notations between the bass and treble clef." His teacher made flourishes, showing Benny the treble and bass clef. Then he drew a circle with a stem like a germinating seed. "That is middle C." He scribbled in a string of notes along the sides. "You read this upwards and downwards. You will learn the circle of fifths. The circle of fifths is a circle of intervals above middle C that increases, then drops the number of sharps and flats until it returns to middle C which has no flats and sharps."

Benny looked perplexed. "I don't understand . . ."

Mr. Marcopolis rose and moved his fingers up and down the keys showing Benny the circle of fifths. "Music isn't just about sound, about pleasure and entertaining. It is also about order." Mr. Marcopolis slid his fingers through a series of chords, built upon the circle of fifths. "You need to understand how the world started. You see, I believe the universe began with a collection of molecules and into those molecules a wave came that reverberated like a tone, and that tone set everything in motion. It all began with music."

Benny shook his head. "I'm not sure what this has to do with what I just played for you."

His teacher ignored the comment. "That is why when you look at the circle of fifths, you see that music and its harmony comes at perfect intervals, that everything is a circle, that all things go back to the beginning. It starts at middle C, then ripples out from there. The world finds its power in roundness and that roundness"—he drew another circle on the page—"that sense of return began with music. It is the source of the perfect order of the universe."

His teacher paused, sighing. "It is like religion." Benny didn't take his eyes off of him. "But somehow you understand this intuitively. It is where your perfect pitch comes from. You know how everything is in order and all things return to where they began." Benny shook his head. He had no idea what he was supposed to learn here. He was about to ask when Mr. Marcopolis rose and showed him to the door. "That's enough of a lesson for one day."

In the afternoons when he practiced, Benny resisted going into the sewing room for as long as he could. He portioned out his time. If he went right into the room, he'd lose precious moments at the piano. And vice versa. He found himself pulled in these two directions. No matter what he was doing, he had to listen for Hannah's footsteps when she came up the stairs. As soon as he heard her, he had to shift quickly from the blues to Beethoven. Or he'd have to rearrange the basket of scraps on the floor.

Benny noticed that the contents of the basket were dwindling. This was cause for concern. He thought of going to Abramovitch's Dry Goods and buying some fabric, cutting it into squares, but only Hannah would know what kind of cloth she used to make their shirts and pants. More and more Benny tried to stay at the piano and resisted opening the sewing room door. In this way his piano playing improved.

Nine

≡

In a jailhouse in New Orleans Joe "King" Oliver was planning ahead. He'd been sitting in a stinking cell for a night and the better part of a day. Because he'd argued with the cops, they'd stuck him all alone. It was Saturday and he was fairly certain that no one would spring him before Monday. So he had plenty of time to think. The night before a fight had broken out in the honky-tonk where he was playing. When the police arrived, they arrested everyone—including the band.

Ever since he returned from Chicago, Joe Oliver had had nothing but trouble. He spent enough nights in jail over the years to know that he didn't want to spend many more. The South wasn't safe for a black man. Train porters brought down copies of the *Chicago Defender*. He'd read of the Mississippi boy whom some white gentlemen had burned at the stake. Another boy who'd had his fingers and toes chopped off. Joe Oliver shook his head as if he could make those thoughts go away.

As he munched on a crust of bread, a mouse scurried into his cell. It came right in front of him and stood on its hind legs. Joe laughed. He held out a few crumbs and the mouse snatched them from Joe's palm and raced away. Joe rubbed his gums and spat onto the floor. Even a mouse wouldn't keep him company. His gums were mushy and in his spit he saw blood. He wanted to get out of the

South while he still had his chops. He was almost forty years old and he didn't know how much time he had. Jazz was migrating. Music was what the black man could do. It was his ticket. He'd go wherever it took him—even years later to Savannah, where he ended up a janitor with a pushcart and broom.

As soon as Joe Oliver got out of jail, he packed up his wife and little girl and headed back to Chicago. His band would come with. Maybe even that street urchin who blew the cornet like he was talking to the angels (or maybe the devil) would join him one of those days. That boy who walked all over him when he let him sit in. King Oliver would form the best band that there ever was. And he'd bring that rascal—the one they called Dippermouth—north with him. Some people have great talent. Others are born to recognize great talent. Joe Oliver had made his peace with the fact that he was the latter. In a few weeks he landed the gig at the Lincoln Gardens. He brought a sound with him that no one had ever heard. And they came from all over to listen.

It wasn't long before Benny was standing outside the Lincoln Gardens, listening to King Oliver's band. He hardly went to school anymore, and when he did, it was mostly to sleep. Benny liked to say that he was going to night school instead. The Stroll was his classroom. And he was studying all the time. Every chance he got, Benny traveled down Satan's Mile. He didn't mind the stench or the grit. He didn't mind being the only white boy for blocks. In fact, he welcomed it. And some even joked that in summer he turned dark enough; he could pass.

During the days in the cutting room Marta stared at him. He tried to avoid her gaze. She looked at him as if she saw right into him. She knew what he thought about her. What he did to her in his mind when he was alone. When she looked at him, he grew hard. He imagined all the ways he would touch her if he could. And now he thought that she might want him to touch her. Perhaps she longed for him the way he longed for her. Then he would have to do something. Something that despite his seventeen years he could only imagine but not quite believe.

He grew more and more shy of her, and the shyer he grew the

more scraps of his mother's cloth he tossed out the window into the garbage cans below until he began to worry that his mother might start to miss them. He began to scrounge around the sewing room, looking for bits of cloth he could throw in. He cut up what he thought was a scrap of denim until Hannah shouted at them in the evening that someone had taken a scissors to Arthur's new jacket. As he watched the scrap basket go down, Benny had no idea what to do.

One day when Benny was going off on a delivery, Marta motioned to him. "Come here," she whispered through her gold teeth. Her heavy breasts rose and fell. She looked flushed, blotchy. Feverish almost. He trembled. She was going to tell him something. She was going to tell him that she knew. Or perhaps she'd ask him to meet her after work. How old could she be? Twenty-five, thirty at the most.

Perhaps he'd meet her in the alleyway not far from Lehrman's Caps and lift her skirts, crushing her against a wall. Or in a room she stayed in nearby. But when he saw her face, he knew she would not ask him anything of the kind, and yet he also knew that he would do whatever she asked. Her eyes were red and puffy as if she had been crying. Then she asked him, "Can you do something for me?"

"Whatever you want," Benny said.

"I have a sick child at home," Marta began, her voice speaking to him for the first time in a barely intelligible English. "And she needs some medicine. She is alone and I am worried about her." It never occurred to Benny that Marta had a child or that, when she came to work, she worried about her. That those breasts he'd wasted his mother's cloth scraps on had suckled a baby. Though he didn't realize this yet, he would never think of her in the same way again. Whenever he started to imagine her, coupling against a doorway, lying half naked across the sewing bench, he would see the child.

"If you could take her this candy and this syrup." Marta whispered her request. She gave him the address. "Go to the fifth floor. Knock once. Wait. Then knock three times. This way she'll know I've sent you." There was a soft, pleading sound to her words. If Benny could just go after his deliveries into the old Slovakian neighborhood on the West Side, until he came to some dilapidated buildings she described. Hers was the third on the left, then up five flights, just take one transfer, not so far out of his way, really.

She handed him a small sack and a slip of paper with the address. Benny looked at the address. It was far out of his way. And he'd have to take two streetcars home, but Marta had such a worried look on her face. Her eyes begged him to go.

The streetcar toward Cicero was packed with women in babushkas who resembled Marta. Some got on with wailing children. Others carried oily fish, wrapped in newspapers. Their long skirts flopped across their wide hips. One woman got on with a squawking chicken. "Hey, lady, no live chickens on this bus," the driver told her. The woman spoke only Polish. Someone translated for her. With a shrug she snapped the chicken's neck in two.

Benny gazed at uninhabited lots filled with trash and broken glass. Children in rags played barefoot in the ruins. Benny felt the horror of these open spaces. It was in a lot such as these that Harold had disappeared. Some of the children had running sores, snot dripping from their noses. Men sat slumped in the entrances to buildings. When the driver announced his stop, Benny got off. A cold breeze blew across the vacant lots and down the alleyways. Glass shards cracked under his feet. Mangy dogs cowered.

He peered up at a building. Its ground-floor windows were boarded up as if there had been a fire. The façade was crumbling. He walked into the dreary entranceway and climbed up slowly, one step at a time, until he reached the fifth floor. The smells of lard and garlic weren't familiar to him, and his stomach began to turn. When he reached Marta's door, he knocked once as she'd told him to do. Paused, then knocked three times.

A girl opened the door. She had sallow skin, and her eyes were dark pits. When she coughed, he said, "I brought you some things from your mother." He wished he were on the Stroll, listening to some jass. But when he handed the child the candy, her eyes lit up. She invited him inside. Except for some breakfast dishes, the apartment was neat and clean, but tiny. Damp laundry hung on a line.

There was a cot in the kitchen where the child slept. Another cot sat in a corner of the living room and a curtain divided the space in two. Without going any farther he could see that there was no other room.

Each time the child coughed she clutched her chest. "Here, I brought you some medicine, too." Benny searched for a spoon and gave her the syrup that she took without making a face. After a few moments her cough seemed to lessen. There was even some color in her cheeks when she handed Benny a book. At last the girl spoke. "Would you read me a story?" Then she took his hand and led him to the couch.

He read her a story about a brother and sister who spend a day skating on a pond. Benny kept expecting something to happen— one of the children falling through the ice, a bad man coming. It wasn't much of a story really. Still it made Benny wish he could take the child skating. He wondered if she even knew what skating was. He imagined himself, gliding back and forth with her and the child laughing, a muffler around her neck.

He stayed with the girl until the early evening when it was already dark. Marta should have been home by now. Benny wondered if he should wait. But the girl had been alone when Benny got there. Surely she could spend time alone until her mother arrived. His own mother might be worried, but he couldn't help himself. There was a pot of soup on the stove. It was a watery bean soup with grease floating on the top. He wanted to taste it, but feared it was seasoned with lard or salt pork—meat that had never touched his lips. He heated the soup and fed it to the child who ate with a loud slurping noise. Then she lay down to rest. Benny did the dishes. He washed whatever was in the sink.

When he left, he put his hand on her feverish brow and kissed her on the cheek, and she smiled. He made his way down the dark stairwell. At the tram stop Benny gazed up and saw the child in a top floor window. He waved and she waved back. When the tram pulled away, the girl was still there.

Benny was planning on going home. He had every intention,

but he couldn't. He couldn't go back to that dreary apartment. He couldn't go back to his mother with her silent anguish and his father with those judgmental eyes. Or the brothers who acted as if he wasn't there. He'd tried, but he couldn't live up to what they wanted. He thought, I should go home. Instead he transferred to the streetcar heading east, then south, and hopped off at Twenty-Seventh Street. Music came from behind every door as Benny roamed, popping his head into clubs. Girls beckoned from alleys. He was tempted by "the white plague" as it was called down here. Women selling their bodies to satisfy white men's yearnings.

He listened for a piano player with his ear to the door. If he liked what he heard, he talked the bouncer into letting him in. It was easy because they didn't see many white boys in that part of town. He peeked into the Firefly Lounge where he heard a good stride piano and bribed the bouncer. The Firefly had tiny white lights flickering over the ceiling and the walls, blinking from under the dance floor. Benny had never seen fireflies, but in school he'd read about insects that illumined meadows and forests on a summer's night. This must be what a field of them looked like.

It was a mostly black crowd. Women in short dresses with fishnet stockings kicked their legs, shook their backsides, dancing the Slim Betty. They swayed as arms flew in the air. Nobody seemed to mind that a white boy stood in their midst. A good band was playing—a few horns, drums, piano, and bass. They were from down south and there was Dixieland in their beat. Benny listened, but he couldn't get the girl with her sallow skin and deep cough out of his mind. The band grated on him now. It was playing honky-tonk too loud and the air was thick with smoke and laughter. He left in the middle of the set and kept going south.

On the Stroll the lights were bright, and black men in shiny suits and spats ambled with pale-skinned women in furs, cloche hats pinned to their heads. He paused at the Lincoln Gardens where King Oliver had just opened for a three-month gig, and they were playing up a storm. But he wasn't in the mood for that up-tempo. He cut down a side street, thinking about where he wanted to go, when he heard that other horn. It wasn't like the Dixieland he'd listened to at the Firefly or outside the Lincoln Gardens. This was a mournful sound as if somebody was lost and couldn't get back.

The piano came in slowly. He was striding with his left hand while the right found a melody, just one note at a time. Then the beat picked up and the trumpet came back in louder and more sure. They were talking to each other. Looking up, he saw the cock's comb, blinking red. He'd heard that trumpet before. This wasn't the first time he'd stopped here to listen. He was drawn to the lilting horn and the easy pace of the piano. The huge bouncer in a red coat with gold buttons was only letting blacks in. Benny waited for him to make eye contact. He rolled up his sleeve. "Hey, look, I'm black."

The bouncer laughed, but still ignored him. Benny held out fifty cents, but the bouncer still acted as if Benny wasn't there. Finally he pulled out a dollar. The enormous man looked at it disdainfully. "Time for your music lesson, son?" he asked.

Humiliated, Benny put his money away. But the bouncer opened the door anyway, and when Benny just stood there, he said, "You see me holding this door open for someone else?" Benny shook his head. "Now gimme that dollar."

Benny thrust it into the outstretched fist and rushed down a narrow corridor, painted black with almost no light at the end of it. The corridor led into a smoky, gin-soaked room with black walls, a single amber light above the bandstand. Waiters in white shirts carried trays with drinks and sandwiches. Black men in gray fedoras and women in sequined dresses with feathered hats drank whiskey and tapped their cigarette holders to the beat.

Benny stood in the back for the first set, but he wanted to see. During the break he elbowed his way to the bandstand, and when the trumpeter came back on, he glanced at Benny, who hunched down. The piano player was off-beat and didn't do quite what he was supposed to do. Benny listened as the left hand wandered up and down the keys. The right hand held the melody but in a strange way, sometimes smashing down two keys next to each other. Benny liked the fact that he didn't know where the piano was going to take him.

The trumpeter was a fat man who could blow. He picked up on

the piano's tune, then went off on his own. He puffed up his cheeks, pursed his lips, and stretched for some high notes Benny didn't know existed. Benny didn't understand how so much sound could come out of three valves. He closed his eyes and listened as the trumpeter bent notes, then reached for a sad sound. Empty rooms, lost dogs, late-night bars all came into his mind.

But then the music seemed to go off and laugh at itself as if it had all been some big joke. It honked and oinked. Screeched as if cops were on your tail or you'd fallen down drunk. There was always something to laugh about. He reached for another high note, flubbed it. Then just to let you know he'd done it on purpose, hit it dead center like a bull's-eye.

Even though Benny was jostled from side to side, he stared up at the bandstand as if nailed to the spot. Everything he'd ever known about the world—that gravity holds you down and mothers are there when you get home, that baseball has nine innings, and sleep awaits you at the end of the day—was turned upside down. He forgot about his brother lost in the snow and the dead girl he'd danced with when the *Eastland* went down. He forgot about Marta's child, home alone and sick. He even forgot he was a person in a crowd, not a very old person at that, just a boy. His arms and legs all melted into one. He wasn't anywhere but inside the music he was hearing. It took him to where he wanted to be. On a train, heading out of town. Away; that's where it took him. He went away.

Ten

When the knocking began, Pearl was sweeping the floor. She was making a dust pile in the center of the room. She enjoyed helping her brothers in the saloon after school, washing glasses, polishing the bar. As she dusted and swept, she hummed the refrain Napoleon said he was writing for her. For the past two years he'd had been coming to the bar on Monday nights with a piano or bass player. He arrived like clockwork at eight o'clock and stayed until midnight, when he packed it up and headed back to the South Side to jam with his friends. At Chimbrova's he tried out a lot of his jazzy numbers. But he was writing his "Night Owl Blues" for her. It was a variation on the tune he'd played to lure her down the stairs when she was afraid to sleep in her own bed, and she sang it to herself as she swept, dancing with her broom.

The saloon didn't open until four, but the banging persisted. At last when Pearl cracked the door, Gwendolyn Walenski, the butcher's wife, stormed in. Half a dozen other women followed. They were her neighbors, and she greeted them even as they rushed past her, kicking up the dust pile she'd just made. They knelt in the middle of the saloon floor in their gray wool dresses, opened their tattered black Bibles, and began to beat their breasts in prayer. Though she asked politely, Pearl could not get them to leave.

Anna was beginning the arduous task of cleaning the house with a feather for Passover when Pearl came up to tell her that the praying women were back. Pearl had never actually seen them before. They had stayed away for months after her father died. His death remained a mystery. The police claimed he was drunk and stumbled in front of an oncoming car, but Anna swore he never touched a drop. Few Jewish *randars* did. That's what made Jews good saloonkeepers. But no one could explain how he'd fallen behind the garbage cans. Or why a shiny nickel was pressed into the palm of his right hand.

After the *Eastland* the praying women seemed to drift off for good, but now they were back. "They won't leave," Pearl said.

"We'll see about that," Anna replied, racing downstairs where Gwendolyn Walenski and her followers were on their knees, Bibles raised in clenched fists. "I need you to move out of the way, Gwendolyn," Anna said, "so our customers can come into the bar." Gwendolyn Walenski knelt in the center of the saloon, shaking her Bible and praying that the Chimbrova family would accept the drys—despite the threats by Anna's older boys that they'd lift Gwendolyn Walenski up and remove her back to the street.

But the round, squashed-looking woman, refused to budge. She'd had her own share of grief. A drunk for a husband, a half-dozen children who hadn't survived past the age of five, though she still had as many at home. "When we get the vote," she threatened Anna from the floor in her plain gray frock, "the first thing women will do is abolish the liquor that takes our men into the bars."

"Well, you should know, Gwendolyn," Anna said, taunting her with the fact that her fat, blood-soaked husband, the butcher, was a regular at the saloon. "Maybe if you kept your husband happy, he wouldn't have to come here." But the woman wouldn't get up. As Anna looked at her neighbor on her knees, pounding her Bible, she grabbed Pearl by the shoulders and pulled her to her chest. "Here, Gwendolyn," Anna said, giving Pearl a shake. "If your work is charity, then why don't you take a few of these home?"

Her mother's fingers dug into her flesh. Anna held Pearl out for the butcher's wife to see. As Gwendolyn Walenski looked her up and down, Pearl trembled, thinking she would die if this woman offered to take her home. But the butcher's wife rose and they all left.

Afraid she would be sent away, Pearl grew more restless. The memory of her mother, dragging her along the shore, had never left her, but it had never been articulated either. It was like a dream, something she couldn't be sure of, but she knew. It was true. It shaped itself inside of her into a round, brown nut, a stone that took the form of silence.

At times she seemed to drift to the brink of despair, and her sisters nudged her, asking what was wrong. At night Ruby prodded. "Tell me, Pearly. Something is bothering you." Though Ruby tried, night after night, Pearl had developed a stubborn streak. She could not, or would not, say what she feared. Who would believe her anyway? She had learned to keep this to herself. And many more things.

Though she was on the brink of adolescence Pearl acted like a child. She clung to Anna, terrified that her mother would get rid of her as she'd tried once before. She would make her live with the butcher's wife. The smell of red meat sickened Pearl. Anna had to pry the girl's fingers off of her in order to get any work done. Pearl took to hiding in closets, avoiding her mother's gaze, thinking that perhaps it would be best, instead of making her presence felt, to make her mother forget about her altogether.

Anna was too distracted by the costs of keeping the family intact to notice what was happening with Pearl. She tried to send the girl out to play, to wrest her off her arm when she clung, to scold her for spending her time hiding in the cedar closet. One day, exasperated, Anna turned to Jonah, "Why don't you take her to the beach?"

But Jonah had never gotten over his fear of water. "Ask Moss," he said. And Moss, who spent his nights pouring drinks at the saloon but had little to occupy himself during the day, said he would. Now Pearl was all the more frightened. The last place she wanted to go was to the shore, but Moss agreed to take his restless sister to the lake for a swim. Maybe a trip to the beach, it was reasoned, would calm her down.

Pearl liked her brother Moss. He had a big smile with white teeth that were very straight and a nice square jaw. In winter he took her for sleigh rides without her having to ask. He was handsome, the way a tree trunk is handsome, sturdy and straight, and Pearl felt she could count on him. Yet she panicked at the thought of Moss taking her alone. Was he part of some secret plan to forget her? To leave her there? Or worse. Pearl was plagued by a memory that felt more like a nightmare. Of her feet at the shore's edge and her mother's hand resting on the small of her back.

Perhaps Anna had decided it was time to let some of the children go. Pearl had heard stories of families with too many children who left one on a streetcar or in an amusement park. Recently identical twins were found in a trash can with a note pinned to their shirts. Other mothers had drowned their children in basins like kittens. And Moss was the perfect one to take her, wasn't he? The gentle Moss whom she trusted above all the others, not like Jonah who had slept in that morning as his brothers drowned. He would be the one to leave her there. Pearl pleaded with her mother not to send her. "What a stupid girl," Anna said, shaking her head. "She doesn't want to go for a swim."

Anna suggested Moss take Opal and Ruby as well—an idea that immediately made Pearl feel relieved, for surely her mother wouldn't try to get rid of all three of them at once. And even if she did, the gem sisters could fend for themselves. But Ruby, who had begun painting small canvases of bowls of fruit and landscapes of forests with strange beasts, didn't want to go, and Anna had second thoughts that the sun would burn Opal's fair skin or darken it with freckles. So Pearl borrowed a bathing costume from Ruby, and Moss took her alone.

They rode the streetcar from Douglass Park to the Twenty-Fifth Street Beach. From time to time Moss glanced at Pearl with her eyes closed, her head down. "Pearly," he'd say, pointing out the window, "look at that policeman with his funny cap." But Pearl would not lift her head or open her eyes. She rode with the same sobriety and resignation as someone heading to her own demise.

The lake wasn't far, just a streetcar ride and a transfer away, but Pearl had never really seen it, except on her birthday, that day when the *Eastland* went down—a day she preferred not to recall. Except for that day, Pearl had never been more than a few blocks from home. Nor had she wanted to. Now the streetcar rocked back and forth, and she grasped the armrest as Moss, having given up trying to make conversation with his sullen sister, rode silently beside her. There was a sandbox in the middle of the car that children played in. Whenever someone threw up, the conductor took a scoop of sand and tossed it on the vomit.

When they reached the lake, Pearl stopped on the sidewalk, stunned. The morning when her mother had dragged her to the shore, the lake had been gray, and her eyes had been fixed on her mother's mad stare. Now it was a sunny day and the water was the color of marbles. The world had turned itself upside down and heaven was on the ground. She could not believe the expanse of blue, the mirror-like surface of the inland sea that stretched before her. Pearl kicked off her shoes and ran across the sand. Her feet burned as she raced toward the water. "Pearl, wait," Moss shouted, panicked that she'd dive in and drown. He ran to catch up, grabbing her just as she was about to fling herself into the breaking waves. He took her by the hand.

The sandy bottom gave way under her feet. For a moment she was afraid she would sink. She clutched his arm, but Moss held her firmly, guiding her into the water. He splashed water on her face and she splashed him back. Then he held out his arms and tilted her back. He kept a hand cupped beneath her head as he moved her through the water and glided her across the surface of the lake. She stared up at the clouds, and beneath her the water seemed like an enormous cool bed, one she'd never have to share.

That night Pearl slept as she hadn't in years—as smooth and untroubled a sleep as the water where she swam. She slept with her legs straight, her arms stretched out, nestled between her sisters, floating as Moss had taught her. Every day after that Pearl begged Moss to take her again to the lake, and Anna told him he should because it made her sleepy. But Moss had to tend the saloon and promised to take her again on Friday if it didn't rain.

On Friday Pearl was up early, dressed in her bathing clothes and towel. "Please, Moss. Let's go." She tugged at him to hurry and polished the bar and stacked glasses on the shelves to help him. They took the same streetcars they had earlier in the week, and this time Pearl memorized the route. It was the last time she'd need someone to take her. Once again Pearl raced to the water, but now Moss was at her side.

He taught her to put her face in the water and blow bubbles as he counted to ten. He helped her lie on her stomach and do the dead man's float. He kept her from sinking. Then Moss dove and disappeared. Pearl screamed with glee when he threw himself up out of the water like a giant fish. He showed her how to blow bubbles and breathe until she ran out of breath. The first time she found herself underwater, Pearl came up gagging, but Moss told her to keep her mouth closed and her eyes shut. She pinched her nose with her fingers. Something was different, but she couldn't explain. She dove again and for a moment did not breathe. This time she opened her eyes. Everything was blue. She dove once more, now without her fingers on her nose, her eyes wide open. There in the water, before she came up coughing, Pearl found what had been eluding her for so long.

She plunged deep, her hands dipping into the silty bottom, and stayed under until Moss began flailing about, searching for her. She rose up, laughing, water splashing everywhere. From then on, whenever she could, Pearl went to the lake whose steely blue-gray had frightened her so long ago. Except when ice floes clinked on the surface, Pearl dove into the chilly waters of the inland sea. She found what she had been searching for in closets, under beds, and the bar beneath the stairs. In the cold and turbulent waters of Lake Michigan, Pearl discovered the absence of sound.

Eleven

As Napoleon Hill walked out into the city, a light snow fell. It was the first snow of the season, and it was early this year—a harbinger of things to come. He'd never gotten used to the Chicago cold, the harsh wintry winds that blew down from the Arctic and landed at his front door. He opened his mouth and caught flakes on his tongue as if he could win them over. He was humming his "Night Owl Blues," the tune he was still trying to get right in his head. He liked going to Chimbrova's saloon. He didn't mind playing for white folks, though he knew the owners of the Rooster wouldn't like it.

Napoleon had his ambitions, and he was getting ready to move on. He just had to come up with a plan. He wanted to play some of the fancier places, like the Apex or the Rendez-Vous Café. Walking along, he tightened the wool scarf around his neck. The snow made him shiver. He needed a drink. Maybe two. He could use a little bourbon. Something to warm his insides. The cold was in his bones. It took hold of him like a woman who won't let you go. At times he couldn't shake them off either. He had to sneak away and hide. Underfoot the ground was slick. He watched his step as he went. He was a big man, and it was a long way down.

Coffee, crackling bacon, the scent of baking bread wafted his way. The sounds of eggs frying over and easy. Wrapping his coat around him, he tried to resist stopping at the diner as he passed.

Maddy would have breakfast waiting when he got home. But that white boy had unnerved him. The way he sat, staring straight ahead. He'd didn't come for a good time the way most boys did. He sat with his arms folded as if he'd come for his history lesson.

"Kinda early for breakfast," the waitress said, taking a pencil from behind her ear. She was blond with a plump ass and skin white as snow. When she tilted her head, he saw the dark roots of her hair. Still he liked what he saw.

Napoleon shrugged, still humming his "Night Owl Blues." "It's my time," he said.

She looked at the horn case. "You must be a musician? Only musicians order eggs and grits at three a.m."

"When does the rest of the world eat breakfast?" Napoleon asked. Napoleon liked white girls. He was drawn to the paleness of their skin. Maybe it was because of his high-yellow mother.

"Oh, around eight, when I get off work."

"Then I'll have to come by around eight sometime."

She gave him a nod, almost a wink, and went to clear a table. "Why don't you do that?" she said.

"I think maybe I will." As she walked away, he tried to imagine that jaunty backside tucked under him. His thoughts shifted to Maddy. Though he often wished she was, Maddy wasn't this kind. She was a large woman, and he'd never been drawn to large ones. She had a birthmark on the side of her cheek that in a white woman would have been port-wine red, but in a black woman was a shade of evergreen. He'd never wanted her in the way a man should be to a woman. Nor she him, for that matter. Not as far as he could tell.

Maybe because he hadn't, he'd lived with her since he came north. She took care of him when he needed taking care of and he helped her in the ways a man can help a woman around the house, without having to be a real man.

It was one of those "meant-to-bes," as Maddy liked to say. He thought that as well, ever since a few years ago when he'd climbed on the Panama Limited with his duffel, his horn, and a cold fish sandwich. Senator Sam with whom he'd come to play had sent him his ticket, one way north. He settled in the colored section across the aisle from a large black woman with three children. It was a cool night for New Orleans, and Napoleon kept his coat on. He stared out at the station. A sliver of a moon shone overhead.

The engine started up. A long whistle, then a toot. He'd worked the rails and been on trains for years, but he always got the same thrill. The chug of the engine. The way the wheels started slow, then faster, building. The steady 4/4 time. As the train pulled out, he saw the windy streets, the flickering lights of New Orleans. The old crumbly buildings with the wrought-iron balconies, the arched porticoes. Soon they were passing the shores of Lake Pontchartrain, the kudzu-choked bayou, past the cotton fields and catfish ponds, the dirt-floor shacks and barefoot childhoods.

With his finger to his lips he'd kissed it all good-bye. He'd wake up in a place he'd never been. That was all right with him. He'd improvise as he went along the way he always had. He never knew what he was doing from one day to the next. He never did the same thing twice. Still as the train gathered speed, he thought maybe he was making a mistake. Leaving home. Not that he had much of a home to leave. But the woman who sat across from him made him miss something he'd never had.

It wasn't long before he sniffed what she had in her carpetbag. His mouth watered as she began to reach in and as if by magic pulled out a bucket of potato salad, buttery corn bread, still warm in a towel, a tub of three-bean salad, a thermos of chicory coffee, beignets, and enough fried chicken to get them to Canada and back. Napoleon held his fish sandwich in his hand. It felt cold and limp as he watched those children bite into the corn bread that brought steam to their faces.

He couldn't bear sitting there with those smells rising from the woman's tubs. He couldn't help himself. He glanced her way. She wore a thin, brown dress that was too tight. Her stomach bulged. The dark shawl she wrapped around her shoulders was frayed and her hair flecked with white, but he didn't think she was older than thirty-five. She had thick arms and, as she opened the tub of chicken, he forced himself to look away. But she turned to him. "Can you blow more than your nose?" she said.

Startled, he nodded. "Yes, ma'am, I believe I can."

"I heard you once on one of those riverboat cruises. You're good," she said. "You are very good." She told him her husband had just passed on (which was a lie because she'd never married the father of her children nor was he dead, but she'd never bother to correct it), and they were moving north to live near her sister. Then she put the bucket of chicken and three-bean salad and corn bread on the seat beside her. "Help yourself," she said. He moved across the aisle, cradling the bucket of chicken in his lap. The chicken was still hot. Salty grease slipped down his throat.

He reached for another piece, then another. Maddy saw right away that you couldn't share with him. He had to have it all. After he finished off his third piece of corn bread, Maddy said, "I'm afraid I'm going to have to ask you to pay for this meal."

Napoleon looked at her, stunned. He had enough money to get him to Chicago, but not much more. "I'm not sure I can now, ma'am, but . . ."

"You can pay me by blowing something on that trumpet of yours."

Napoleon's face lit up. He rubbed up his lips to warm them, then took down his horn. Clearing the mouthpiece, he blew his spit valve a few times on the floor. He ran up and down the scales, then entertained the whole car by playing "Bayou Blues," then "Wild Bird" and a few songs of his own. When he put his trumpet down, it was close to midnight, and the passengers were starting to drift off to sleep. Already the children were huddled inside their coats.

He played one last tune, a lullaby his grandmother used to sing that he riffed on. Then he put his horn down and curled up against Maddy Winslow's warm side. He hadn't meant to spend the night there, but found he couldn't go back to his seat either. It was soft against her fleshy arm, and he fell fast asleep. It grew colder in the night, and the coldness entered his bones. When his head slumped on Maddy Winslow's shoulder, she tried to push him away. But he weighed twice what she did, so she let him sleep and wrapped some of her shawl around him.

He slept with only the sense of the train and its trajectory north. He was aware of softness, an oily smell, flesh, and hair. It was the longest he'd ever stayed beside a woman at one time. He woke groggy, amazed. Outside everything was flat, stretching as far as he could see. A whiteness burned his eyes. He had never seen snow before and now he saw miles of it. Putting his fingers to the window, he shook with the cold. His breath made a circle on the pane.

Maddy poured him some of her chicory coffee, which was still warm, and Napoleon drank that and munched on a beignet. At noon the conductor called out "Cairo, Illinois" in his throaty, singsongy voice. They were in the "Egypt" part of the state, and Maddy gave him a shove. "Get up," she said. "Go to the club car. You're in the North now."

"What do you mean?"

"You're across the Ohio. Go order a sandwich. Sit next to a white man. Do whatever you want."

Napoleon looked at her, surprised. "You mean I can go anywhere?"

"Anywhere you like." Maddy nodded. But Napoleon had no money for a sandwich and he didn't want to leave her. He'd tasted her chicken and stared into the greenish-black birthmark on her face. He stayed at her side, like an animal in the warmth of its den, until dusk when the conductor called out, "Last stop, Chicago."

As he stepped off the train, the icy wind from the lake stung him. He'd been many things in his life, but he'd never been cold like this. His hands went numb as he helped Maddy Winslow and her children get off the train. Maddy's sister was on the platform, waiting for her. She leaped on them with hugs and had winter coats which she threw over the children. No one was there to meet him. He thought Senator Sam or one of the boys might show, but when no one did, he figured he'd find a rooming house for a night or two. As they walked off, Napoleon stood shivering on the platform, icy shards stinging his skin, his horn case dangling from his hand. The platform was freezing and deserted. When Maddy paused and looked back at him, Napoleon just stared. "Well," she said, "are you coming or not?"

As Napoleon made his way up the stairs, he heard the rattle of dishes, water running in the sink. Maddy was getting up. She rose by five every day to get the kids off to school, then on to the hotel where she worked as a maid. She also got up at five to give Napoleon the bed.

It was the bargain they'd struck when he'd followed her to her sister's place and later to this cottage. The first few nights she'd given him the couch. But when she noticed him getting home after four, Maddy had said, "You know, I'm crawling out of bed at about when you drag yourself in." So it began. He slipped into the sheets as she slipped out. Once in a blue moon he slept with her, but not as man and woman exactly. For years they'd danced around each other, being cozy, wrestling, almost becoming lovers before settling into the comfort they knew now.

The Cuddle Inn was what Napoleon liked to call the room he inhabited with Maddy. It was more like mother and son, and it suited them both. When the chill got into his bones and he couldn't shake it, she let him huddle against her flesh. When he had too much to drink and couldn't lose the bad thoughts that swirled in his head, she'd hold him until it passed. But most nights, just before dawn, she was up, making sandwiches, straightening the children's rooms, waiting so she could leave for the hotel when he came home.

For years now they'd lived in a cottage along the railroad tracks—one of those cottages blacks had been taking over since they began moving north. It wasn't the best place, but it wasn't the worst either. They'd gotten used to the rumble of the trains and the smoke. And Maddy was happy to have a man living in the house, especially when she left for work if the kids were home. They were like a family, not a real family, but a makeshift one. As much family as Napoleon had known in a very long time.

Inside the yellowed walls of their cottage Maddy stood at the stove. A cold wind seeped in, making her shiver. She was still in her robe, heating up biscuits and gravy, when Napoleon walked in. She had a pot of rice and red beans warming. "Morning, Miss Rice and Red Beans," he said, the way he did every morning as he staggered in.

"Morning, Your Majesty," she said, poking fun at his nickname, scooping his biscuits onto a plate, ladling the gravy, pouring him a mug of coffee. "I bet you're hungry after your show."

"I could eat a cow and more," Napoleon said. "Especially if you fixed it." It never mattered that he had just eaten. Napoleon had an appetite he couldn't explain. He had to control himself, but controlling himself wasn't what he did best and he knew it. Some nights when he played, it was nothing for him to have a fried chicken and mashed potato meal at six, a plate of meatloaf and pork pie at eight, then steak and eggs at midnight, not including desserts and all the ice cream he could eat. And still have room for breakfast when he got home.

He could always eat again. He could drink a fish tank of coffee and still go to sleep. "So will you be here when the kids get home?" she asked, as she did each morning.

"I'll be asleep," he said with a laugh. "Just like always."

Maddy was fretting about the children being alone that evening. A few nights a week she worked a second job in a restaurant, tidying up the bathroom and handing white ladies paper towels, wiping their toilet seats dry, for tips. She kept air fresheners and perfumes, combs and hand lotion in the bathroom, too, and the women were always appreciative and she did all right with her tips. Those nights the kids were on their own. "Don't worry," he said, "I won't leave them before eight."

They should have made more of a life together, Napoleon thought as he watched her getting ready to leave for work. Perhaps things would have been different if they'd had a child. He would have liked to have had a son. Not a girl. He could not bear to think of a daughter with a man who took advantage such as himself. But a boy would have been different. He could teach the boy whatever he knew. But it hadn't happened. Not with Maddy nor with another woman.

"You'll be back by midnight?"

She nodded, rifling in the drawer for something. She was always rummaging around. Her cottage of two bedrooms and a kitchen was crammed with sepia prints—old pictures of her with her pretend husband and the kids on picnics, wedding pictures, crushed bouquets, locks of hair tied with ribbons. She was always searching for something she couldn't find.

With a sigh and a shake of the head, her gaze fell on the postcard of Idlewilde taped above the sink. Idlewilde was a resort in Michigan where blacks could go, and Napoleon had sent it to her when he'd gone to play a gig. It was a picture of a clear, blue lake, surrounded by pines, and a hotel on the water. On the back he'd scribbled how the moon glistened and fireflies lit the woods like lanterns. Black children jumped off docks, shouting, and the air smelled of citronella candles and ribs. You could drink cocktails on porches, and the music came from everywhere.

He wanted to give Maddy what she'd given him. Something they could call home. One day he would leave the Rooster. He planned to leave soon, though when he'd asked the Gianellis, who owned the bar, they'd laughed in his face. They'd tried to frighten him by sending a few thugs around, big vault-sized men who hung out at the door. But when the time was right, he'd move on. He'd head over to Dreamland or the Grand and get a better gig. He gazed at the card again. He circled a bungalow with a front porch, right off the lake. He'd buy it for her one day.

Maddy sat while he slopped up the gravy with his biscuit. "There's this white boy been coming around, listening to us play. I think he's stealing."

"What you got worth stealing?"

"I got my tunes."

"Maybe he's taking some of that." She gave him that fake scowl of hers. "Or maybe he just likes to hear you play." Napoleon pondered this as he wiped his plate clean. It was a possibility he hadn't really considered. He and Maddy paused, listening as the first morning train rumbled by, shaking the cottage. It was her alarm clock—

the moment she knew she had to start leaving for work. He kissed her on the cheek and, while Maddy dressed in the kitchen, went whistling his tune into the room they shared. She'd pulled up the covers so that the bed wouldn't be cold when he crawled in. The sheets were still warm from her body and that warmth soothed him as he slept.

Twelve

Ever since he could remember, Leo Lehrman tossed all night. When he was a boy, he would wake up and cry. He was stricken with night terrors. He could imagine a million things gone wrong even as a small child. His father walking out on them again and again. His mother never home when he returned from school. The beatings he took with his father's belt or, even worse, the back of his hand. He imagined all kinds of impossible things. Insects that laid black eggs on his arm. His head stuck between the slats of a fence. Once he saw his own head, impaled on the top of a pole, wearing one of his caps. And then there were the very real dreams of running out of money, his family with nothing to eat. He woke from all these dreams, shaking. He never shared any of them with a soul.

It was rare for Leo to sleep through the night. On this night he'd woken, preoccupied with trying to convince baseball teams to put the designs on their caps. He had heard that Detroit already had an orange tiger on theirs, and he was afraid the idea would catch on fast. He wanted to be in the forefront. He'd overextended himself with a ten-thousand-dollar loan to purchase embroidery machines. He wanted the women to work faster, more efficiently. Then they could make more caps. But the women didn't like the machines. Their fingers were accustomed to frilly work, stitches made one at a time.

Orders weren't pouring in. Though he had canvassed all the major Chicago teams and had even tried the Negro League, there wasn't been much interest in his caps with trademarks. The managers thought they were too fancy, and the players seemed to agree. But Leo was certain its time had come. He had to be patient and persevere, but he wasn't sure he could even meet the interest on his loan. He tossed and turned, trying to find a place to rest away from Hannah's small, brown body. He had loved another woman before her. The woman he had loved had large round breasts that he'd hold in each hand. He had never warmed up against his wife's thin, bony flesh.

The mattress was too soft, the pillows too fluffy. Leo sank in the feathery down until he thought he would suffocate. Besides he had his problems. The pressure in his bladder, the gas that plagued him in the night. He got up to check on his boys in their beds. He'd liked it when there were four little boys. He had enjoyed their heavy breathing, their night sweats. The covers pulled up to their chins. He'd liked the roundness of the number four, the evenness of the six of them. The way they'd fit—three in front, three in back—into the Model T.

When Harold died, there was suddenly an empty bed. Hannah said they'd keep it for guests, but Leo couldn't bear the sight of its emptiness. The oddness of the number three, the unevenness of the breathing, the fact that now all the boys rode in the backseat of the car, the parents up front. The boys no longer slept as they had: Benny and Ira in one room; Art and Harold in the other. For a time Ira seemed to float around, moving between his old room and Harold's bed so that sometimes Leo's breath was taken away when he peered into Art's room and saw that two boys were tucked in bed.

After a while the boys began to sleep that way, the middle boys sharing a room. Benny never said anything about it, though he and Ira had shared a room all their lives. The empty bed in Benny's room was eventually moved into the sewing room for the guests who never came. Only Benny slept alone as if he were a kind of pariah. He was put into solitary confinement as punishment for his neglect.

Leo roamed, hoping to relieve his gas or empty his bladder, taking sips of cold milk, and when that didn't work, he poured himself a brandy. He paused at Ira and Art's room where they lay in their beds. Then he peered into Benny's. Benny should have been asleep, but he hadn't come home. Hannah had fretted, wringing her hands. Leo was certain that nothing was wrong, but she'd been worried enough to cry herself to sleep.

The overstuffed chair was Leo's favorite place to sit. It was green velvet with big arms, and he sat in that chair like a king, as if he ruled from there. He often fell asleep in it. But mainly he listened to sounds in the middle of the night. Carts wheeling by; bakers opening their shops. He listened for creaks on the stairs and banging doors. He'd listen, if it took all night, for his son to come home.

From the street Benny saw that the living room light was on. He hoped his mother had left it on for him or perhaps his father was sleeping, as he sometimes did, in the chair. He assumed, for whatever reason, that his parents didn't notice his nightly wanderings. Or if they did that they didn't care. Quietly Benny made his way up the stairs, putting his key in the door. He wore a thin jacket and, even though it wasn't yet winter, was shivering. He needed a new coat, but had no money for one. He didn't dare ask his father. Perhaps his mother could sew a new lining in this one. Flakes of snow were melting in his dark brown hair. The apartment was silent, but when he walked in, he heard his father's voice. "Benjamin," his father boomed, "come here."

His father never called him Benjamin. All his life he had been Benny. He thought for a moment, I don't even know who Benjamin is. When his father called again, he followed the voice into the living room where his father sat in the dim light.

Now Benny stood in front of him.

"Where have you been?" His father looked bloated, his skin ashen. But a fire raged in his eyes.

Benny thought of a dragon—the kind that frightened him in children's stories. In the silence of the room Benny could hear his father breathing. It was not a normal breath but a deep, wheezy sound. Benny pondered telling his father the truth about where he'd been, but he was afraid he would get Marta in trouble. There were a dozen lies, but which one would be better? "I was playing ball with the guys. Then it got late and I went over to Moe's for a card game. I fell asleep over there."

"No, you didn't. I saw them in the lot and you weren't there. And I walked over to Moe's. You weren't there either."

Benny looked out the window where the sky was growing light. A violet hue hung over the buildings.

"Didn't I tell you never to lie to me?"

Benny heaved a heavy sigh. "I went to listen to music."

"What kind of music?"

He couldn't bring himself to look his father in the eye. He feared he'd start to stammer. "Music I like to listen to."

"And what kind of music is that?" Benny just shook his head. His father knew. Benny could tell by the way he pursed his lips. His father held a piece of paper in his hand and he was folding it and unfolding it, making small animals out of paper. "Were you drinking?"

"I don't drink," Benny said.

His father nodded, taking this in. "Have you been doing something with that woman at the factory? That slut you're always hanging around?" Benny winced at the word "slut" but said nothing. Slowly, methodically, Leo folded and unfolded the slip of paper. Everything he was he'd made happen himself. Another man would hear his own father's voice, telling him what to do, but Leo heard none. His father, a forger of art objects and religious artifacts, had fled to Palestine when Leo was still a boy in Russia, leaving behind his debts and a memory of beatings. His mother, a woman he remembered only for her smell of soap and her rough hands, died soon afterward. He'd forgotten his siblings long ago.

Leo had been raised by cousins, then he'd made his way to America. No one had ever helped him out. At each step he had met with obstacles—businesses gone bad, a child lost, women who had left him. But he had struggled on until now he found himself standing before his oldest son in a rage over where he wandered off to in the night. Surely another father would know how to handle this better than he. But all Leo knew how to show was his fury.

"I haven't been doing anything I shouldn't have," Benny replied.

His father, who was not a large man but was strong, rose up. "And how do you know what you should or should not be doing? I will decide that. As long as you live under this roof, I will make that decision." Leo felt the anger rising in him, an anger he didn't know he could feel for anything, let alone his son. Now all the things he'd once blamed on himself he blamed on Benny. All of this had somehow become Benny's fault.

"I . . . I think I'm old enough . . ." The words were stuck in his throat.

"I don't care what you think. This is my house." Leo was trembling now, a wave building inside. "I'll tell you when you're old enough."

As the hand made its arc, Benny did not flinch. Even as his father's open palm smacked against his face, he did not move away. Tears stung his eyes; his cheek burned. Deep inside his bones throbbed, and a darkness grew around him. Leo stood, shaking while Benny waited to see if the blow would be repeated. When it was not, his face smarting, he went to his room.

The following day, his cheek swollen, his eye darkened, Benny climbed the stairs to Mr. Marcopolis's dreary rooms, where his teacher waited for him. His teacher took one look at Benny, then tilted his head in his direction. "What happened to you?"

"A baseball," Benny replied.

Mr. Marcopolis nodded thoughtfully. "Well, you're going to have to stop that if you want to protect your hands."

Benny stared down at his hands. He hadn't thought about protecting them before. He had been working on his reach. He could slip a twelfth now. It wasn't as long as Honey Boy's, but it was big just the same. Now he had to protect them.

Mr. Marcopolis sat on his chair beside the piano bench, sipping his tea. "I'm tired today, Benny. I'd like you to just play for me."

"Play for you?"

"Play your own music. Don't worry. I won't charge you for the lesson. I want to listen."

So Benny sat at the bench and, as it happened to him whenever he sat down at the piano, he forgot about where he was or who was listening. He just played. At first he was aware of Mr. Marcopolis's foot, tapping along, but then he didn't think about it again. The notes came to him. One tune blending into the next. He began with a melody he'd heard, then improvised on that. He broke the chords down, inverting them. He slowed the left hand down, letting it come in late, then sped it up. He went off in directions he had no idea how he'd resolve, but came back to where he'd started. He played by instinct, the way he always had.

When he was finished, he looked up and saw his teacher, sitting with his eyes closed, his light skin paler than it usually was. It seemed as if he was not even breathing and for an instant Benny panicked. But slowly Mr. Marcopolis opened his dark eyes and peered at Benny once again.

"I don't suppose you've ever heard of Abraham Abulafia, Benny, have you?" Benny shook his head. "He was a mystic who lived in 1280. I know about him because I have a small interest in the Kabbalah. Abulafia believed that to find God it was necessary to 'unseal the soul; untie the knots which bind it.' Are you following me?"

Benny nodded, letting his fingers drift along the keys. Though he wasn't really following and he wondered what this had to do with music, Benny was used to Mr. Marcopolis's mind drifting off onto strange philosophical tangents. He tried to listen.

"Untying the knots is what you are learning to do, Benny. Abulafia taught the method of Hokhmah ha-Tseruf, The Science of the Combination of the Letters. The Kabbalist took the letters of the name of God and meditated on them by recombining the letters in different ways. Abulafia himself said this was reminiscent of musical harmonies in which the letters of the alphabet take the place of the notes of a scale. Are you paying attention?"

"Yes, I am." Benny had a sense that this would be his last lesson, so he did his best to understand.

"What I am trying to say, Benny, is that Kabbalah is like jazz." Benny could not hide his surprise. "Yes," Mr. Marcopolis went on. "I've been listening, too. I even went to hear some music in one of those clubs where it is played. It's not a musical form I particularly enjoy, but one I am beginning to admire. So, Benny, what you are doing is this. You are improvising on the name of God. Isn't that what you want to do with your music? In this way, Benny, though you may not know it yet, you are coming closer to God." Then Mr. Marcopolis handed Benny a small notebook with musical lines. "This is a present for you." Without another word, he ushered Benny to the door and said good-bye.

The leather-goods shop was on his way home. Benny passed it dozens of times over the years, but had never so much as glanced in the window before. He'd never noticed the briefcases and wallets, the belts and purses dangling from mannequins' arms, all artfully displayed. Now something caught his eye. In the middle of a display of shoes and purses was a red leather suitcase with a shiny zipper that glistened in the sun.

He went inside. The store smelled of dead animals and what he imagined pigs smelled like, but he girded himself and asked the aging owner to see it. The man had other suitcases for sale, but Benny wanted the one in the window. The man shrugged and groaned as he pulled the suitcase out. He put it on the counter with great flourish, and Benny ran his hands along the warm leather. The man unzipped it. Inside it smelled fresh and new, ripe with possibilities.

It had a zipper compartment along the top, and he opened this, too. It was lined in red silk, the color of blood. Benny asked the old man how much, and the man told him seven dollars. Benny had been saving his tips over the years, and his life savings amounted to a little more than twelve dollars. He went home, got his savings, and bought a suitcase he hadn't known he needed until he saw it.

The day after Benny bought his red suitcase he ran into Moe on the street. As he saw Moe coming, he was struck by how much they looked alike. They were both dark, small boys, who were sometimes mistaken for brothers with their black wavy hair and long arms. And they both liked music. Moe's mother still made him play the French horn, but Moe was teaching himself the slide trombone. "What's up, Benny?" Moe gave him a half punch in the arm.

Benny hadn't really planned to say anything, but the words slipped out. "Hey, Moe, I'm leaving town. I gotta get out of here." Moe cocked his head, still smiling, taking this in. "You wanna hop a freight?"

Moe was used to Benny's talk of getting away, though usually no farther than the South Side. "You serious?"

"I'm serious."

Moe didn't have to think about it for long. He had a father who used him as a punching bag and thought nothing of slugging his mother, too. He had lost interest in school. He was playing the trombone and wanted nothing more than to be on his own. Moe was happy to accommodate Benny by coming along. "Just say when," Moe shouted as he veered off.

That evening Benny packed his red suitcase with a few shirts, a pair of trousers. When he was done, he ran his hands over the fine leather and shoved it under his bed where weeks would go by and it would gather dust. Then Benny practiced the piano until his father told him it was late and he should go to sleep. When he went into his room, his father stuck his head in and told Benny he had never played the Beethoven so well. It brought tears to his mother's eyes.

Thirteen

The floor of Lehrman's Caps was dusty with cuts of cloth, scraps, and thread. The room was a buzz of grinding machines. The Slovakian women muttered to one another with their heads down, shawls draped across their shoulders as a cold draft blew in from the lake. As Benny stopped in to pick up an order of caps, his father called him into his office. "I have something to say to you, Benny," his father said. "I'm taking you off deliveries. It's time for you to learn the ropes."

"But I want to stay on the streets." Benny stood in his father's office amid an array of invoices and ashtrays, scraps of cloth, and crumpled-up designs that would never see the light of day. Just as he was contemplating getting away, his father was taking him off the streets.

Extending his arms, Leo replied, "This will all be yours one day." On the bench the Slovakian women were hunched over their machines. Across the room on a long table the cutters who were mostly men worked on the heavy cloth. At the end of the day their fingers were raw and wrapped in gauze. They left spots of blood on the fabric that the women scrubbed clean. Benny was content spending his days delivering caps, wandering the perimeters of the South Side, at night slipping into the clubs. As long as he got his work done and made it home before ten, his parents did not seem bothered by his comings and goings. But now his father was taking him off the street. He was taller than his father. More powerful in his limbs. Yet he still trembled before him. At one time he'd believed that the caps factory was his only prospect. Now he dreaded the thought of it. "I don't know . . . It's not what I want to do."

"What do you mean . . . it's not what you want to do?"

"I mean I have other plans for myself."

"Well, those can wait. You need to learn a business. And this one is as good as any other."

His father put him to work with a scissors and cloth. "This is how I learned," Leo said. "From the ground up. If you're going to work in the caps business, you've got to know how a cap gets made."

Benny became a cutter on the floor. As his father berated a slow worker and shouted at his bookkeeper, Benny cut denim patterns out of cloth. He followed the loosely drawn shapes. He snipped until his fingers cracked and bled; hard calluses formed where he gripped the scissors. He watched the women, sewing designs into caps, their fingers red and gnarled. At work Benny rubbed his hands with lanolin the women kept in a big jar. At the end of the day Hannah soaked them in warm water with peroxide, then massaged them with linseed oil.

On his breaks he took out the small notebook Mr. Marcopolis had given to him and, as he sat off to the side eating a sandwich, scribbled down the music that was inside his head. He ignored Marta and the other women who teased him. His hands were stiff and covered in sores after he had worked on the floor for two weeks. As he held a pen, his fingers ached. One evening on arriving home, he took the red suitcase out from under his bed. He dusted it off and packed two more clean pressed shirts, an extra pair of pants, clean socks, and his only silk tie. He packed his postcards from the *Eastland*. He'd heard he could sell these for a nickel or even a dime. He wanted to be ready when it was time to leave.

Then he went into the sewing room and looked at the photo of

Harold's beaming face. He took the picture and put it in his suitcase as well.

That night Benny was back, knocking on the tavern door. "Well, look who's here," Honey Boy said. "If it isn't the Professor," which was what piano players were called down in New Orleans. "Come on in," he said, with a little bow. "I thought you'd flown the coop."

"I did," Benny said. "I went away for a little while. I had a gig down south."

"Oh, a gig." Honey Boy chuckled as if he knew better, then offered Benny a platter of food. "C'mon, kid, eat with me." Benny stared at what was put before him, afraid it was pork. "What's the matter? You don't like frog legs and rattlesnake tongues? Make you popular with the ladies." In truth it was red beans and rice with gravy stew, and Benny was surprised at how good it was, how it filled his belly. When they were done, Honey Boy ordered Benny to sit down. "Let's see what you've learned." At first Benny was nervous, but he'd been practicing some of the New Orleans–style pieces Honey Boy had taught him. He thought he could lead in with that, then improve on the rhythm and the harmonies. He dropped his head and picked up the beat. He took a few pieces he'd heard and blended them into one. He held his chords in the right hand while he let the melody rip.

When he paused, Honey Boy stood beside him, mouth open but saying nothing. He made a motion for Benny to scoot over while he played a long complicated number he called his "Funky Butt Boogie." He let Benny sit back down again and rough it out as well. Benny held to the tune, then added some harmonies of his own. And he played it back. When Benny looked up, Honey Boy wasn't smiling anymore. "You're making progress, kid." He laughed an uncomfortable laugh. "Looks like I'm going to be taking lessons from you one day." The caramel-colored man went to the jar of poppy seeds and grabbed a handful. "Here, have a mouthful of these." The tiny black seeds settled between his teeth. Honey Boy flexed a biceps. "Be glad it ain't those frog legs or rattlesnake tongue."

———

The next day after work Benny hurried home. If he was lucky, his mother would be out shopping and his brothers not back from school. He could practice for an hour or so. He ran up the stairs two at a time, slipped his key into the door, and was enveloped in a soothing calm—the quiet of unoccupied rooms, the steamy aroma of chicken in a pot. He was alone.

Benny sat on the bench, his head down, trying to recall what Honey Boy had done. He played straight chords as he roughed out the melody. He began with what he remembered, then began to digress and his fingers roamed. He noodled with the rhythm, hesitating, and then he let it go. He forgot that he was in his parents' living room with its brown sofa and his father's beige chair in the middle of the day. He forgot that it was a cloudy day and he hadn't seen the sun. Everything came to him bright, in colors. Flashes of blue and orange. If someone interrupted, he wouldn't know his own name or where he lived. All the songs became one as his fingers traveled wherever they wanted.

Benny wasn't aware of the darkness that filled the room. He didn't hear his mother's feet on the landing or her key as she slipped it into the door. For an instant he froze, then switched to a Bach partite that he hadn't played in years. Hannah stood in the dim light of the entranceway, her hat pinned to her head. Slowly she put her grocery bags down on the dining room table. "Play what you were playing again." He played a few bars of the Bach. "No, not that," his mother said, shaking her head. "Play what you were playing while I was standing outside on the street."

Benny looked at her, and then arched his fingers over the keys. He tapped out four beats with his left foot, and played whatever came into his head. His fingers jumped all over the keys. When he was done, his mother said. "Who taught you that?"

"Nobody. I just picked it up."

"And how did you pick it up?"

Benny shrugged. There was nothing he could say. "I listened for a long time."

Folding her arms, a stance Benny rarely saw, she spoke firmly. "And where was that?"

Benny put his head down. He'd never been very successful at lying to his mother. "When I made my deliveries. Sometimes I heard music there."

She pursed her lips. "Well, don't let your father hear you playing that Negro music around here."

"It's called jass, Ma."

"I don't care what it's called. I don't want to hear it again." Then she carried her groceries into the kitchen, where he heard her putting them away.

When Benny knocked on the tavern door, Honey Boy told him it was time to become a man. "You can't play jass and still be a kid," he said. Honey Boy explained that there were a few things he had to do to be a great musician. He had to drink a pint of whiskey, smoke some gunge, and be with a woman. Benny didn't know what gunge was, and Honey Boy and the girls laughed. "The ofay doesn't know what gunge is," Honey Boy said. "It's gauge, muta, muggles, rouch, grefa, grass, weed. I'm going to give you the best gold leaf, no salt and pepper for you." Honey Boy took the weed out of his pocket and began rolling a joint for Benny. Honey Boy said the whiskey first, then the weed. Velvet would oblige with the third.

"I'm not sure about this." Benny was suddenly afraid.

"Well, then, you better get out of here and don't ever come back. We don't want any woosy ofays around here."

"All right," he said. Honey Boy set up a glass of the amber liquid, which Benny took back in one slug. A burning shot down his throat. Honey Boy set up one more and Benny drank that back, too. Then he lit the cigarette, took a puff, held it in his lungs, and handed it over to Benny. He took a drag, coughed, then thought his lungs were on fire. Heat rushed through his veins. His head ached, but after a while he couldn't feel it. Benny wanted to play. He staggered over in his stupor, settled down at the keys.

"Oh," Honey Boy said, "wish your daddy could see you now."

"Well, he can't." Benny's fingers fiddled with some chords. "My father's dead."

"I'm sorry. I didn't know . . ." Honey Boy looked as if he suddenly felt sorry for the boy. Benny wondered why he'd said what he had. Of course his father wasn't dead. He was alive and well and working at Lehrman's Caps, but to Benny at that moment his father felt dead. *I wish he were,* Benny muttered under his breath.

"My father is dead," Benny said again. When he said it this time, he knew it was so. His father was dead—at least to him. The room he was in seemed far away. Nothing was quite where it should be. His hand reached for tabletops and missed them. Walls didn't seem to be at the end of the floor. The keys on the piano swirled; black mixing with white. A hand tugged at his arm, leading him away. In the background a bluesy number played. Benny had heard it before and tried to give it a name, but he couldn't. Honey Boy gave a flash of his diamond stud. His face looked fat and contorted as if it were dropping off his jaw. Money changed hands; Velvet led him upstairs into a room he'd never seen before.

Everything was soft in there. The rug, the bedspread he sat down on. It was as if he were floating on a cloud. Or he was a baby again, swaddled in a crib. He wanted to sleep in this room. He thought if he could just sleep, he'd wake up and everything would be clear. He was aware of sounds—a car rattling past in the street, the blues coming from down below. The room was dark, though it was day. Then he made out the velvet curtains, the red velvet spread. Everything in the room was red velvet. So that must be why they called her by that name.

Velvet moved her fingers across his buttons, helping him off with his things. He was ready to sleep on that soft spread in this cool, dark room where everything came at him red. Sleep for a little while. Not too long, just until the things stopped moving. Until the room stood still. But he didn't like it when he closed his eyes. The room spun, and a swirl came from inside of him. When he was naked as a baby, Velvet helped him lay back gently on the bed. Her hands rubbed his back, massaged his buttocks, his thighs, turned him over, and rubbed his chest. Her skin was soft and smooth as fresh cream. And when he reached down, when he put his finger between her legs, that was velvet, too.

Hannah didn't know what to make of her son as he staggered up the steps, said he was sick, and went to bed. She brought him a bowl and tried to ladle chicken soup into his mouth, but the fat coated his mouth and he spit it into the bowl. He vomited into the bucket she placed by his bed until she thought he'd spew his guts out. "He's drunk," Leo said.

Hannah shook her head. She knew it wasn't just drink that made the dark bile pour out of her son with the stench of sulfur. "He must have eaten sausage from the filthy Poles." Hannah spoke in Yiddish, which was her language for secrets and curses, and Leo seemed to believe her. But even Hannah didn't believe that this was just from eating something in the street. This must be the devil's work. Someone had cast a spell on her son. She made him packs of ground onions, cayenne, and baking soda to draw the sweat. She spoon-fed him warm milk laced with honey to coat his stomach and this he kept down. The next day she fed him chicken broth.

For three days he rocked from side to side. His head was going to split in two. He felt as if his insides were gone. Even in his delirium, he swore he'd never smoke reefer. He vowed he would never touch another drink. Hannah watched him, troubled by what had become of her boy. Leo sat with Hannah at their son's side. When he was well enough to work, Leo made one concession. He wouldn't put Benny on the floor where he could ruin his hands. But he wouldn't give his son the South Side either. He kept him on the Near North where his caps went to bakeries, not saloons.

Then one wintry day a delivery boy called in sick, and Leo had nobody to make the run down to the stockyards so he told Benny to go. It had been months since Benny had walked those bloody streets. Even in the cold wind off the lake he smelled the rotting meat. Blocks away, Benny heard the animal cries. As he brought his caps to the loading dock, the black workers taunted him. "Hey, honky, where ya been?"

"To hell and back," Benny shouted at them. When he finished his run, he took the "el" north, but only as far as Thirty-First Street. Buttoning his jacket and pulling his cap down against the blistery chill he walked the icy streets to the tavern. Twice he slipped on black ice and almost fell. He came to the door, but it was padlocked. He looked around, up and down the alley. Perhaps he had the wrong place. He knocked hard. But no one was there.

A woman stuck her head out of the window upstairs. He'd never seen her before. She said that those other people were gone and good riddance to them. "Nothing but trouble." She told him to get out of here, too, and she spat down at him.

Benny stepped off the curb to avoid her spit and walked back over to State. Honey Boy and Velvet were gone, making him wonder if they'd ever really been there. He started walking and kept heading north. On his way he passed the redbrick building that seemed to offer people a second chance and read the inscription above the door. TO THINE OWN SELF BE TRUE; THERE ALL HONOR LIES. It was Jane Addams's Hull House. Pausing, he heard music coming from inside. The sweet sound of the clarinet. Another Benny was taking lessons there. He was only eight years old, but in six years he'd be playing with a band. "My namesake," Benny Lehrman would one day joke. Another Chicago white boy, Benny Goodman, was practicing inside.

That night he sat down at his mother's piano and played a perfunctory Beethoven, but his fingers kept slipping into honky-tonk. Hungry, he went to his mother's pantry. Rummaging through he found a jar of poppy seeds. Benny reached his hand in and pulled out a fistful. He thrust them into his mouth. They were gritty between his teeth, but the black seeds tasted crunchy and sweet. He licked his hand clean.

Fourteen

≡

Over the years Pearl had taken to ignoring her birthday. While other siblings celebrated theirs with cakes and cards, Pearl had chosen to forget about hers. It was a date filled with sadness and grief and, since she seemed content to let it pass unnoticed, her brothers and sisters tended to forget it as well. She no longer thought much about why she didn't celebrate or that she'd even had one in the first place. She viewed the birthdays of others with their cakes and gifts, their parties and songs, as curiosities, rituals, as foreign as Christmas. But each July she became aware of some subtle change that was taking place in her life that she marked silently, without fanfare, simply acknowledging herself to be one year older than she'd been the day before.

But now Pearl felt herself easing into womanhood. Her body was plump but firm, filling in her blouses and her dresses. Her periods came every thirty days with the full moon, the same as Opal and Ruby, with whom she still shared a bed. When she paused to admire herself in front of the long mirror Anna had kept in the hall, Pearl saw her trim waist, her ample breasts. She wore long green or gray dresses, cinched at the waist. Her skin was clear and olive, and she made a point of staying out of the sun except when she went to the lake. Her lips were full and so red she didn't need lipstick, not that she would dare to wear any. Every morning her sister, Fern, who had just opened a beauty salon in a colored neighborhood, ran a brush through Pearl's sleek, black hair, then pinned it for her on top of her head. Pearl liked what she saw.

It was a hot summer, but Pearl couldn't go to the beach. That July a black boy named Eugene Williams was floating on his back, his eyes closed, relaxing in Lake Michigan. He didn't notice that he drifted onto a white Chicago beach where he was struck with a stone and drowned. The riots that ensued tore the city apart. White thugs beat black youths with baseball bats. An old white lady was dragged off a bus and had her head bashed in. Pearl couldn't get the image of that boy out of her mind. His startled face, his hands groping, flailing. Gasping for breath. At times she thought about drowning. What it would be like to feel the tug of the water on you, pulling you down? Your lungs filling with water?

The White Sox were losing the World Series and some suspected they were throwing it. In a year women would vote. Meanwhile men had discovered that women enjoyed pleasure, and F. Scott Fitzgerald declared that the Jazz Age had begun. The praying women who'd flung themselves on the floors of saloons and beat their breasts for temperance won. In the fall the Volstead Act was passed and the city dumped gallons of beer into the river. The police commissioner posed with giant padlocks he intended to bolt on saloon doors. Clubs were raided and closed, only to be reopened hours later on "technicalities."

As bulletins were posted on telephone poles, Lev Walenski, the butcher, wept at the bar, cursing his wife who was marching through the streets, waving the banners of her victory. Mrs. Baum's dead husband appeared for what he assumed was his last drink. Bud Hansen and Bert Winkler placed bets on what the Chimbrovas would do. As the neighborhood mulled over public notices, and Moss and Jonah debated whether to turn Chimbrova's into a café that served tea and finger sandwiches, Pearl was upstairs making curtains out of green damask. She had learned well in the hours she'd spent listening to the ragtime and jazz that seeped up from the saloon. More and more musicians were moving north.

Since the day she'd dissuaded her mother from drowning her and

Opal in the lake she'd come to love, Pearl had a plan. While Jonah pondered how the family would live, Pearl saw the opportunity. The rallying cries of the suffragettes inspired her. Women would soon be voting. Why couldn't she run a business? She was good at math and she had an ear for music. Sometimes she knew when the piano was flat even before Vlado Slovak, their soused piano tuner who got his drinks on the house. She'd come to know when a musician had great chops and when he didn't. She hadn't spent years on the stairwell listening to Napoleon blow without learning a few things.

Since Anna's death the year before, the candy shop had been neglected. Even when she was alive, she lost interest. Anna, who'd never recovered from the loss of her boys, didn't seem to die as much as fade away. The lemon drops and sassafras balls left in their glass jars had turned into sugary bricks. Dust coated the counters. Doing what her mother never would have approved, Pearl had her brothers build a sturdy door with a slot that slid open between the candy shop and the saloon. This way they could see whoever was trying to get in. They could also bolt it shut if need be. If barbershops and shoe repairs and, Pearl had heard, even police stations were fronts for saloons, why not Anna's candy shop? Pearl had the candy jars scrubbed, the counters washed clean. She set Opal to work making sponge taffy and peppermint canes.

With the death benefit they'd received from Western Electric, Pearl convinced her brothers to refurbish the bar with Honduran mahogany. They put in a rococo glass chandelier and purchased French bistro tables and chairs that she placed along the wall. They had the oak floors polished and a small raised platform built, large enough to hold the piano, drums, and some horn players. Above the bar Pearl hung that old picture of her mother standing in front of the first Ferris wheel at the 1893 World's Fair.

Off to one side Pearl created a space for dancing, but not too large because dancing would cut down on the drinking. They hired a small band that came with a redheaded cabaret singer named Fifi La Belle who went from table to table singing "Yes, We Have No Bananas" and "I'll See You in My Dreams." If the saloon was to earn a living, its customers needed to sit and drink, and Fifi kept them in their chairs. Then Pearl made a deal with a druggist around the corner who was selling bathtub gin from his back room, and deliveries began on a regular basis to the saloon.

Pearl entreated Ruby who was by now always sketching and drawing to paint a mural in honor of her brothers who had drowned. She wanted a forest scene, filled with birds and wild things. And scattered on the forest floor, as if from a jeweler's pouch, would be the semiprecious stones. The gem sisters. Opal, Ruby, and Pearl. Ruby began sketching while Pearl removed the old CHIMBROVA'S SALOON AND SWEETS sign that had hung in front of the saloon since their father had run it years before. She wanted to give the place a real name and decided to call it the Night Owl Saloon in honor of a tune Napoleon had written for her when she was a frightened, insomniac girl.

When Napoleon came in one night after hours, Pearl told him the new name. Thinking he'd be pleased, she was surprised when he frowned. "You can't call it that." He rubbed the gris-gris bag around his neck. "It's bad luck. It's bad for my music."

Pearl remembered her own mother who spat into the air to keep evil away. "Well, what should I call it then?"

Napoleon took a look around. He gazed at the mural with the woodland plants and birds, the magical, twisted trees, and the shore that opened to the lake. Boats painted into the sky. Musical instruments woven in. Mirrors that reflected the gold and silver strobe. The bandstand with the set of drums, the old upright piano. "Ain't no place that looks like this one. Looks like a jazz palace," Napoleon said. "That's as good a name as any if you ask me."

And Pearl agreed. While no sign would hang above the door, soon everyone on the North Side knew where the Jazz Palace was, and anyone you asked could direct you there.

Fifteen

The posters of shrieking women and swarthy men graced the walls of the Regency Theater. Most of these posters had been up for years. Benny had walked by them dozens of times, so it wasn't the posters that made him pause. It was the sign taped across one of them. PIANO PLAYER WANTED.

Milo Peyton, who was chief operator, ticket taker, and projectionist, explained to Benny as he purchased his tickets that the woman with the chopsticks in her hair had quit abruptly the week before and given no notice. Benny sat through the silent film, made all the more silent because no one played the trills, but he couldn't concentrate on the movie. It was a boring series of images, building pointlessly on the next, without tunes to hold it together. When the film was over, Benny went up to Milo Peyton and asked if he'd hired a new piano player. "It's better with music."

"Don't you think I know that, kid. But after all these years that gal just walked out on me. Know anyone who can?" Peyton asked, chewing on an unlit cigar.

Benny took a deep breath. "Well, I play . . . ," he said.

Peyton knew Benny. He'd been coming there for years. Peyton considered himself someone who had an eye for such things and doubted that the boy could play honky-tonk rags. "Is that so?" Peyton said to humor him. "Okay, let's give it a try." Peyton put on the house lights. "Play something for me."

"You mean, right now?" Under the harsh lights Benny saw how shabby the Regency was with its tattered sheet, its crumbling walls covered in a coat of black paint. Dust and soot and stale popcorn coated the floor.

"Now's as good a time as any." Peyton spat onto the floor. He went to the projector and put on a film that Benny had seen half a dozen times before. Then he snapped off the house lights and sat back to listen. In the dark room, illumined only by the light from the projector, Benny fumbled with the greasy, yellowed keys which sounded flat; a few of them stuck. He didn't think he could get much sound. He struck a chord, did a glide. He smelled Peyton sitting in the first row of folding chairs. Though Benny couldn't see him, he could hear Peyton's foot tapping the floor. Benny wanted to forget about him. He didn't want to think about someone sitting there.

On the screen a girl on her way home paused at the railroad tracks, looking both ways. The man crouched beside a shack, eyeing her. Benny looked for a rhythm to follow along. Nervously he tried to remember some of the first numbers he ever learned. As he worked his way through "Maple Leaf Rag," Peyton coughed and shifted in his seat. Benny ground his way through a few other Joplin numbers and went on to popular tunes he thought Peyton would like to hear. He played through "Livery Stable Blues" and a little "Darktown Strutters' Ball."

An amber light flared in the darkness as Peyton lit his cigar. But Benny didn't care about Peyton or the bitter smell of cigar smoke that filled the air. He was listening to himself play. His sound lay dead by the side of the road. How soon could he get out of here? He flubbed notes, missed chords as Peyton puffed on his cigar. At any moment Benny expected Peyton to walk out of the room. He would if he had to sit there. Benny moved on to a few numbers Honey Boy had played. He improvised on the melodies he'd heard in the garbage-strewn alley of the South Side. But none of them felt right.

Benny stopped and shook out his hands. He took a deep breath. He forgot about what he was doing there. He picked up the sounds he'd heard on the Stroll, but then he took off and went beyond what he remembered. The movie danced in black and white against the sheet. The girl let herself into her house. The villain followed. Benny anticipated a fall, a dive, a plunge, a knock, a clap, a scream. The refrains weren't written down and didn't seem to come from anywhere. He was inside a globe like a paperweight and around him the music swirled, shaking, and what had been outside was inside of him now. It didn't matter if someone was listening or if he was alone. He moved away from a world where mistakes happened and things went wrong. A mistake was just his next chord. He went wherever it took him—out of this dingy building, out past the city and into the world.

When the film ended, Benny sat back, trembling. He was out of breath as if he'd been running for miles. When he looked up, Peyton was sitting very still. He didn't speak until he was sure Benny was done. "Come back tomorrow and I'll run a few more pictures for you. You gotta work on your slaps and claps. The sound of somebody falling down. Playing with the picture. Practice a little; then you start next week. You work nights and weekends and matinees. I'll give you a penny on every two bits I earn," Peyton said. "The more people who come here, the more you get."

"That's it?" Benny asked, incredulous. "I have the job?"

"That's right. You have the job. But you can't be late and you can't miss a show." They shook hands, and that was the deal.

It was dark as Benny made his way home. He'd gone into the theater during the day, and now it was night. There was a lightness in his step as he hummed. With his palms he made a clap noise, a knock, a slap. He'd dredge these sounds from the piano. He would do this job for a few months and then, when he had some real experience, he'd take his red suitcase and his friend Moe and get out of town. They'd go to St. Louis. Or New York. Maybe down to New Orleans. And they'd make music.

Benny wondered how he'd tell his father that he was leaving the job at the factory. He'd found another one, and it was something he wanted to do. For years now it had seemed to Benny that there was no reason not to do what one wanted in this world. He would explain to his father that he planned to play piano in a darkened movie house. And a man named Milo Peyton would pay Benny to do it.

But Benny never had the opportunity to tell his father because, when he walked in, he found him in the living room, the newspaper folded on his lap. "Benny, sit down," his father said. "I need to talk to you." Benny pulled out the piano bench. "You see," Leo began, "I missed a payment on a loan for those embroidery machines. Just one payment." Sitting in the armchair, his father looked like a diminutive version of himself. His nose hairs were black in the light, and something about him made Benny want to laugh, though he resisted. "Twenty years with the same bank and they threaten to foreclose on you for one payment."

A cousin had paid off the loan of ten thousand dollars so that Lehrman's Caps could stay open, but he'd have to scale back and fire the Slovakian women. Leo would now be indebted to his cousin for the rest of his life. All the boys would have to work, and even Hannah would have to take in sewing.

Benny told his father he'd already gotten a job, managing a small theater, and that he would be paid about a dime a night.

"That's not enough," Leo said.

"I can still work for you during the day. This would just be extra." Benny told his father perhaps he would help run the business. He was good at math. He could help with the books. His father seemed pleased that this was one less thing he had to worry about, so Benny went to the Regency where every night he played to an almost-empty house. At the end of each show Peyton gave him a few pennies or a nickel for his efforts most of which Benny placed in the jar in the kitchen, as did his brothers from their paper routes and shoeshine stand. He also added a few quarters that he'd kept from the piano lessons he'd never taken, and that his mother had never mentioned. Slowly he would pay her back.

Benny didn't mind that he couldn't keep all the money from the Regency for himself. He loved to be in that theater with the dank smell of crumbling plaster and mildew, of cat piss and back-alley trash, of stale popcorn and spilled ginger ale. In that darkened room he could play the way he wanted, and he was paid to do it.

On Thursday afternoons Benny went to the Regency, and Peyton screened for him the weekend's film. With a small pad on his lap, Benny sat at the piano, scribbling notes. He jotted down themes for heroes and villains, a lover's disappointment, a victory march. Sadness came in minor chords, a fall down a well with a big downward glissando, a slap became any quick chord. Alone in the theater Benny felt an impending sense, a supplicant before his calling.

One night he looked up and saw that the room was full. Even the balcony, which had always been empty, was packed. He was surprised because he hadn't noticed all those people come in and it didn't seem to him that the film was any better than before. But there must have been seventy people crammed into that shabby room. He was halfway through the first film and didn't miss a beat. He became aware of the sounds around him. A lady's gasp, a cough, the shuffling of feet, stockings rubbing together, random thoughts, a kiss in the back row, the memory of a ball game, an argument someone was having in the street, a baby's cry, a trolley passing by. He heard it all. A horn honking, a siren rushing to a fire, someone's loss—and the whole city and the whole world and the lake against the shore all became a part of the music he played. *This is who I am*, he said to himself as he pounded the keys, never coming up for air. *This is the best I'll ever be.*

That night Benny got fifty cents. He stared at the coins, sitting in his palm. "It's too much, Mr. Peyton," Benny said, but Milo Peyton shook his head.

"Don't be an idiot. You've earned it." The next night and the nights that followed—despite the same dreary saga about a girl who was abducted and locked in a room—the movie house was packed. People leaned against the back wall. They sat cross-legged in the aisles. It was standing room only. They kept coming until Milo had to turn them away.

When Milo Peyton offered Benny a flat fee of five dollars a week,

Benny was amazed. It was more money than he'd ever earned in a month. "You don't have to do this, Mr. Peyton."

"I know I don't have to, but I'm going to. Why do you think all these people are coming here, Benny?"

"To see the picture, sir?"

"Naw, you think they're coming to see that same dumb show, night after night?" Milo Peyton tipped his hat back as he spoke. "They're coming to hear you."

Every night Benny performed. He didn't pay much attention to the picture or even the story line. He only vaguely followed "The Wandering Hand," about a murderous hand that strangles unsuspecting victims. Or the ongoing episodes of Ken and Shirley. He was indifferent to the women who came back week after week to see what would happen to them.

He stomped his feet, one, two, three, found a rhythm, and played whatever came into his head. At first he followed the story, but then he just took off. He built up the tension slowly, easing his crescendos to a climactic moment, then went flying in whatever direction his fingers took him. When the movie ended and the lights came on, he was exhausted, spent. He never had any idea how long he'd been playing. He was lost, and it surprised him when he came back. Often he didn't know where he'd been. But one evening he couldn't lose himself. He felt someone staring at him. His eyes scanned the darkened room. In the back a small man in a gray fedora seemed to be leaning against the wall.

His father stood, staring at Benny. Benny blinked, looking twice to make sure that he was there. Without so much as a nod, Benny turned back to the screen. When he looked up again, his father was gone. When his gig was over, he didn't want to go home. He had no idea what he would say to his father. He had no idea if Leo would be angry or proud. Or if he'd tell Hannah where their son was working. Instead Benny headed downtown.

A bone-chilling wind blew off the lake as he hopped the tram that took him down Ashland to Division where he transferred to the streetcar that would take him to the Loop. As he waited, a cold Chicago Arctic wind came down from the north and hit the corner where he stood. Benny's teeth chattered as he tried to find refuge from the wind. His jacket was old and threadbare. Hannah had promised to make him another, but he never sat still long enough for her to measure. It was almost spring, but in Chicago there was little mercy. In the Loop he changed to the Alley. Every time the doors opened, the frigid air blew in.

Hands thrust into his pockets, he went down to those blocks between Thirty-First and Thirty-Fifth, the street of streets, the Black Light District, the Gay White Way. White not because white people went here, but because it was illumined with blazing lights. If he had a dollar or two (or maybe he could get the bouncer to look the other way), he'd go in and listen for an hour, and still be home before midnight. He moved from club to club, standing outside, listening to the bands. If they let whites in, he paid the cover. He snuck into the Pompeii and the Deluxe. He ducked into the Firefly just to see its ball with a million tiny mirrors and little lights under the stage and to hear Senator Sam and his Dixieland band.

Then he cut over to the Rooster. There was a no-name quartet with a pianist, a drummer, and bass player, and the trumpeter with big cheeks and thick pink lips, a towel flung across his neck. The trumpeter gave Benny a glare that let him know that he thought the kid was slumming and maybe stealing. Benny curled up in a booth in the back, sipping his cream soda. He liked the music. It wasn't that wild, frantic beat. They played just to play, dreamy melodies that traveled into space, then came back around fast like a boomerang.

The breaks were long and extended themselves into solos. He listened as the pianist played one melody after another. Benny heard the notes in his head. Then he started to work with them. He roughed out the chords, figured out the changes. Before the second set was finished, he was on the Alley. The next day when his mother went out to run her errands, he fiddled with what he'd heard. He picked up the melody, played a few bars. Once he got it, he let it rip. Before his mother returned, he had a whole number down.

That evening Benny slipped back into the Rooster for a song, and the trumpeter began to taunt him. "That boy's back. We had that white guy Al Jolson here last week. He was stealing. And Sophie

Tucker, she's been stealing, too." Benny sat, impassive. He knew that whites went to black establishments to lift arrangements, but that's not why he was there. He came to listen. And to learn. That the same as stealing, wasn't it? He kept his eyes on the piano, watching those hands rove the keyboard as the trumpeter came in for the head.

The piano man called out to him. "Hey, white boy, you keep coming around. You learning our licks?" Benny sat still as the man poked fun at him. "You must wanta sit in," the man said.

Benny pursed his lips, shaking his head slowly. He didn't want to be singled out. "No," he replied. He had seen other men sit in with these two and if you didn't play it right, the trumpeter would not hesitate to say, "That's not how we do it here."

"I guess the boy's just slumming and don't know how to play. Or else he's a chicken shit," the trumpeter said.

At last Benny spoke. "I'm not a chicken shit," he said. "And I can play."

"Well, let's hear what you can do." The trumpeter lowered his horn. "If you've got something to say, come up here and say it." Actually Benny was a bit of a chicken shit and wasn't at all sure that he wanted to get up to jam with those guys, but they'd called his bluff. He had no choice if he was ever to come back here again. He stood up and walked over to the keyboard, his long arms and fingers flexing as he crossed the room. The piano man slid over to the bar, grabbed a beer, shaking his head, laughing. He couldn't wait to see Benny fall on his face.

"What'll it be?" the trumpeter said. He unhooked his mouthpiece, let the saliva in it drip to the floor. He blew hard until it was clear, then rubbed his lips.

"You start . . ."

"You're the one who's sitting in here." Laughter rose from the bar.

"How about . . ." Benny didn't know the names of all the songs he played, but he knew the melodies. He'd heard something just the other day on the radio so he ran his fingers up and down the keys, roughing out a little refrain, "This in G?"

"That's 'Wild Boy Stomp'?" The piano player shouted from the bar, and more laughter rose. "And I don't know what key you're play-ing in, but that's not what we do around here."

The trumpeter blew a few notes, then put his horn down. "I want this kid to do my taxes, don't you folks?" he said. Once again laugh-ter filled the room. It was true Benny looked more like an accoun-tant in his jacket and tie than a stride piano player. The trumpeter drummed his valves. "Only ofays play like this."

"Okay," Benny said, understanding that he was an ofay. He wouldn't ask what key it was in again. He didn't need anyone to tell him it was E-flat minor. He had been listening for years and playing for almost as long. He had a job at a movie house, but he'd never sat in before, never like this. The trumpeter was just trying to give him a hard time. He ran his fingers up the minor scale, transposing the chords from what he knew until he was sure. "Let's go."

Benny hunched over the keys as if he were taking a test for which he wasn't prepared. He arched his long fingers and settled into some easy chords. With his left foot he marked the beat. He began quiet as a whisper, the way he always did. He liked to get the feel of the water before he plunged in. His opening was nothing fancy—a pro-gression built around a simple melody. The trumpeter followed, then filled in notes, adding some trills of his own. He waited for the boy to improve on it. It was a contest and Benny knew it.

They played off each other for a few bars. Then the trumpeter put his horn down, and Benny let his fingers run across the keys. The drummer and the bass stayed in right behind him as Benny picked up the tempo. He struggled to keep his tongue in his mouth, though it crept out when he played, then snapped back like a lizard's. Then the music happened to him the way it always did. He forgot that there was an audience listening or anything he had to prove. He started floating off in space, just tuning in to what they were playing. He picked up on a refrain, then went with it. He built on what they gave him until, with a nod, the trumpeter and bass dropped out. The drummer was just marking the beat as Benny took a chorus on his own.

He gave his fingers their full reach and took over the whole key-board. He riffed on the melody, taking it way up to the treble, then down again to the bass. Benny altered the changes, liked them, and tried them out. His mind drifted as he let the tune take a sad turn. It made him think of the gulls circling the dump near his house at dusk. Wind blowing through the empty lot, devoid of boys. He saw Harold's dimpled face drifting away. His father, standing in the back of that theater.

He was aware of silence around him. He kept thinking he'd hear glasses clinking, voices, but it was only silence, and he stayed inside his almost-sad song. He didn't want to bring everyone with him there so he didn't stay too long. He warmed it up, brought it back to earth. He heard the crack of bats, bonfires in an open field. He was lying in bed on a spring morning with the windows open. A breeze blowing in. Boys shouting below. Then he started coming out of it, gathering speed. And soon he was flying over rooftops and prairie. If nothing brought him back, he'd be heading out to sea. He soared until he was almost gone.

The trumpeter was slow in picking up his horn. He'd heard white boys play before. Most played cornfield music or New Orleans tunes. Some were good, but not like this one. This boy played like a black man. Negroes had nothing to lose and they knew it. That was how they played the blues. They gave it their body and soul. But white boys always had something that was theirs, and if they played the blues, it was because they'd lost it. They were children who'd had a toy taken away. They never could reach into that place where you'd nothing to begin with. They didn't know that sadness dwelled in the bottom of a deep well. Or that if you dug around, you could bring up something so beautiful.

He'd heard them play from memory or mimic. He'd say, "Oh, look, the mockingbird's gonna play." A mockingbird is a copycat that takes what it wants from other birds and it sings into the night. They are the tricksters and pranksters, the con artists who come to pilfer arrangements and steal songs. He'd been fooled enough times not to want to be fooled again. He never named his tunes and he played with a handkerchief draped over his fingers. When a white man came by and asked to record him, he said no. And he didn't want any white boys taking what he'd worked so hard to figure out for himself.

But he'd never heard anyone off the street who could dredge it up like an old wagon in the swamp and bring it back. Bring it up for air from down below. Boys came and went in a joint like this, but this one had something. Maybe it was meanness, maybe it was greed, or maybe he was just a bottom feeder. But he could play the blues.

Then they all came back at the head, not missing a beat, as the trumpeter said to himself, *That boy's no mynah; he's his own thing.*

"I thought we were going to have to gong you," the trumpeter said when they finished the set. Benny gave him a puzzled look. "Hurl the cymbals to get you off the stage, but the joke was on us." He held out his hand. "Napoleon Hill. Pleased to meet you."

And Benny held out his hand in return.

Sixteen

There were clubs where you danced the Slim Betty, the Charleston, or the Black Bottom, like the Lincoln Gardens and the Firefly, and others where you just listened, like at the Red Rooster. In some places you went for the girls and the bootlegged whiskey. In others you went for the band. Kids came to listen and party, driving their flivvers with flasks filled with rotgut. Hipsters, they were called, always sipping from the flasks tucked in their hip pockets. The music was faster now. Social reformers had declared slow dancing immoral. The Juvenile Protection Agency ordered the dance halls to speed things up. Nobody could do the toddle or the shimmy slow. Now everything was played in double time.

The Jazz Palace was more a listening kind of place with a gambling room off to the side, though Pearl had arranged the tables so that the hipsters could get up and swing. Moss made cheese sandwiches with mustard, which were sold for a dollar with a bottle of home-brewed beer. Opal, with her wispy blond hair and wraithlike body, served the beer and sandwiches on plastic red trays, carrying them with a flourish of one hand. Jonah poured the rotgut liquor that they kept under the bar, and Fern, who had opened the small beauty salon on the South Side, managed the household upstairs.

At night Pearl dabbed a touch of Anna's rosewater behind her ears and helped run the saloon. Jonah kept the books and bought bootlegged liquor. They served whiskey or gin or beer that was thirty percent ginger ale with a little air pumped in. Once in a while a cop came in and yelled at them, but Pearl slipped the cop a shot of the expensive whiskey, not the bathtub booze they usually served. Jonah never discussed with his sisters or with Moss where the beer and whiskey came from. The less people knew the better, but each morning a milkman arrived, dropping off silver canisters of liquid that would be siphoned into bottles, the empties left out on the step the next day.

It was no problem, really, keeping the saloon open in this way. Alcohol was no more difficult to procure than hard candy; it flowed like water. In Italian neighborhoods truckloads of grapes were dropped off daily and wine was picked up the following week. William J. Harding served wine at the White House. And the mayor of Chicago, Big Bill Thompson, owned a boat called the *Fish Fans Club* whose purpose was to support the fish in Lake Michigan. To celebrate Thompson's reelection so many members showed up for a drink that the *Fish Fans Club* sank.

It was rumored that gangs of thugs were driving around Chicago, demanding protection money from the speaks and tonks and illegal clubs. From time to time Pearl wondered why no one ever came to demand protection money from them. Perhaps the Jazz Palace was a forgotten place, neglected by the authorities as a harmless distraction. Or perhaps they were too small to be noticed, though Balaban and Katz, theatrical entrepreneurs, never forgot them. They were no longer the bedraggled boys who had taken free hot dogs when offered. Now they were rich men.

Every Wednesday evening a black limo pulled up in front of the candy store, and the two men in their pinstriped suits got out. Though they now owned theaters throughout the city, they still made their weekly stop. They ate hog dogs and drank sodas as they had since they were boys when Anna had only charged them a penny apiece. They talked to Pearl about the most ordinary things, even the weather or how those White Sox were doing. "Can you believe it?" Balaban said. "They threw the Series."

Though she didn't follow baseball and this would never have occurred to her, Pearl nodded. "I believe they did."

As they were leaving, they always asked the same thing. "Is there anything you need?" and Pearl always said no. "We're just keeping our promise to your mother," they told her. Then they disappeared back inside their limousine and drove away. Pearl was left to finger the envelope she kept in a drawer with the crisp ten- and twenty-dollar bills. She assumed that eventually someone would come in, demanding the money, but no one ever did. "I think we're already protected," Jonah said.

Napoleon continued to play on Mondays, and he was showing up on his off-nights too. The Red Rooster was his steady gig, but it was closed for repairs. Recently the club had come under new management. The light fixtures were removed and a crystal chandelier that cast amber light was hung. The big, cracked mirror over the bar was being antiqued and new porcelain toilets and sinks were installed. They kept the old cherrywood bar but brought in new stools. Some fancy tables and chairs were brought in, and a dance floor was laid along with a platform for the band. Napoleon was informed that the next time he came back to work he should wear his best suit.

So he was showing up more and more at Pearl's. He wouldn't allow her to pay him, though he'd never say no to free whiskey or tips. He brought musicians with him whenever he could. He told Pearl that there was a kid who'd been jamming with them. "A white boy, if you can imagine that." Napoleon laughed, shaking his head. Pearl told him that whenever he wanted he could bring the boy around. And Napoleon said that he would.

That summer on a hot August afternoon a man in a white linen suit slammed into a taxicab. He stumbled from his car, pulled a gun from his vest pocket, and threatened the driver. When the police arrived, they arrested the young man for drunk driving, disorderly conduct, and carrying a concealed weapon. He had a slash across his face that he would never explain. The business card he presented to the cops read "Alphonse Capone—secondhand furniture dealer." He had never dealt in secondhand furniture. He couldn't tell an antique from a ready-made chair. John Torrio, head of the Chicago syndicates, had hired this bookkeeper from Brooklyn whose real job was running two brothels.

He apologized to the driver for his outburst. He told a joke and made the policemen laugh. He was an affable man. He shook hands. Back in Brooklyn he was known for being a gentle boy. Despite his stocky build, he was a good dancer. He had rhythm and was light as a bird on his feet. He dressed well and was a family man. He sent his mother flowers for no reason. He did not know that he was suffering from tertiary syphilis, which was affecting his brain. This arrest would be the first time Al Capone's name appeared in the news, but not the last. The charges would later be dropped.

That same month a black boy named Louis, with a horn and a Star of David around his neck, bought a one-way ticket from New Orleans to Chicago. He wasn't really a boy. He was twenty-one years old, but people still called him "boy"—though Joe Oliver called him Dippermouth because of his big, wide grin. King Oliver who told Louis that the music was happening up north had sent him the money for the fare. Lately there had been more lynchings in the South. Even worse had been done to young black men.

And now his wife, Daisy, was running around, looking for him, with a razor blade. She'd slashed a man's throat before. Nothing was to stop her from doing it again. He was ready to leave. He wore the Star of David in honor of the Karnofsky family for whom he'd once delivered coal. They treated him like a son. They gave him his first cornet. The ticket was a gift from Joe "King" Oliver who asked him to play second cornet with his Creole Jazz Band. As the train pulled out, this boy knew that everything was about to change.

The cotton fields receded. Cities and farmlands came into view. The farmlands went on and on as if they'd never end. The ride seemed to be taking forever, and it was. The train would be hours late when it finally pulled into Union Station. In the stuffy compartments the young man sweated. His shirt was soaked and he'd brought only one change of clothes. When he reached Chicago, the air was sweltering, and no one was there to greet him. He walked up and down the platform, not knowing what to do. He had no money. He had nowhere to go.

An old black porter was walking toward him on the platform, and the young man stepped out of the way. But the porter kept coming toward him, and the young man wondered if he'd already done something wrong. "Excuse me," the old man said, tilting his red cap back, "but are you Mr. Armstrong?"

"Yes, sir," the startled cornet player replied, "I am."

"Well, King Oliver is sorry he couldn't meet your train, but he's expecting you. He asked me if I saw you to give you this." And the porter handed Louis two dollars to take a taxi downtown. Armstrong rode, his face pressed against the glass. They reached a street of blazing lights, and he saw the Stroll. He blinked and wiped his forehead. He wasn't sure if this place was real or a dream he was still having on a moving train.

At the Lincoln Gardens, a three-hundred-pound bouncer stood at the door. The music was the sweetest he'd ever heard. Armstrong touched the Star of David, certain that this was all a mistake. He stood in the doorway, sweating even more. His shirt was soaked. He needed a bath and something to eat. In his hand he clutched his cornet. The music paused and a man stepped out the side door of the Gardens. He lit a cigarette.

When he saw the boy, standing there, sweating, clutching his horn, Joe Oliver started to laugh. It had been four years since he'd heard the ragged kid playing at the brothel in Storyville. That horn had stopped Oliver in his tracks. He'd never heard anything like it, and he never forgot it. "What are you waiting for?" Joe Oliver asked. Armstrong looked perplexed. Oliver pressed his tongue to his gums. When he emptied his spit valve now, he saw blood. He looked at this boy with his portly build and bangs. "Get in there and go to work," King Oliver said. And Armstrong picked up his horn and went in.

An enormous crystal ball dangled from the center of the room, shooting a million rainbows of light. He thought he would be blinded. A thousand people were dancing. He'd never seen so many people in one room. He'd never been inside a room this big that wasn't a barn. White couples danced alongside blacks. Joe Oliver put him up on the bandstand before he had time to wash his face. The band started up and Armstrong followed. The crowds were dancing.

Drinks were clinking. It was at least a hundred degrees in that room. It smelled like a cave. Oliver pointed to Armstrong, and, trembling, he stood up to take a solo. Everyone was moving; then Dippermouth hit a high F sharp. The crowd came to a halt. It was a sound no one had ever heard. The band members stared. For an instant nobody moved. Then the crowd started shouting as if they had gone insane. King motioned for the band to come back in and they were all dancing like crazy again.

Chicago was a swinging town. Every night the clubs were filled. Benny went to the Lincoln Gardens every chance he could. That F sharp rang in his ears. Wherever the music took him, that's where Benny went. He picked up gigs here and there. He worked as a sideman for some bands. He was looking for a more permanent gig. Moe was still talking about putting together a band, and Benny thought maybe he'd join. At dinner he tapped out rhythms on his napkin as platters of chicken were being passed around. He hummed or whistled to himself. He was becoming a nuisance. He seemed to have lost interest in words. At dinner he tended to point rather than say, "Pass the peas." Hannah gazed at her son with a look of concern that annoyed Leo even more. He wanted the boy to snap out of it. Quit keeping his secrets hidden inside. But his mother forgave him. He was her dreamy child.

Seventeen

The Quarters Club was a replica of an old Southern mansion with large white columns. On the backdrop painted with weeping willows and slave quarters, black men strummed. An old woman carved a watermelon. Down four steps was the dance floor, which was also used for floor shows, and a full orchestra that performed in front of large double doors of the mansion. Waiters dressed in red shirts, overalls with suspenders, a bandanna around their necks. They got paid a dollar a night and made good money on tips.

It was one of the few fancy clubs that served blacks. Most of them catered to an all-white crowd, but the Quarters Club was a black and tan that served savory ribs and let in well-dressed blacks with money to blow. The owners, an Italian family named the Sorvinos, ran a few clubs with the philosophy that allowing black customers added to the local color. Blind Johnny and his band had been performing there for months.

Napoleon brought Benny down the steps on his arm. Because he had a white boy with him, they got a table near the front. Blind Johnny, dressed in a purple shirt, an orange jacket, and red-plaid trousers, was in the middle of his second set, but he gave Napoleon a wave. Napoleon waved back. "He's not really blind. Just color blind. Look at what he wears. He prides himself in it."

They sat back, taking in the music of the twelve-piece band.

Napoleon tapped his fingers on the table and smiled a wide grin. "I love this place. Reminds me of home." Napoleon laughed. "Actually I love the music." The cocktail waitress with pickaninny pigtails came by. "Have a drink. It's on me."

Benny shook his head, thinking about the one time he'd had a whiskey. "I don't drink," he said.

"Well, then order whatever that bottle is that you're always sucking on."

Napoleon had a whiskey and Benny sipped his cream soda. They settled back to listen to Blind Johnny and his band play some real jazz. The dance floor, which could hold almost a thousand people, was packed with young couples, cutting up the carpet. Napoleon glanced around, taking in all the other well-dressed white couples. He smiled, his pearly teeth shining as he told Benny, "You know, someday I want to play at a place like this."

"So why don't you?" Benny said.

"Why don't I . . ." Napoleon laughed. "You're Italian, right?"

"I'm a Jew, but it's a secret. Don't tell anyone. I pass for Italian when I need to."

"Your secret's safe with me. Besides I love Jews. They've been good to me. So to answer your question, I don't work here because I'm owned by the Rooster."

Benny put down his cream soda. "You're owned?"

"Oh yeah. The Gianellis own us." Napoleon explained that when he came north two black brothers named Jethrows owned the Rooster, but then they sold it and moved back to Kansas City and the Gianellis bought it. "They bought the club and they bought the musicians with it."

"I don't understand," Benny said, shaking his head.

Napoleon leaned forward to explain to Benny the facts of life. He told him that the Stroll is a big plantation. The musicians had their jazz slave masters, just like in the old days. Because he was under a contract with the Rooster, he could not play anywhere else for profit nor could his children and nor their children and so on. To the club owners he was just a *melanzane*. An eggplant. A black boy to these guys. "If word got out that I wanted to play at the Quarters

Club . . ." Napoleon made a sign of a knife sliding across the bottom of his throat. "And basically it's all run by Capone. In this part of town anyway."

Benny shook his head. "This can't be true."

"What planet are you from? Don't you know that about gangsters? They love jazz 'cause it's got guts and it don't make them slobber." Napoleon laughed, but Benny sensed the bitterness in his voice. "So they own us, man. Just like we used to be owned. We're owned like the Civil War never happened."

"You mean you aren't free . . ."

"You could say that," Napoleon said with a laugh. "I'm not exactly free. But," Napoleon said, making a fist and gazing out across the posh club, "I'm gonna be."

That evening as Napoleon was heading home, the city smelled of trash. As he walked, someone fell into step behind him. He couldn't tell if it was two or three people, but he was certain that they were men. Their footsteps came down hard on the pavement. Napoleon kept walking, but soon it seemed as if they were trying to walk to his beat. Glancing back, he saw two hefty men in shiny suits. He thought he'd seen them before, but he didn't know where or when. Napoleon avoided their eyes. He put his head down and ducked into an alleyway. They didn't follow him. He heard their footsteps receding, but he didn't look back. He never wanted to show a white man that he was afraid.

Eighteen

Since he'd been hanging out at the Rooster, Benny had been writing
down the music he heard in his head. He'd long ago filled the notebook his piano teacher had given to him. He'd gone to a music shop,
purchased a dozen more, and these he'd filled as well. He found that
once he started writing down the tunes that came to him, he couldn't
stop. If he didn't have a notebook with him, he wrote on menus and
napkins, on receipts and newspapers. It was usually just a few notes,
a bar, an opening refrain. He stuffed these scraps into his pockets
where they might be forgotten unless Hannah rescued them from
the wash.

But most nights when he got home, Benny spread them out on
his bed. He drew lines on paper and wrote down the music he made
up. Everything he heard found its way into the notes he made. As
the dawn light crept into his room, he pulled the red suitcase from
beneath his bed. He took the sheets with melodies he'd written,
opened the zipper pouch, and stuffed in the music he'd scribbled.

He wrote all the time except during those late-afternoon hours
between night and day when he didn't know what to do with himself. When work was over and the evening hadn't yet begun. He saw
people going about their business, on their way home on the streetcars, walking with the evening newspaper in their hands. He looked
at the dull gray of the city as it settled to dark, the clatter of dishes,

children's heads bent over books, cooking smells—chicken, stews, soups—drifting into the street.

It was in the pauses, in the space between notes, in the slips and breaks, a kind of slow steady interval as if one thing could lead to the next. As if you could go to sleep and wake up and it would be a new day and somehow things would be different than they'd been before. But Benny knew otherwise. Life didn't get better as it went along. It got narrower as if you were walking through a tunnel that was closing in on you, toward a distant beam of light that kept receding. Life got slower and the pauses got longer. Benny didn't mind the day when he was busy, and he waited for the night when he'd go somewhere and listen or play if they let him. It was the in-between time when he felt lost.

He started a song about that as well. He called it "Twilight Blue." In motion he was fine. It was when he stopped that the gray limbo settled around him. It would go away for a time. Then when he thought it wouldn't come back again, it did. In the chiaroscuro light other people went home, made supper, played cards, read the paper, made love, slept, talked to the children. But for Benny it was the dead time. This is what it's like to move through the world as a ghost. Benny wrote about this too. He scribbled it on his bits of paper, on menus. Across the palm of his hand.

In the Rooster late at night, between sets, Napoleon watched Benny scribbling. He heard Benny sit down at the piano and play what was written on the scraps of paper. Napoleon hadn't ever really wanted to write his music down before. He didn't want it codified or inscribed. He had wanted it to be open ended, whatever he made up in his head. But now there was so much of it and he couldn't remember one version from the next. And, he was beginning to realize, the music would die with him.

"My music," Napoleon said, "once I play it, it's gone."

"I could help write it down for you," Benny offered one night between sets.

"Naw, I don't want you doing that." And though Napoleon didn't want to say this to Benny, he was afraid that if it was written down, white boys would steal it as they had stolen so many things.

"Okay, so I won't." But Benny didn't believe him, and he began transcribing Napoleon's tunes as well as his own. When Napoleon played, Benny wrote as fast as he could. He wrote down what he was able, then asked Napoleon to play it again so he could pick up the rest. Napoleon never asked why. After hours he played a tune maybe half a dozen times before Benny had it right. He heard the music, then wrote it down. But not Napoleon. He had to rough it out, play it with his fingers. There were no colors racing through his head. He had to hear it in his joints, in his bones. But lately those fingers had been stiffening up on him. At times he woke up in the night, not able to find his hands. They stayed asleep long after the rest of him was up and drinking its coffee. Some mornings his fingers felt like wooden sticks. He soaked them in a bucket of scalding hot water. Once he made the water too hot, and the skin peeled off.

Benny wrote down all the music for himself and for Napoleon. He took it home and stuffed it into the red suitcase. He opened the zipper pouch where he kept his music pads and sheet music. He stayed up until all hours, writing from memory the tunes he'd heard Napoleon play and the ones he'd played with them. On the music composed by Napoleon he wrote "Written by Napoleon Hill/transcribed by Benny Lehrman" and the date.

Benny showed up at the Rooster almost every night. He sat in the back, his cap pulled over his head, sipping his cream soda. He never asked to sit in, but when the Judge took a smoke break, something he was doing more and more often, Napoleon gave the boy a nod. Napoleon wondered if this time the boy was here to stay or if he'd disappear again. He could look up any night and the boy would be gone. Past his bedtime, Napoleon thought. "Don't you have a mother?" Napoleon asked one evening between sets. "Don't you live somewhere?"

"I'm an orphan," Benny told him. Though his mother still waited up for him and his father slept in the chair until he was home, Benny thought of himself in this way. As if he lived in the streets by his wits.

Napoleon took this in. "You aren't an orphan," he replied. "Your shirts are too clean. You just act like one."

Benny gave Napoleon a little smile. Strange kid. Outside of the Chimbrova family, the only white people Napoleon had ever met were dead people. That was in New Orleans when he'd lived in Lafayette Cemetery where the bodies were buried above the ground. Otherwise, when the groundwater rose, the bodies floated away. At night when he was a boy who could not afford any other bed, Napoleon lay down on these crypts and slept. Before he drifted off, he looked over the raised graves, rested his hand on chiseled stone. He ran his fingers over what was etched.

These were white people's graves. Black people were buried in open fields with hand-carved cement slabs to mark their graves. Burnt-out trees served as wishing stumps, carrying the hopes of the living to the dead. White people didn't have wishing stumps. They were buried in cement. They didn't fertilize the fields. They didn't play the blues. But this boy did. His arms were long and loose. They reached all over, winding as back roads, twisting as if they could grab and pull you in. Napoleon had seen arms like that before, but he couldn't quite place it. Then as Benny was playing a break, his arms flailing, Napoleon did.

When they finished the tune, Napoleon said, "I got a name for you. You know, I'm gonna call you Moon Jelly. That's the jellyfish we got down on the Gulf Coast. I've seen them on the beach and popped them with sticks. Seen them get caught up in the fisherman's nets. 'Jelly' 'cause you're loose and 'Moon' because you're white and changeable. That's what you remind me of."

"Moon Jelly." Benny liked the sound of it. He ran it over and over in his mind. "Okay, so that's what I'll be." He dropped his head down and started riffing on his "Twilight Blue." He'd been fiddling with the melody for a while but hadn't gotten it right. Napoleon picked it up in G minor and soon they were improvising, letting it go wherever it went. Benny's foot stomped away as he added some changes at the end of the first chorus, and Napoleon took off on that as well. Now they were swinging, eyes on each other, barely coming up for air.

Benny was hunched over the keys when two men in sharkskin suits walked in, but something in him stirred and made him look up. He almost laughed. They were big, like walking vaults. One man's suit was an electric blue and he wore a bright yellow tie. The other was dressed in green with a red shirt. They looked like Christmas ornaments as they ordered lemonade that they sipped through straws. The man in green tapped his hands on the table but not in time with the music. The other was cleaning his fingernails with a knife. Benny switched to "Fat Man Rag" and grimaced as Napoleon flubbed a high note that was well within his reach.

"What's up?" Benny gave Napoleon a look, but Napoleon kept on playing. When they finished the last set, the customers trickled out. But the two men in the sharkskin suits remained. The one in green sipped his lemonade until it made a slurping sound. The other was still filing his nails. He let the shavings drop to the floor. Benny wanted to stay and help close, but Napoleon shook his head. "You'd better get home. You've got a ways to go."

"Remember, I'm an orphan." But Napoleon made a gesture that said "scram."

"You sure?" Benny asked. "You don't want me to stick around?"

"Naw, go on. Take a powder," Napoleon said. "You get out of here."

It was a brisk spring morning, and Benny wasn't in a hurry. The fresh air felt good off the lake. He thrust his hands into his pockets and picked up his step. He listened to the click of his footsteps on the pavement. The sounds of the city rose around him. A car door slamming, a truck making early morning deliveries rattling by. Laughter came from a building above.

But he was uneasy. He'd forgotten something. He had a feeling he'd left something behind. Halfway down the block he remembered his notes for "Twilight Blue." He checked his pockets, then realized he'd left them on the piano. They'd be in the trash by morning. Benny turned and raced back to the Rooster as the cock's comb went dark. He tapped on the window, then on the door, but no one was inside. He banged again, then told himself he'd have to come back in the morning. As he turned to leave, he heard the clatter of trash cans. He thought it was tomcats rummaging in the trash, but then he heard it again—louder this time.

Peering into the alley, he saw the scuffle. The two men were jumping on a third. They were the men in sharkskin suits who'd been sipping lemonade. They were jumping on a man in a shiny pearl-gray suit. Benny poked his head farther down the alleyway and saw that they had Napoleon on the ground. Before he knew what he was doing, Benny rushed into the fray. He was small and wiry but strong. He grabbed an arm, tugging it back as the man tried to slam Napoleon into the pavement. He was amazed at the man's grip. The arm shook him off, flinging Benny against the trash can. Benny returned, laying a punch with his long arms. Something hard landed against his jaw. He swung back, though he was worried about his hands. He curled them into tight balls as he got in a few more punches.

A silver blade flashed. Benny saw the knife coming toward him, and he tried to grab the man's wrist. But the man pushed Benny aside the way a child might discard a toy. They weren't interested in him. They batted Benny backward to get him out of the way, their arms hurling him against the walls of the alley as he flailed like a man who suddenly realizes that he can't swim. Within seconds the men took off, but not before, with a few deft strokes, they left Napoleon bleeding.

They slashed his cheeks, his throat, and his lips. The cheeks and throat were just surface cuts, but his lips were sliced in two. Benny put his fingers on them to stanch the bleeding, but the cut was deep. The puffy lips that he massaged every day with eucalyptus and lard were butterflied like a fish. Napoleon looked up, dazed. He sobbed, sputtering out the words "I'm never gonna play again," as the blood rolled down his chin. "They knew what they was doing. I ain't ever going to play again."

"You will," Benny said, though even as he said it he wasn't sure. "Come on. Let's get this stitched up."

"Jew boy," Napoleon said, "get out of here."

Benny ignored him. He took Napoleon by the arm. He was so

heavy Benny could barely take a step. He'd seen a shingle for a doctor around the corner and he dragged Napoleon there. Benny banged on the door. Sleepily the doctor opened it, but when he looked at the cuts that crisscrossed Napoleon's face, he said, "I can't help you. No one will touch this." Benny had been naïve once, but he didn't need this explained to him now.

Benny thought for a moment. "Tell me how to stitch it up." Napoleon groaned as blood splattered down his creamy silk shirt. "Tell me what to do."

"You have to match the edge of the vermilion border. Where the pink meets the black. Start there. Then sew up and down. Tiny stitches." And the doctor closed the door.

With Napoleon moaning, Benny stood wondering where to go next. Then suddenly he knew. "Stay here," he said, and he pushed Napoleon behind a pile of trash. "I don't want anyone to see you." Benny went to the corner and flagged down a taxi. When the taxi stopped, he motioned for Napoleon to get in. "I'm not taking any . . ." The driver didn't finish his sentence.

"You'll get a good tip. Head towards Cicero." The driver looked back with an angry gaze. "Just drive," Benny said. He hoped he could remember how to get to where he was going. He'd been there only once before. The driver, mad because he had a black man with bleeding lips in his backseat, grumbled but followed Benny's hand motions, wove his way through the streets, heading west. "No," Benny said as Napoleon groaned beside him, "it's farther west." They passed vacant lots, trash-lined streets, packing houses.

He saw two or three buildings that he thought were right, but then he told the driver to keep going. "No, not here."

The driver shook a glance behind him as Napoleon moaned, a bloody handkerchief pressed to his lips. "Don't you dare mess up my cab, buddy," he said.

"Just keep driving," Benny said. He wasn't sure if he'd remember, but he did. He spotted the building with the large, empty lot stretching before it. He saw the crumbling façade, the boarded-up ground floors, and he told the driver to stop. He tossed him five bucks, a whole week's salary, which the man snatched, then screeched his tires as he drove away. Benny led Napoleon up the dreary staircase. He knocked once. Waited. Then knocked three more times. An old woman in bathrobe and slippers opened it, startled to find a white boy in a fedora and a black man with blood drizzling down his chin. Benny told her whom he wanted, and the woman pointed upstairs. He had counted the landings wrong. Napoleon struggled to climb. Tears poured down his face.

On the fifth landing Benny knocked again—once, then three times. The girl in a gray nightie opened the door. She was skinny and frail with dark circles under her eyes. Her tiny nipples budded out from the gown. "I've been here before," Benny told her, but he could see that she had no idea who he was. "Is your mother home?" The girl called out as she let them in.

When Marta came to the door, she stared at him, then at the black man. Her face had hardened and she seemed older. Her fingers were thick and gnarled. She had a shawl around her shoulders. Benny could still see the wide shape of her hips, her ample breasts, but he was long past hiding in his mother's sewing room and tossing bits of scrap cloth out the window that he had moistened with thoughts of her.

Marta held up her finger and told Benny to wait. When she came back, she had on a robe and her hair was brushed. She motioned them inside. The girl was already asleep on the cot in the kitchen behind the curtain. She looked as small as he remembered, and her breathing was so heavy that he could hear it. Benny explained what he wanted done. "He's a trumpeter," Benny said. "He needs his lips."

She looked at the gash, then gave Napoleon cloth soaked in whiskey, which he sucked as if it were a mouthpiece. She woke a neighbor who had a block of ice. After Napoleon finished the whiskey and lay still, Marta held the ice to his lips. While she pressed it, the child coughed. Marta got up, motioning for Napoleon to hold the ice himself. She went to the child, put her hand on her forehead, then pulled the covers up and tucked her in.

Then Marta returned to Napoleon, keeping the ice there until his lips were numb. With a tiny needle and the thinnest black thread, she matched the edge of the vermilion border as Benny told her to do. She stitched up, then down. Napoleon twitched under her needle, but he didn't cry out. Benny held his hand and Napoleon squeezed hard, but not so hard as to hurt Benny's fingers, while Marta made the tiniest, quickest stitches Benny had ever seen.

When she was done, Napoleon's lips looked like a narrow fault line, a crack running through them. Benny rubbed his finger over it until he was satisfied that the suture was smooth and would hold. All night Marta kept ice pressed against his mouth. As Napoleon slept in a drunken stupor, she held the ice until the light of morning seeped in.

Nineteen

When Napoleon arrived at the Jazz Palace with a ragged scar on his lips and a white boy on his arm, Pearl was surprised. It had been weeks since she'd seen him and she'd begun to wonder if he was ever coming back. She worried that something might have happened and she didn't know where he lived. She was beginning to think about going down to the South Side and look for him when he showed up maimed and with a honky, as Napoleon would say, she'd never seen. She pointed to his lips, but he waved her away.

"Cut myself shaving," he said as he led his companion into the saloon. Napoleon had shown up in the past with other musicians, but they were all black men who jammed with him. And they'd all had come up from the South. "Any black man who's been in a town that's seen a lynching is going to get on a train heading north," he told Pearl one night when she asked why so many were coming to Chicago. He'd never shown up with a white boy before.

As they walked in, Pearl was rinsing glasses at the bar. She was holding one up to the light to make sure it was squeaky clean. She rubbed out the smudges with a cloth. Through the refracted light, she saw Benny, but not all at once. He came to her in pieces. Four eyes, an enlarged nose. She put the glass down and he reassembled himself. He had a shy, quiet face and mud-colored eyes she could barely see because of the cap he pulled over them, and a big laugh that came from somewhere deep inside.

As he stepped past the black mourning ribbons that dangled from the doorway, he took off his cap, revealing a shock of wavy black hair. He wore a strange bag around his neck that emitted the pungent odor of stale tea. As he walked across the room, he bumped into a table. At the bar his gangly arms knocked over an empty glass. His hands shook as he fumbled to pick it up and his eyes darted around the room. Pearl had no idea why Napoleon had brought him here.

Benny was wondering as well. He'd been happy playing off-hours in the South Side juke joints and honky-tonks, picking up sessions work here and there. But Napoleon had insisted. "You don't want to be the best-kept secret in town, do you? White folks should hear you play." Napoleon told him he needed to play at the Jazz Palace.

Except for the thin pink scar that divided his mouth in two, Napoleon's lips were healed; *healed but not sealed* is what he liked to say. His embouchure was restored, and he was grateful to Benny. When he found he could blow again, Napoleon had draped the gris-gris bag his grandmother had given him around Benny's neck. "You saved my life, Moon," Napoleon told him. "Here's John the Conqueror. The trickster for when you need him."

"I saved your lips," Benny replied.

"I don't know the difference. From now on you're a brother to me."

As he was listening to the all-black band jamming, Benny fondled the bag. Often he found himself touching it. It seemed to calm him down. He never took it off except to bathe. The group was playing loud and fast, New Orleans style, and the place was jumping, but on their break, Jonah urged him to play. "Go ahead," Jonah said. He assumed this boy was a musician. Why else would Napoleon have brought him? "Let's see what you can do." Benny looked around to be sure it was all right. Most people had never seen a white boy playing with black men, but this didn't bother Jonah. "It's okay. You can sit in here."

The bass player and drummer wandered back in as Napoleon took out his horn and Benny sat down on the bench. Pearl rolled her eyes and thought, *This better be good.* Napoleon nodded. "What'll you drink?" she called.

Napoleon shouted back, "Give me a whiskey, but this boy won't touch nothing."

"I'll take a cream soda," he said, pulling his cap back over his eyes. Pearl shrugged. She'd never known a musician to refuse a drink before, but she sent Opal into the candy shop for a cold cream soda, and she returned, wide-eyed, hands trembling as she placed the drink on the piano. Opal gazed at Benny who stared back at the girl with the golden hair and pale-blue eyes. He hunched over the keys. He curled deep so that his neck disappeared into his shoulders like a snail. He ran some scales and nodded, declaring the piano good. Then his feet started tapping and Napoleon was snapping his fingers. Benny improvised on a jaunty intro while the musicians nodded. Napoleon whispered, "That's it, Moon. You show them how it's done."

Benny nodded and kept playing until he came up for air, and Napoleon picked up his horn. They played a little "Avalon" and "Bugle Boogey," songs anyone would know. And when Benny saw that the crowd was warmed up, he slowed it down and switched to an odd little tune he'd been thinking about. It had come to Benny one day as he watched people dragging their feet, going to work. Not wanting to go anywhere. He watched them on the trolley as he headed to and from his father's caps factory. And as he stood on the street, hesitating before he went inside. He assumed that the rest of the world hesitated too in front of the factories and tailors and retail shops and laundries and butchers. Places where you left a little piece of yourself outside the door. Then in the early evening he watched them coming home, dragging their feet back to cold-water flats and crying babies and wives who wanted more or husbands who wanted less.

"State Street Shuffle" was what he called it. It started out slow, hushed as a secret, and the customers who had been chatting leaned in to listen. Sadness in the notes hung in the air like bad news. No one wanted to be reminded of a cold wind off the lake, a bill you couldn't pay. Or someone who'd be coming home late. Or not at all. Then the melody picked up and the drum came in. People got up and started taking a spin on the dance floor or sipping a glass of gin. The bass picked up the beat as Napoleon waited to come in.

Pearl, who was wiping the mahogany counter, cocked her head. She was listening. And looking. It wasn't so much the music, though she was listening to that as well. She was trying to place him. There was something about his hunched-over shoulders and the way his long fingers moved. The jitters of his arms and legs. She'd seen him before, though she had no idea when or where. He brought with him his melancholy eyes, his tapping feet, and a memory of disaster that overwhelmed her. His apelike arms dangled toward the floor, and his hands were the size of catchers' gloves. She wondered if he was from the neighborhood or had gone to her school. He was too old to be in her grade. Had he been a friend of her brothers who'd drowned? But wouldn't he have said so?

Pearl was trying to remember as he sped the music up. He'd grown weary of the past as he picked up steam. His hands moved faster, the left hand churning like a hamster in a wheel. He hit the pedal, pounding the beat with his foot as his fingers glided up and down. Napoleon came in blasting and the drummer was laughing and hitting his skins. He turned his "State Street Shuffle" into Dixieland and soon feet were pumping, hands clapping.

Opal grabbed up her long gray skirt and clicked her heels in the middle of the floor. Her blond tresses tumbled down while Pearl kept the beat with her palms on the mahogany bar. Benny's hands skipped across the keys. He had dozens of tunes in him and he played them all, leaping from one to the next. He kept going and going and the band stayed with him until he dropped his head down again and as the room grew still, Pearl caught her breath. "It's so strange." She turned to Jonah who stood beside her, beaming at the bar.

"What? The way he plays?" Even Jonah was swaying to the beat.

"No, it's not that. I can't explain it." She stared at Benny, shaking her head. "I feel as if I've known him my whole life."

"What do you mean?" Jonah stared at her, surprised.

"I don't know," Pearl said as Benny hit the keys with a laugh and brought back the beat. "I just do."

Twenty

The next morning Napoleon got up earlier than he had since he was pouring coffee at the Shoestring Diner. He bathed with Maddy's almond-scented soap and gave himself a close shave, then splashed on a stinging aftershave and dusted talc under his arms. Then he put on his best gray flannel jacket, pressed navy-blue slacks, and a fedora, stuck a red handkerchief in his pocket, and walked down the street. It was a crisp day and he took his time. He was about to do something he'd never willingly done in his life. He was going to walk into a police station. It was rare for a Negro, let alone a well-dressed one, to be seen voluntarily entering a police station.

As he approached the building, cops on the sidewalk stared, perhaps taking him for a pimp or a visiting dignitary from a small African nation. One laughed and said, "Where's the party," then asked to see his invitation. A criminal being moved for arraignment shook his head in disbelief. On the first step Napoleon paused. He sucked in the air, filling his lungs. He thought he'd have to say what he needed to say in one long breath, and he wanted to be prepared. It had taken him weeks to gather the courage. But the night before at the Jazz Palace he'd felt his nerve return. After all, it had once taken him weeks to take a trolley to the North Side. Now that he could blow and knew he would go on, Napoleon was determined to right this wrong.

Since "the incident," as he referred to the assault on his lips, Napoleon had changed. It was a slow, tortoiselike shift. Unless it was about a woman, most things changed for him slowly. It wasn't perceptible, really. Not something anyone who didn't know him well, and not many people did, might have noticed. His gaze was more of a stare. His jaw squarely set as if he were biting down on a bone. Something had been growing inside of him like a hard, stubborn seed.

Before he'd allowed life to carry him along. He went wherever the flow took him. From the delta to New Orleans. From the streets in the South he'd made his way north. He found a place to live as soon as he arrived, and he'd lived with Maddy for the past twelve years. He'd helped raise her kids, but he had none of his own. Nothing to hold him down. Nothing to keep him still. Maddy knew that he might wake up any morning and leave. He wouldn't look back. It was as if everything—even his music—had just happened to him.

He'd been the recipient of good and bad through no effort of his own. People he loved died or went away. Others just lingered. He seemed to have no say in the matter. He hadn't really struggled against any demons. He wouldn't know them if they were staring at him from the mirror. But now it seemed they were. For days he'd stayed in bed. He couldn't bring himself to get up, let alone go to work. It was difficult for him to speak, let alone smile. He thought he'd split down the seam. For weeks the only thing he could eat was banana mash and milk with a straw. His face had been blown up like a blowfish. His mouth looked as if a pinprick would make it explode. Even as the swelling subsided, he found it hard to speak, let alone purse his lips around his mouthpiece. When he blew, all that came out was a faint whistle. The air siphoned through like a house with a draft. For weeks he was sure he'd never play again.

Maddy had tried to coax him with warm broths and cold plasters she placed over his lips. She'd rubbed them gently with a salve she made from aloe and mint. When she did, Napoleon kept his eyes closed because he feared what he'd see in hers. It was what everyone knew, but no one would say. He'd never play the trumpet again. Because he couldn't bear the pity in anyone's eyes, he slept with a blanket pulled tight over his head. He didn't know day from night. When Maddy came home, she found him like this.

He'd lain around despondent, smoldering as the rage built inside him, and then one morning he erupted, flinging off the covers and deciding that his lying around was done. Something was shifting. The razor had slashed through more than just his lips. There was a deeper cut that made it clear to Napoleon that he had to do something. A deep ancestral cry rose in his throat. He needed to shout it out. If not from his voice, then from his horn. Perhaps for the first time in his life Napoleon had something he wanted to say. A grave injustice had been done to him.

He had suffered many things in his thirty-six years. He was not a stranger to any feeling. But this one. Injustice. It was a different kind of beast. A multiheaded Hydra. He could not let it live. When the blacks got off the trains that carried them north and away from Jim Crow, they settled by the railroad tracks. They didn't know where else to go. They couldn't imagine anything more for themselves. Now Napoleon was furious. The North was no different than the South. He may as well have been beaten with a whip. The more his lips healed the more defiant he grew.

One morning weeks after his attack he'd thrown off the covers and gotten out of bed. He went to the bathroom where he scrubbed every pore and orifice until he was the cleanest he'd been since the day a skunk ambushed him and his grandmother stuck him in a washtub and went over every inch of him with carbolic soap. In his closet he found a clean shirt and a pressed pair of pants. He pulled up a chair and began making smacking noises in front of the mirror. He went to work on his chops. He didn't know if he'd play again, but he had to give it a try.

He stretched his tight lips with his fingers the way a ballerina stretches her thighs. He massaged them when they were sore. He kissed anyone he could. But when he put his trumpet to his lips, the noise that came out sputtered like an old man's farts. The pain he likened to childbirth, though Maddy shook her head and told him that like most men on this subject he didn't know a thing. Every night he tried to play until tears streamed from his eyes. Nothing came close to music. He tried again the following evening and the one after that. He stretched his lips and rubbed lard and aloe salve on them. He massaged them the way a trainer rubs his boxer's legs. One night when he put the horn to his lips, they puckered, and he found that he could blow. He squeaked out a minor scale. Then he collapsed in sobs because he understood that his life wasn't through.

And now months later he was back and he was prepared. It had taken all of his courage, for what black man would dare to do what he was about to do? A black man who didn't plan to live long was probably the answer. As he stepped up to the desk, the man in uniform was filling out a report. He didn't bother looking up. Napoleon put his hands on the desk and the officer glanced at them with disdain, then shook his head. "Excuse me," Napoleon said, but the policeman ignored him. He waited again, then spoke again a bit more firmly, "I would like to speak to someone."

The officer looked up at him, a questioning look in his eyes. "To whom would you like to speak?" The officer's tone was mocking, as Napoleon assumed it would be. Black men in flannel suits didn't normally come into this precinct, or any precinct, for that matter, unless they were handcuffed. Especially a black man with a slashed mouth. Normally these kinds of Negroes settled their own scores. The officer assumed he'd come to bail out a friend. "The bondsman is down the hall." He pointed, still without looking up.

"I have come to file a grievance," Napoleon said. "I have been assaulted and I would like to fill out whatever form is necessary to aid in the apprehending of the men who did this to me." He pointed a gloved index finger to his face.

The man stared impassively at Napoleon's filleted lips. He gazed at the scar.

"Hey, you're lucky it was only your lips." A rookie standing near the desk giggled. "You musta done something somebody didn't like."

Napoleon didn't flinch. "Yes, I played music in another club. "

The officer shrugged as if to say what did you expect. Then he handed Napoleon the form for a police report, which he filled out as best he could. He described the men who had assaulted him. He could barely see their faces, but he knew their shiny suits. He signed it, then handed it back to the officer who looked it over and grinned. Then Napoleon turned and walked out of the police station, hesitating on the steps long enough to hear the officers laughing and to see the cop crumple his report and lob it into the trash.

Napoleon wouldn't give up. He'd find a way to handle this himself. He began doing calisthenics. He did push-ups and pull-ups on whatever rafter he could hang from. He made muscles in front of mirrors, examining his rippled arm. He'd be ready for them when they came next time, but, as he tugged himself up and down from the rafters, Maddy worried that he was going to pull down the whole house. He stopped drinking whiskey. He drank unsweetened lemonade and black coffee instead.

A few nights later Napoleon was back on the Stroll. He took whatever gigs were offered. As far as he was concerned, the only thing he had to lose was his life, and his music meant more. He played at the Rendez-Vous Café. He played at Dreamland and the Quarters Club. When he arrived at a gig, he never looked around to see who might be sitting in the audience. It was his funeral, as Maddy liked to remind him. He'd come to play and he'd play wherever and whenever he wanted. His fame grew. Everyone wanted to see the man with the scar on his lips. They'd heard about the Defiant Black Man. That's what the black press had begun calling him. The Defiant Black Man.

Every Monday Napoleon arrived at the precinct where the officers were getting to know him. They greeted him with waves and slaps on the back. Once they invited him to sit in on a hand of poker. One or two came to hear him play after hours in one of the South Side clubs. His fame grew. They liked him at the police station, but clearly no one would touch his complaint with a ten-foot pole. Each week he asked politely if any action had been taken on his behalf. He was told it was an ongoing investigation. He was told it was being looked into. He was asked to fill out a new complaint, as the old paperwork had been lost. That paperwork was quickly lost as well. When the police did nothing about finding the thugs who'd cut him, he asked for Benny's help. He told Benny that he wanted to write a letter.

Napoleon dictated to Benny. "In the spring of this year two men came to the Red Rooster Lounge as Napoleon Hill was closing up for the night. They had heard the rumors that Mr. Hill was looking to play in other clubs. With evil intent and knowing that he is a musician, and specifically a trumpeter, they sliced his lips. He was fortunate, however, to have had a friend with him who knew what to do. Mr. Hill has resumed his musical career. It should be noted that black men are no longer slaves and they should not be treated like slaves and this includes the circumstances of their employ. We have earned the right to be free and so we shall be."

In the morning Napoleon put on his best gray suit with a snazzy purple tie, shiny black shoes with spats, and a fedora with a purple band. He rubbed the salve on his lips and cologne behind his ears, then set off, walking south. It was a long walk, but the weather was fine. There was a cool breeze off the lake and Napoleon took in great gulps of air. He reasoned that this might be one of the last morning walks he'd ever take so he wanted to savor the moment.

He walked until he came to the old synagogue that had recently become the offices of the *Chicago Defender*. Napoleon took a deep breath. He straightened his tie and his fedora and walked in the door. He stood for a moment in the large open newsroom, filled with black journalists who were writing copy, editing copy, writing headlines. Slowly the newsroom came to a halt. One worker after another looked up and stared. Then they rose in recognition of the man their paper had dubbed the Defiant Black Man. The glass door at the back of the editorial offices opened and a portly black man in a three-piece suit walked into the hushed newsroom. He moved toward Napoleon, his hand extended. "Mr. Hill," Robert S. Abbott said, "to what do I owe this honor?"

Napoleon collected himself. He had no idea that he was this famous. He had no idea that Robert S. Abbott, editor and founder of the most prestigious black newspaper in America, would know his name. Napoleon cleared his throat. With his lips cut he had to be careful not to spit. "This is my manifesto," Napoleon said. "Please print it." There was a risk and Abbott knew it. The Chicago Outfit, as they were becoming known, thought nothing of firebombing a speakeasy. Surely they wouldn't think twice about destroying a newspaper. Yet he had spent his years as a journalist campaigning for blacks to leave the South. He'd convinced thousands that the opportunities were in the North. He could not ignore what was happening now in the city to which he'd urged black men and women to come.

The next day the story ran, "Defiant Black Man Throws Down Gauntlet." It got picked up in the white press. The *Sun Times* ran a story as well, but it didn't call him the Defiant Black Man. Because of the way his lips looked, they referred to him as the Black Butterfly instead. "Black Butterfly Defies Mob." When Napoleon saw the name, he liked it. It was strange in a way he enjoyed. "Black" and "butterfly" didn't seem to belong in the same phrase, but in this case they went hand in hand.

From then on Napoleon announced himself onstage by his sobriquet. All the posters and advertisements, announcing his performances, referred to him as the Black Butterfly as well. He got asked to play more clubs than he could handle. He never said no to a gig no matter how small. He played all the white clubs and the black and tans. He was at the Orchid and the Diamond Club while still doing sets at the Rendez-Vous Café and Dreamland. He was a spectacle people came to see. They wanted to hear the Negro play whose lips had been cut in two. People came just to hear the Black Butterfly jam. Men in zoot suits and girls in flapper dresses and fox shawls, wearing cloche hats and strands of pearls, stopped perfect strangers in the street. "Do you know where the Black Butterfly is playing tonight?" they'd ask.

It was a novelty in a world that seemed constantly in need of more novelties. He became a celebrity in his defiance. "Black Butterfly Emerges from His Cocoon," headlines read. "Black Butterfly Defies the Odds."

Twenty-One

≡

It was a warm evening of Indian summer as Benny headed through the vacant lot, kicking a stone. He didn't like walking across the lot after dusk. And he wasn't sure why he was going this way now. The four of them had once played together here in the summer and those early evenings when their homework was done. They played ball until their mother called them to come home. Sometimes Benny thought he heard Harold—his high-pitched shout. A voice that had never changed.

He didn't notice the dark figure coming up beside him. He leaped with his heart in his throat. "Hey," Moe said, "what's with you?"

"You spooked me." He placed a hand on his heart and another on his friend's arm.

"Sorry about that." Moe fell into pace beside him.

"So," Benny said, still trying to catch his breath, "where've you been keeping yourself?"

Moe gave a wave of his hand. "You know. Around." He paused. "Say, Benny, I'm still waiting. When are we going to strike out on our own?"

"On our own?"

"You know, get a band going."

Benny smiled as he stayed in stride with his friend. "Sure, Moe. We could."

"I mean look at those boys from Austin High. They've got a band and they're doing all right." Scheming and dreaming, that's how Benny thought of Moe. Moe was the one with the plans. He'd long ago stopped caring about his family or supporting them. But Benny was different. He had responsibilities. Or they had him. Deep down, though, Benny knew that it wasn't just that. There was a loneliness in him that he couldn't name. At times he wanted to form a combo. The Benny Lehrman Trio sounded good. But he didn't know if he would. He was more of a sideman. Or he'd go solo. He'd join other people's bands, but he didn't think he could form one of his own. He was too much of a lone wolf. That's what he'd always been. But had he? He tried to remember back to a time before Harold died. But he could never get there. It was as if his life began and ended on that day.

"I'm moving into a place downtown. There's room for you. It's not far from the Board of Trade. I bet my uncle could get you a job there. We could walk to work. And we could do music whenever we want."

Benny thought about the gray walls of his parents' apartment, the worn-out overstuffed chairs. The smell of soup that lingered in his clothing. He wanted to go, but he couldn't. Benny was still his parents' son. "I'll think about it," he said. "I promise I will."

"Thinking about it means you aren't going to do it." Moe shook his head of dark curls that had thinned over the years. "You'd be welcome . . . We never did leave town, did we, Benny? But we still could, you know."

Benny nodded. "Yes. Maybe we will."

"One of these days, right?" Moe jabbed him in the ribs.

"That's right." Benny jabbed back, and Moe pretended to duck. "One of these days." The two friends shook hands as if they'd just sealed a business deal. Then Benny strolled along Lawrence Avenue. He breathed in the clean fall air. Above him gulls squawked. He laughed at their raucous sound.

It was quiet at the Jazz Palace as Benny walked in. He shouted a hello to Jonah and greeted Pearl at the bar. "The usual?" Pearl asked, giving him a nod.

"That would be swell." She went into the candy store for his cream soda. "Hot for this time of year, isn't it?" he said as she returned. "Hot or cold, that's Chicago."

Pearl stood by the door, fanning herself. "Yes, it is." He took his cream soda and leaned against the lintel. "Maybe that's what's keeping the customers away." Pearl sighed. Since Benny had been playing here, the place was usually packed. But tonight you could hear a pin drop.

He pressed the cold bottle of soda against his brow. "Let's get some air." He touched her arm, leading her to the tavern door. She was surprised at how cool, almost clammy, his hands were. There was hardly a breeze as they stood outside. When he spoke, she listened to the lilt in his voice, the familiarity in his eyes. "We've become good friends, haven't we, Pearl?" She drew back as he said this. It wasn't what she wanted to hear.

"Yes, I suppose we have . . ."

"How old are you, Pearl?"

She was surprised by the directness of his question. "Well, you tell me first. How old are you?" she asked.

"I'm twenty-three. It's easy for me to remember. I'm as old as the century. Now you tell me."

Pearl had to think about this for a moment, since she'd hardly marked the years. "I'm just twenty," she said.

Benny laughed. "Oh, I thought you were older than that."

She winced at this. At times even to herself she seemed older than her years. It was as if she'd had to grow up suddenly and too quickly. She wondered if there wasn't something or someone who could make her young. "Well, you must think I'm an old maid then."

"No, no. It's just that you seem more grown up." He patted her hand, then let it go.

She tried to determine if this news disappointed him. "I suppose I am. I've had to grow up fast." She gazed up at the lintel of the Jazz Palace.

"So have I," Benny said. "Ever since I lost my brother."

"Oh, I'm sorry to hear that." Pearl gave him a look of concern. "I didn't know. Do you mind if I ask what happened?"

Benny shook his head. "He got lost in the snow." He realized that this sounded strange. How could a boy get lost in the snow? "There was a blizzard." He couldn't bring himself to explain to her about the rope that held his brothers together. How it was his responsibility to make certain the rope was taut.

"It's terrible. I understand," Pearl murmured. "I lost three."

"Really? I'd wondered . . ." He shook his head, following her gaze to the tattered black cloth. "Was it the influenza?"

It was easier to lie. The truth would have required a long explanation. It would have led to pity and sadness. But she decided against it. "No, but they died suddenly. Our mother was never the same."

He wanted to tell her about Harold's smile. How he'd been the favorite and gotten lost in the snow. He wanted to tell her how he'd tried to save others, that his first dance was in the arms of a dead girl. He had never confided about this to anyone. He wished he could now. He thought perhaps he would, but Pearl put her hand on Benny's arm. "Let's not talk about this," she said. "It's too sad."

Benny agreed. "Let's not talk about it again."

Customers trickled into the Jazz Palace as Napoleon arrived in a new yellow jacket and a cream-colored tie and walked right past Benny and Pearl at the entranceway, tipping his hat. On the bandstand Napoleon whispered into Benny's ear. "I see you're spending time with my night owl."

Benny nodded. "She's just a friend."

"Well, you should make her more. She's a strong girl and she's prettier than you think. You gotta look at her right."

"And how is that?" Benny laughed.

"Don't look at her straight on. That's not her best angle."

Laughing, Benny shook his head.

"Look at her sideways," Napoleon said. But Benny didn't know how.

Sitting on the bench, Benny tapped his foot. His pink tongue curled in his mouth, flicked out like a lizard's. He hunched over. His fingers skidded across the keys, then he jabbed at them, the way you might poke at a sleeping beast. He settled into some chords as he found a tune. A quiet came over the saloon, the second silence Pearl had ever heard there—the first when she was a girl of twelve and the sounds of Napoleon's trumpet snuck upstairs and wrapped themselves around her bed.

Pearl froze in midmotion, wiping the bar with a cloth. She tried to put her finger on what she was hearing as she watched him drift into the music. It wasn't just playing that Benny did. It was going away. Even he might have called it that if anyone asked. He went to a different place. He wasn't in the room. He wasn't anywhere. He was gone, lost inside something of his own making. At the bar Pearl caught Napoleon by the arm. "Tell me. Where did he learn to play like that?"

"He's not playing." Napoleon reached for his horn. "He's howling at the moon."

Dropping his head, Benny tapped his foot and slipped into a few standards like "St. Louis Blues" and "Wild Boy Stomp." Then his fingers flashed with his "Small Potatoes" as he got the joint jumping and segued into his newest number, which he called "Satan's Mile." Once he knew he had them, he quieted the place down with that tune he'd been struggling with. His "Twilight Blue." He noodled with the opening bars. The tune was hushed as a baby sleeping, and the saloon grew still. He began with the melody in the right hand, and slowly he brought in the left. It was as quiet a melody as anyone had ever heard, and it drifted off so no one was sure where it had gone or if he was done until he stopped.

Benny looked up, blinking like a sleeper in a strange hotel who, startled upon waking, has no idea where he is. His eyes landed on Pearl, who stood behind the bar, and he had a stunned look as his eyes made contact with hers. Her dark hair, her olive skin. The almond eyes. He looked at her the way a person might if he has just stepped off the edge of a building and realizes his error. She hadn't moved since he began. "That was good," she said. "That was very good."

"It was," Opal chimed.

His eyes rested on the golden-haired girl. "Well, thank you." There was a twinge of irony in his voice. "It isn't finished."

"I could tell," Pearl said, patting her brow with a hankie. "It sort of just goes off, doesn't it? But you'll finish it." She paused. "I know you will."

Benny nodded, smiling, as Pearl handed him another cold cream soda. Sweat dripped from his forehead as they edged to the door. She fanned herself with her hand. "It's so hot."

"That it is." Benny was wiping his brow.

"Shall we stroll?" she asked. On a whim she slipped her arm through his. His muscles were taut, but his arm quivered as if a part of him could not sit still. He downed his soda, and they walked outside. It was a moonless night and the city was choked under a blanket of stale, humid air. A heaviness hung as they walked to the corner, then continued up the block.

Trash was piled high, and the sidewalk stank of rotting fruit. A trolley clattered by and dust got in their eyes. Their feet moved in a rhythm, one step at a time. This is what happens to people. People who are getting to know each other and share confidences. People who will be in love and destined to be together. Ever since her mother tried to drown her, ever since she'd gotten them back on a streetcar and made her way home, Pearl had to be certain of where she was going. Now, as she walked with her arm through Benny's, she was. "I'm sure I know you from somewhere," she said.

"It's possible. We could have crossed paths." He nodded thoughtfully. "I feel as if I know you all." It wasn't the answer she wanted and he knew it, but it was what came to him.

"I wish my mother were alive," she said. Pearl rarely thought of her mother and did not really wish she was alive because Pearl had remained afraid of Anna, but now she did. "She'd remember."

They passed an ice-cream vendor who was closing up his cart, about to head home. "Would you like a cone?" Benny asked.

Pearl laughed. "Yes, I would."

The vendor raised his scoop. "What flavor?" Benny asked. "Chocolate? Strawberry?"

"Oh, no, not strawberry." Pearl's throat constricted. "I don't like strawberry."

Benny shrugged, "Really?" He seemed surprised. He was about to say more but didn't.

"Vanilla," she said. "I'll have vanilla."

The vendor dipped into his bins and scooped out a cone for Pearl. He gestured toward Benny, who shook his head, then pushed on, his ringing bell receding in the night. As the cart passed, Pearl licked at her cone. "I've got to eat this fast." Rivulets slid down her wrist.

In the dark of a summer's night Benny listened to her speak. He couldn't remember names, faces, or directions. At times he forgot where he was. Streets he'd walked his entire life could suddenly become unfamiliar. But he never forgot a voice. His perfect pitch translated into remembering. Listening closely, he heard it in her voice. But it wasn't a good memory. It was one of cold, greasy water and ships going down. It made Benny shiver, but he knew that Pearl was right. They had spoken before.

Twenty-Two

The gem sisters were outgrowing their bed. They slept, arms and legs entwined like some strange subterranean beast—the kind you'd only find at the bottom of the sea or in the deepest of caves. There was an odor about them and about their room. It was a mingled scent of oil and sweat and blood. At times they talked of moving into the extra room where the brothers who drowned used to sleep, but they never did. It didn't matter how crammed they were into their Murphy bed; it would never occur to any of them to sleep elsewhere.

But on this night, her wrists still sticky from ice cream that she didn't want to wash away, Pearl couldn't sleep. And it was impossible for her to toss and turn, wedged as she was in the middle. She tried to ignore Ruby's heavy breathing and Opal's nighttime coughs. Pearl had stayed up until the bar closed, and she was so tired she could hardly stand. But still she was awake. She longed to shake her sisters and talk to them. Especially Ruby. Surely Ruby harbored her own thoughts about young men, though she'd never said. She'd know what to do. But both girls were sound asleep. Pearl jostled Ruby who slept hard and was slow to wake. "Ruby," Pearl said, "I want to ask you something . . ."

But Ruby grumbled, turning her face to the wall. Pearl's limbs were prickly as if she couldn't stay inside her skin. It wasn't a feeling she'd known before. It wasn't love. It was more like danger. Something you were supposed to stay away from but could not. She thought of Benny, bent over the keys. That flicking tongue. The long reach of his fingers, those slow tempo climbs.

Whenever she could, Pearl went to the lake. She wanted to get away from the din of the house. The clatter of plates, the clomp of shoes, the whispering that never stopped. She found that when she was down there, she could forget whatever was bothering her. Lake Michigan never looked the same. When it was still, it was green as a frog pond, and before a storm, it turned a shade of muddy brown. At times it was a steely gray; at others it was the deepest blue. The lake had its moods as Pearl had hers.

She took a streetcar to the North Avenue Beach where the white people swam. The blacks stayed on the South Side. It was hard to believe that there were still beaches only for white people and others only for blacks. No wonder Napoleon wouldn't go near water. She recalled the summer when Eugene Williams drowned. Nothing had changed. She wore a bathing suit underneath the clothes she quickly peeled off. The cold of the lake startled her as she dove deep and did a long breaststroke under water. She dove and came up again, opening her eyes in the murky water.

When she dove into the water, she drank it in. She took big gulps, pulled the lake into her body. She liked the fact that it was fresh, not salty. She couldn't begin to imagine the oceans and their briny taste. Yet her lake, as she'd come to think of it, was still so big you couldn't see across it. Pearl had developed a thirst she couldn't quench. Though she drank all the water she could find, glasses and glasses of it, and peed until Fern thought she had a kidney problem and took her to see Dr. Rosen, there was nothing wrong with her. She just wanted to drink. She swam in long, even strokes as if she were swimming toward something that was just beyond her reach. She loved the lake for its sudden changes, its unpredictability, its unseen dangers. It was along this lakefront that Pearl came to understand that there could be places you never wanted to leave—places that seemed as much a part of you as the color of your eyes, the curve of your spine.

The water was warm for this time of year and greasy. She preferred it in the late spring when it hadn't lost its winter chill. At times even in May it could be freezing. She swam, up and back past the lifeguard's stand. At first she counted her laps, but then she gave herself up to the water. Even as her arms ached, she kept going. The dark water. At times she gulped for air. She knew there was nothing in the water to hurt her—to nibble at her toes, to pull her into the deep. Still she couldn't get it out of her head that something lurked below her. Something could come out of nowhere and tug her down.

She wanted to forget about the piano man who kept her up at night. She wanted to forget his name. His familiar ways. Who made her long for something she'd scarcely ever thought about before. Pearl was a practical woman. She wasn't the type to want something she couldn't have. But she wanted Benny. She swam as if she were swimming away. As if she could keep going, farther and farther out to sea—even as she hugged the shore. She didn't notice the shadows grow long. It wasn't until she heard the lifeguard's final whistle that she stopped.

As she dragged herself to shore, the sun was dipping behind the buildings. A chill was in the air, and she stayed on the beach until a breeze came up. She walked to the trolley stop, smelling of lake water, sand clinging to her skin. She rode with sea grass in her hair, her nipples tingling and erect, past merchants, ragpickers, and hot-dog stands along the bustle of Halsted Street, where she'd once struggled to bring her mother and Opal safely home, then walked west to the saloon with Benny still on her mind. Nothing had willed him away.

When she got home, Opal was napping in their bed. Since she'd stopped sucking her thumb, Opal slept with her head tilted back, her mouth wide open, making Pearl want to drop a goldfish down it. They hardly spoke these days. The sisters found themselves locked in a silent battle neither could explain, nor even discuss. Pearl paused, staring down at her sleeping sister. *Sleep looks so much like death*, Pearl thought, walking by.

Rudolph Valentino was coming to Chicago. He was going to dance the tango at the Trianon Ballroom with his lover, Natasha, who would soon become his wife. Valentino had come to America from Italy where he couldn't find work. In America he bused tables. He became a taxi dancer at Maxim's in New York. This was where he learned to tango. In Hollywood he did the tango in a silent film and became a matinee idol. Everyone wanted to see him. Everyone wanted to touch him. Valentino and Natasha were coming to promote Mineralava Beauty Clay. Opal begged Pearl to let her go.

Opal wanted to dance. Rhythm was in her blood. She wanted to kick up her legs and flap her arms the way she'd heard the Ziegfeld girls did. When she felt the beat of the band downstairs, she couldn't help herself. She had no choice but to move. It seemed as if no part of her was ever still. She practiced when no one was around. She stretched her legs far above her head and lay in splits, splayed like a rag doll, her head sweeping the floor.

At night she danced in her nightgown before Ruby made her go to bed. On Saturday afternoons she snuck out when her siblings were napping or at shul and entered contests that were held in the city's ballrooms. She strutted the Buzzard's Glory, the Big Apple, the Stevedore's Stomp, the Black Bottom. She could keep up with the finest of the rug cutters, but Pearl made her stick to a curfew. Home by nine. But she was wild as a colt. No mother had raised her, and now she was a feral creature no one could contain.

The best contests didn't even get going until one or two in the morning. Some of the winners went on to become professional dancers. Or taxi dancers, earning a nickel a song to dance with the male patrons. Opal thought she was good enough to be one of these. In the clubs strangers picked her up and spun her over their heads or slid her on the floor between their legs. She needed a partner as lithe and limber as she. Someone who could hold his own. And stay out all night.

Pearl wouldn't hear of it. "You're just sixteen," Pearl hollered at her. "You are not going to be out until all hours."

"I'm old enough, and I want to dance."

"You can dance at home." So Opal danced in the living room and downstairs in the saloon. She twirled and kicked her legs, working on her Slim Betty and her Bunny Hug. In the saloon she danced all night. When she asked Pearl to let her go see Valentino, Pearl agreed, but she couldn't go alone. On a cold Sunday in February the two sisters, dressed in long wool dresses, wrapped themselves up in Anna's old furs and set out for the Trianon. They arrived hours early and were among the first people in line. They stood shivering, huddling against each other in the Chicago wind.

As the doors opened, six thousand fans stormed the room. The throng pressed against Pearl's back. "Opal," Pearl called out as they were swept into the giant hall. Women screamed as they were thrust against the stage. Others were almost trampled. The lights dimmed and, dressed in spurs, sombrero, and chaps, Valentino swept onto the stage. Natasha, in a long red gown, was at his side. He gazed at her with his dark, Latin eyes. He lifted her into his arms and turned her so that they were cheek to cheek. His face was sweaty, and his pancake makeup streaked as he led her up and down the stage. In three years he would be dead of a ruptured appendix, but for now he exuded heat. Pearl was so close she could smell his cologne. They danced for four minutes. In the crush of bodies Pearl swooned. As Valentino was autographing slips of paper, the hems of skirts, and the arms of girls who swore they'd never bathe again, she fainted and Opal had to follow as two attendants carried her outside for air.

In a matter of moments Pearl recovered, but it was too late to go back inside. Instead they made their way home where Opal sulked in a corner, and Pearl stood in her slip in front of the mirror. She struck erect poses, kicked a leg up behind her. She cupped her breasts, ran her hands along her thighs. In her nightgown with broom in hand, she danced. Downstairs the next evening as she poured drinks and kept the tabs, she imagined Benny, guiding her across the floor. His hand at her waist. He'd whisper, "I didn't know you could dance like this."

"There's a lot about me you don't know," she'd reply.

Pearl was gliding across the barroom floor when she heard

Benny's shave-and-a-haircut knock. But it was Opal with shrimp-pink lipstick and hot-red nails who raced to the door. Opal who had fashioned a red blouse from some old damask looked as if she were on fire. The sweat seeped through Pearl's pores as she pulled Opal aside. "What is wrong with you? You look like a slut."

"You aren't my mother," Opal shot back.

"You're parading around like a whore." And Pearl handed Opal a rag. "Wipe your face." Then turning to Benny, "What'll it be, Benny?" Pearl patted her hair. "The usual? One round if Benny plays." Benny was surprised because Pearl never served drinks on the house.

"The usual," he said.

He pulled back the bench and ran his fingers across the keys. He struck a few chords, then launched into "Wild Man Stomp." Opal leaned across the piano, her fingers tapping out the beat. Her smile softened; her eyes were bright. She was listening not just with her ears, but with her eyes and her hands, with the curve of her mouth, with her hips. She threw her head back and began to sway. She was moving. First her legs, then her arms. Then the rest of her. She pushed away from the piano and danced fast with a cigarette in one hand, a drink in the other. Beads of sweat covered her face. Pearl glared at Opal. She'd tell her what she thought later. For now she turned to Ruby. "She's making a fool of herself," Pearl said.

"Yes, she is," Ruby replied. But Opal wouldn't stop. She was unaccustomed to the scent of men. She wasn't used to the clomp of shoes, to deep voices at the dinner table. She was young when her father died and not much older when her bird brothers drowned. And Moss and Jonah were nocturnal creatures whom she rarely saw and who trudged upstairs just before dawn. She had no memory of strong arms carrying her from the sofa to her bed. She'd never felt a man's beard scratching against her cheek as he tucked her in or sniffed the strange mix of tobacco, beer, and sweat that made a man what he was. All she knew were the soft hands of sisters, the rise and fall of their breath, the gentle strokes of a hairbrush, and the edge of the bed from which she struggled not to slip onto the floor and into darkness.

Benny was playing a melody at full tilt. His right hand was flying across the keys, improvising as his left marked time. He let his breaks last longer and take him wherever they went. He was making it up, bar after bar. Opal kicked her leg high. Benny could see the place where her garters met her stockings. She took off her shoes and put them on top of the piano. Dark circles of sweat clung to her bloodstone dress. As she slapped her backside, then the soles of her feet, she moved with the precision of a Swiss watch and the surety of a snake.

His foot started tapping as he jumped into "Small Potatoes." Balaban and Katz who'd come for their usual hot dogs and soda started clapping, and Lev Walenski, the butcher, banged on the bar. Mrs. Baum's dead husband leaped up and grabbed Opal by the hands. He hadn't danced since his wedding, but his feet and arms entwined like a contortionist's as he threw Opal out, and then pulled her back in. She tossed back her head of golden flax and roared.

She caught the beat. It came easily to her as if it were in her bones. Her arms and hands flew. Sweat poured from her brow and her golden hair tumbled to her waist. As she fluttered around Benny like a hummingbird, Napoleon caught sight of her. She was cotton candy with hair of spun gold. He'd never seen a girl move like that— all arms and legs, and the beat coming as if it was inside of her. She didn't stop until the music was done.

Twenty-Three

≡

It was dark on the road to the Indiana Dunes. If it weren't for the moon, they'd only have had their lights to guide them. It seemed as if they'd been driving for hours. Benny was beginning to think they were lost. Perhaps they had taken a wrong turn. There were no signs of other cars on the lake road. No headlights coming toward them from the distance. But the moonlight shimmered on the water to his left. This was the only road that followed the lake.

Anyway it didn't matter if it was the right road or not. He'd follow it wherever it took them. He liked the feel of the car he'd borrowed from his father, the snow crunching beneath the tires, the light of the moon to guide them. He breathed her perfume. Laughter spilled out of her like splintering glass. She was young. But not that young. He squeezed her hand as he told her that he was glad Pearl let her come.

"So am I." Opal breathed a sigh of relief. "I didn't think she would." She smiled at Benny. Of course it was a lie. She hadn't told Pearl anything at all. Pearl never would have let Opal come. Though she'd convinced Benny that she was eighteen, in fact Opal had just turned sixteen. As soon as she'd heard that Benny was going to the Golden Door, she was determined to go. She wore a yellow silk dress with a pattern of blue cornflowers that matched her eyes. She'd stolen it from Field's. She wore yellow slippers that she'd shoplifted from

Carson Pirie Scott. The cloche hat and clutch purse she'd taken from there as well. She'd gotten them over several visits. Opal knew better than to take too much at once. And she always bought a little something first—a slip, a pair of silk hose. Her girlfriend Rita had taught her this trick. This way people weren't watching her that closely.

The yellow slippers pinched her toes. She hadn't been able to try them on before she lifted them and now wondered if she'd be able to dance. Her dress smelled of licorice and lemon drops, for she'd been hiding it in one of the old candy bins. She'd dressed at the back door of the candy shop, then waited, shivering in the cold before Benny could honk the horn. Her hair was tucked and pinned under her hat. Fern had refused to cut it even when she'd begged. These days everyone was cutting their hair. Fern had even cut Pearl's into a bob. When Opal complained, Fern said, "When you grow up, I'll cut your hair." So Opal had piled hers on the top of her head and tucked beneath her hat instead.

She'd pay for this when she got home, but it was a small price. *Let her beat me*, Opal said to herself. Pearl was worse than any mother could be. At night in their bed Opal felt stifled. She gasped for air until Pearl put a warm poultice on her chest. Lately no matter where she was—in tight corners, in crowded "els," though never on the dance floor—Opal wheezed. If she listened, she could hear her own lungs. She could almost hear the blood coursing through her veins. It was as if another person were inside of her, clambering to leave.

Opal wanted to wear short dresses, ride trains, and see the sunrise before going to bed. She wanted to eat because she was hungry and not because the food was prepared and the table set. She hated house rules and picture albums and hand-me-downs. She hated sitting around the kitchen table as her siblings discussed a bill that needed to be paid, a shipment of booze that was delayed. She wanted to run away and keep going. New York. Hollywood. She could be an actress. She would dance in films that one day Pearl would have to pay a nickel to see.

The flickering yellow lights of the Golden Door appeared ahead. The club rose up from the horizon and illumined the coast. It was an old beach resort, lit like a fairy castle, beaming on the shore. Husk

O'Hare's Wolverines were playing. Word was spreading about the young cornet player they'd recently hired. Already a drunk, rarely sober, Bix was said to play like a black man. Some people claimed he had to be black. Some said he'd made a pact with the devil to blow his horn. The Indiana Dunes were farther than Benny liked to go for music, but he wanted to hear Bix. And Opal had begged him to take her along.

A valet took the keys to Benny's car. Against a dark façade the gold door shimmered. A sign read NO JEWS OR DOGS ALLOWED. Benny chose to ignore it, and Opal didn't notice. Inside everything was glistening and yellow, and milky white, including Opal in her flapper dress that set off her blond hair. Benny took her by the arm. As the door opened, music seemed to spill out. As they made their way to the bar, Benny smelled her lavender perfume and smoke. "I'm going to celebrate," he said. He ordered two whiskey sours.

"But you don't drink."

"Well, tonight I do." Benny rested on his elbows so he could see the bandstand. As a dark-haired, slightly chubby Bix stood up to take a solo, he looked like a kid, not even Benny's age. His tux rode up his ankles, and he was wearing white socks.

Opal laughed, pointing. "I don't know what the fuss is about. You can't even hear him."

He played a soft horn that was hard to hear, but Benny cupped his ear to listen. "You're wrong," he said. "He's quiet, but he's good." There was more to that horn, and Benny recognized it. Cornfields, the flat lands, a father's contempt, and a defiant son. His parents had sent him to the Lake Forest Academy that was known for turning disorderly boys into men. But every chance he could, Bix took the Chicago Northwestern and then the "el" until he found himself on the South Side outside the Lincoln Gardens.

When Bix was a boy in Davenport, he wandered down to the river. He lay on the banks, listening to the riverboat bands that came up from the South. That New Orleans rhythm got into his veins. As the Mississippi flowed, he heard a high-pitched horn. It pierced the night and went straight into his heart. He'd go wherever it went. Despite his parents' efforts, he'd been following it ever since. Here was another white boy who could play and who had a father who hated him. Benny wanted to shake his hand as Bix sat down after his solo. He dropped his head as if he'd just exposed the most private part of himself, and the band came back at a feverish pitch. Opal clasped her drink as her legs were pumping and she couldn't sit still. "Come on," she shouted, downing the whiskey.

Opal forgot about her tight slippers and her pinched toes as she pulled Benny to the dance floor. Her supple body caught the beat while he fumbled like an aquatic bird that glides and skims on water but is graceless on land. At the piano he could make two different rhythms happen with his right and left hand, but he was lost when it came to his feet. Opal laughed at his arms that flailed like a drowning man's. As she shimmied and turned, Benny got caught up in his own legs and thought he would topple over. She was trying to teach him a new dance called the Charleston when a half-dozen men walked in. They were huge, all dressed in brown and black suits. Two stood blocking the door. Two more followed. One wore an electric-blue silk suit and a scarlet shirt, shiny blue socks, a pearl-gray fedora with the black band, and a diamond stickpin.

"Machine Gun" McGurn, as he would soon be known, dressed like Capone. The same tailor made him his custom-made suits of purple, yellow, electric blue. He liked his accessories—his fedoras and stickpins, his spats and cane with its silver knob. He was tall and wide as a vault. He weighed over two hundred and fifty pounds, but he could move like an alligator at lethal speed. He was known for his big tips, his dashing good looks, and the blade he carried in his inside breast pocket. Benny recognized him as the man who'd filleted Napoleon's lips. He wondered if McGurn would remember him.

His real name was Vicenzo Gebaldi. He became a psychopath after his father was murdered. He'd been cheating the mob to save money for his family. A nickel was found in his father's right fist. Whenever McGurn killed someone, he left a nickel in the palm in memory of his father. McGurn was a high-ranking associate of the Capone brothers. A silent partner, he orchestrated events behind the scenes. It was his expertise with a knife that made him famous.

McGurn knew how to peel back the skin on a man's face, not to kill him, but to teach him a lesson. Once he'd sliced the vocal cords of a singer who tried to move to a new club.

The band came to a halt. Dancers stopped dancing as if frozen in place. McGurn cleared away a table at the front. But not before he took care of their bill. The golden doors swung open again. Two of the men, carrying tommy guns, stood sentinel on either side of the room. Suddenly a short, stocky man, wearing a green silk suit, sauntered in. He had a cigar in his mouth and a scar carved across his left cheek. Everyone gasped. Some looked away. The man motioned to the band. "Keep playing," he said.

Al Capone lived on Prairie Avenue. He shared his house with his wife, Mae, and their only child, Sonny, but he worked out of his office at the Metropole Hotel. It wasn't unusual for him to show up at one of his clubs. When he did, the doors were locked. No one left until dawn. Wherever he went, Capone was a celebrity. Police officers and politicians raced to shake his hand. Bands struck up the songs he loved to hear. He was affable and generous when he wanted to be. He wore cashmere coats and the finest silks. He loved handkerchiefs, fedoras, fine pigskin gloves. He required six bodyguards including two with machine guns. He was often seen at the opera and the symphony. He had rhythm in his stubby fingers and his feet. He loved jazz musicians. When musicians played for him, he stuffed C-notes into their pockets. Once he made a trembling surgeon sew back on a bass player's thumb.

Capone took his seat at the table in the front. He waved his arms in the air. The band played faster. A bottle of whiskey was placed on his table. Capone didn't look at it, but he picked up his glass when it was filled. He could make a bigger profit on milk, but he enjoyed the clubs. People needed to have fun. Music and booze, that's all it took. He kept his gaze fixed on the dance floor. Girls were being dipped and spun overhead. They slid between men's legs and twirled in their hands. His eyes came to rest on the girl with golden hair. She was dancing like crazy with a partner who could barely keep up. Her hair flew. Her arms and legs went everywhere, but she followed the beat.

Capone was a family man. Every night he dined with Sonny and Mae. He called his mother once a week. Still, he had his girls on the side. He had them whenever he wanted them the same way he had whiskey and cigars and automobiles and front-row seats when he wanted them. They were his for the asking, to be paid for, and delivered. Usually it wasn't that difficult. Girls waited for him inside clubs. They slipped him their number as they sold him cigarettes. Everyone knew who Al Capone was. Nobody refused him. They didn't dare.

On the dance floor Opal spun. She flung her legs back and forth. Her blond tresses shook free. Benny was starting to get the hang of it, but it seemed as if McGurn's eyes were on him. Perhaps McGurn did remember him. He tried to dance faster as if that would make the evening over sooner. Benny didn't know that McGurn had never seen his face that night in the alley. It was Opal he was watching. Capone was watching her, too.

Suddenly Capone stood up, and his men did as well. But he told them to sit down. He motioned to the band to keep playing as he walked across the dance floor. Tapping Benny on the shoulder, Capone made a gesture that he wanted a dance with his girl. Opal looked at Benny with watery eyes. Benny couldn't say no. Capone took her in his arms and planted his hand on the small of her back. When the first chord was struck, he started to move. Despite his bulk, he was graceful and light on his feet.

He tilted back and forth like a metronome until he caught the beat. Then he was whirling. He swung to the music. He threw Opal out, and brought her back. He kicked his feet, paused at the beat, then swung her out again. The whole club was watching. Opal wondered if this was what it would be like when she was famous. For a moment she was frightened, but she went with the beat. His hand was firm and moist on her back. Sweat seeped through the yellow silk of her dress. His moves were smooth and even, and he never missed a beat. His steps grew more complicated. She twirled around and around as they sashayed across the floor. When he dipped her, she relaxed in his arms. If she'd never danced before, she'd have been able to dance with this man.

A strip of orange cut across the sky as Benny and Opal stumbled out of the club. The sun was rising as they followed the lake. Laughing, Benny told her that she'd danced with Al Capone. She took off her yellow slippers and rubbed her aching feet. Her ankles were raw, and she had blisters on her toes. She rested her head against his arm. Her breathing was labored as she drifted in and out of sleep. She snored lightly in a way that amused him. Benny drove fast, trying to stay awake. He wanted to pull over and go to sleep, but he kept driving. Opal was light and feathery as a bird. Her bones barely pressed into his flesh. Her breath was shallow. It reminded him of Marta's little girl. As he pulled into the alley, he nudged her awake. "Your sister is going to kill me." He kissed the top of her head.

Opal yawned and stretched like a cat. She kissed him on the lips, and then slipped out of the car. As he pulled away, she waved with the shoes that she carried in her hand. Before she went inside, Opal looked up at the morning star and made a wish. She wished that she could see the lone star every morning, and that she could stand outside in her stocking feet as the rest of the world slept and breathe in the fresh air.

Carefully she opened the door, tiptoeing inside as if she knew every creek in the floor. In a corner of the candy store she took off the yellow silk dress which now smelled of cigar smoke, rum, and sweat—the scents of men that she'd never known—and slipped back into the plain skirt and blouse she'd worn the night before. In a bin she stashed her dress and cloche hat and fishnet hose and the yellow slippers in which she'd danced with a gangster. They were sacred relics to her now. She slipped into bed beside Pearl, who never said a word.

Twenty-Four

Opal sat on the edge of her bed, thinking that she barely remembered her mother. But she did recall one thing. Anna was afraid of mirrors. There was a tarnished silver mirror in Opal's hand, and she stared at herself in it. Her mother had feared that she would suddenly find herself reflected in someone else's life. Opal was not afraid of that. She welcomed it.

She'd been an orphan for as long as she could remember. When she was a little girl in shul and with Pearl and Ruby on either side, clutching her hands, they listened to the men recite the Kaddish, the Orphan's Prayer, and Opal thought it was a prayer for her. She'd been just a child when her father was killed and not much older when her mother died. Now she was sixteen. When she was very small, she'd believed that Pearl was her mother. It was Pearl who had led her by the hand across streets, Pearl who had wiped her bottom and fed her food. She'd cried when Jonah told her that her real mother wasn't Pearl. It was the old woman with the bloated legs and spider veins who stood at the sink, spitting in the air to ward off evil spirits.

Now Pearl moved through their rooms, putting laundry away, changing sheets, as oblivious to Opal as if she were a ghost. Even if Opal said such mundane things as "Pass the salt," Pearl pretended not to hear. If she cornered Pearl in the bathroom or barred her entrance into the saloon, Pearl waited as if all that stood in front of her was air.

As Opal brushed her white-blond hair that she lightened now with lemon juice and peroxide and applied cream to her milky skin, she wondered whom she resembled. Some claimed that she was a pale version of Pearl, a phantom of her older sister. In truth she bore no real resemblance to any of them. At times Opal felt as if she'd been kidnapped and left behind by a troop of gypsies. Certainly no one would ever take her for a Jew.

On the dressing table she had assembled a tray of lipsticks and rouges, tortoiseshell combs and sable-hair brushes, perfumes in bottles of cut glass—most of which had been left from Anna. Nothing belonged to Opal. It was all borrowed or shared or handed down. When she looked at the clothes in her drawers and closet, there was nothing new. It was all discarded skirts and dresses that Pearl had remade for her—cutting old cloth to fit Opal's delicate bones.

Now she had something that she didn't have to share with anyone. It was a secret, festering inside of her. At the Golden Door something wild had been set loose. She drank gin and danced with a gangster. She stayed out until dawn. The caged creature had had her taste of freedom. And she vowed never go back inside again.

The next time Benny showed up at the Jazz Palace, Opal moved the chairs out of the way so she could dance. He didn't play with his head down. He kept his eyes on this dancing girl, his head thrown back. A cigarette dangled from his lips and, as Opal flung her arms and legs, dipped her head, he laughed. When she went behind the bar to make herself a whiskey sour, Benny said, "I'll have whiskey, too."

"You don't drink here," Pearl told Opal. But Ruby took her aside. "She'll just drink elsewhere."

"She is shaming us," Pearl said.

Ruby shook her head. "You're the one who spoiled her."

Pearl poured Benny his drink from the best whiskey that she kept under the bar and placed it on the piano top. A little of the brown liquid splattered on the keys. He whisked the moisture away with his fingers, licked it off, and kept playing, pausing only to take sips that stung as he swallowed. Opal clasped her glass with her moon-shaped nails, filed just so, and polished red as she leaned across the piano. As he played, her feet started to move. She swayed. She tossed her head back and shook her golden curls. Her arms moved in rhythm with her feet, her hips. It was more as if she were flying than dancing. Watching her, Benny played like one possessed. He pounded the keys until his fingers were numb, and then he played some more. He hit the keys hard, then soft as his fingers made easy runs up and down. He took on standards and requests. But mostly he went with whatever tune popped into his head.

He was covered in sweat and his fingers ached when Pearl said she was closing. He said good night, then stumbled out into the cold alley. The ground was slippery. It was almost spring, but still fresh snow was falling and his boots made a crunching sound as he walked, huddled, with that biting dog of a Chicago wind at his face. He was tipsy, but his body felt warm. He'd had too much to drink, and he had to get home. Even sober the cold could be deceiving and he knew they mustn't dally for his own brother had frozen to death on a winter's morning and Benny lived with the fear of the cold taking over his limbs.

As he stumbled down the alley, he heard his name being called, but he thought it was the wind. "Benny, Benny," she shouted again. Turning, he saw Opal racing toward him with just a shawl around her arms. "You forgot your hat." She slipped as she rushed to him and he caught her, gripping her tightly. Covering her mouth as she coughed, she tumbled against him.

He slipped his hand around her waist. "What are you doing?" he asked, a scolding tone in his voice. "You'll freeze and your sisters will never forgive me."

"Oh, who cares? I am having fun." Her breath was hot against his cheek. They huddled, bent over, scarves around their necks. It was March, but still icicles hung overhead, and Opal, laughing, reached for one. She plucked it as if from the sky and gave it to Benny. "Suck on it," she told him. She plucked another for herself, holding it as if it were a cigarette.

He pulled on his icicle as well. "Wonderful." Benny laughed.

She put his cap on and gave it a tug. "I can hardly see your face." Opal reached up and pulled it off his head. Her laugh was tipsy, and as Benny grabbed into the air, she dashed behind some garbage cans. "There," she said, "now I can see you."

Benny ran his hand along his head. His ears were numb. His head felt naked and exposed. He reached for his cap once more as Opal tugged it on to her head. He gazed at her in her scarlet coat and shoes, his gray cap on her head. "You look good in it," he said. "You can keep it." Opal laughed, clasping her arm tightly through his.

A blast of cold air struck them, and she pressed against his shoulder. He led her trembling to the end of the alleyway. At the streetlight he paused, and his lips came down to hers. It was a brief, burning kiss, but it left a feeling, moving through him like a locomotive, starting up slowly as it gathered speed.

Across the prairie, wheat blew in the wind. There were miles of it, tall and waving, seas of winter wheat. When it was ready, the farmers of Illinois, Nebraska, Iowa, harvested it, separating the grain from the chaff. Then they drove their truckloads to the grain elevators where the farmers were paid by the bushel. Winter wheat was bought in autumn. September wheat was sold in July.

The farmers were never happy with the price their crops bought. They grumbled and complained among themselves but in the end had no choice. They took what was offered whether it was a dollar or seventy-five cents to the bushel. They accepted this because, months before, some manufacturer had speculated on the price of wheat. Pillsbury or General Mills purchased the grain to make bread and cakes, store-bought items, and what had once flowed like a sea was now shipped to the mills.

As Benny sat in the order booth, he tried to understand the journey of the wheat. How it was so young and went so far. How so much happened to it in its short life. He pictured wheat in fields and silos, on trains and mills, being fought over and bargained for, and he was filled with envy. Thoughts of a girl got caught up in the wheat. Not Pearl, whom Napoleon wanted him to like, but Opal—that porcelain doll with the yellow hair.

If Opal was thirsty for men, Benny was searching for his muse. The music had come so easily to him. He feared it would leave in the same way. By stealth. In the night. He'd wake and find it gone. He feared that it was a guest who'd stopped on its way somewhere else. He couldn't explain this to anyone. How dead he felt, how ordinary he was when he wasn't playing or thinking about playing or composing a tune or tapping out what was in his head. He wondered how normal people went about their jobs in factories or at an office, how they put soup and bread on the table, dressed their children and took them off to school, how they got through their days with nothing to elevate them beyond unmade beds and meals and doctor's visits.

He couldn't find his inspiration in the chicken-scented hallways, in Harold's empty bed, at the caps factory, and now at the Board of Trade. He didn't find it being with a woman, but by imagining being with one. It wasn't the real flesh and blood that he wanted, but a vision of one. That was why he couldn't be with Pearl. There was nothing to imagine. He couldn't uncover the mystery there. Because Benny didn't have another word yet for what he felt for Opal, he called it love. It must be love if it kept you up at night. Even though deep down Benny knew that this was something else.

He was thinking of the wheat and its flow and the girl with corn-silk hair who brought him his soda as his hands shot up from the booth and the orders came in. "Buy" and he waved toward his chest. "Sell" and he pushed it away. A closed fist meant a dollar. Five shakes of the fist, five dollars. Thumbs up was seven-eighths of a dollar. And Moe and his uncle shot back the same signals, confirming purchases and sales.

With his big, sure hands, Benny learned the signals quickly. Moe told him he would when Benny had gone to his friend one afternoon and said he needed a job. Milo Peyton had sold the Regency to Balaban and Katz, and they were refurbishing it for a vaudeville house.

He couldn't watch his father, sitting up night after night, counting his debts, knowing he'd never make payroll. It became clear to Benny when he returned home from the clubs and found his father still awake, or collapsed in a chair, a pad and pencil in his hand, that he'd have to keep working days.

The booth was small and cramped, but he was grateful to Moe who'd gotten him the job. They went to work in two-toned jackets of tan and blue and spent the day, taking orders, carrying messages from the traders. Benny found the work tedious, and the noise in the pit grated on him.

He answered calls, shouting back while his unresolved melody, "Twilight Blue," was floating in his head. He fiddled with it. He tried to make it better, but some refrain eluded him. He couldn't get it right. The final phrase of his song and the face of the girl all intertwined. How long would it take for Opal to grow up? The thought of her brought heat to his veins. She made the hair on his neck stand up and his nipples go hard. It felt like love, didn't it?

Besides, she was a Jew who looked like a shiksa, a word his mother roughly translated as "lizard." What more could a Jewish boy—or his mother, for that matter—ask? Never mind that her laughter was out of proportion, her gaze never seemed to let him go, and he began to wish that her brain matched her blue marble eyes. Or that Pearl was the one with the golden hair. Why couldn't he take the two girls and fold them into one?

Moe's uncle was shouting at him. "What about the order, Benny? Do we buy or sell?"

Benny fumbled through the sheets in front of him. Buy or sell what? He couldn't remember what he'd just sent to the floor. "Sell." Benny pushed his hand away from his chest with a thumbs-up as the music in his head slipped away.

That evening Benny packed up his red suitcase and walked the streets with it clasped in his fist. He was looking at postings until he found a laundry with a sign in a window on Ashland. ROOM TO RENT. A thickset Polish man led him up a steamy stairwell that stank of cleaning solvents into a spare but clean room. It had a bed, a dresser, a washbasin, and a mirror. There was a water closet in the hall. The view was of a billboard of a girl with a blond-haired bob, puffing a Lucky. Smoke came out of her mouth. The sign read REACH FOR A LUCKY INSTEAD OF A SWEET. It had been proven. Girls who started smoking lost weight. The room rented for two dollars a week. "I'll take it," Benny said.

The decision had come to him easily. He'd fought with his father when he'd gotten home late the night before. He promised his mother that he wouldn't go far. Still she'd wept and slipped a cheese sandwich into his bag. He put the suitcase on top of the dresser and opened it. He unpacked two clean shirts, a couple changes of underwear, socks, a pair of slacks. Benny put all of this into the chest of drawers that he inspected for dust and mouse droppings with a bare hand. Then he put the suitcase, with all of his music still inside, on the upper shelf of the closet and closed the door.

In the evening he went to the Jazz Palace and pulled Opal aside. "I've rented a room on Ashland," he told her.

"What kind of room?" Opal looked at him wide-eyed.

"One I plan to live in for a while," he told her.

"Take me there." And she put on her wrap. When Pearl had her back turned, they slipped out the door. They walked down Ainslie and around the corner until they got to the laundry building. Benny let them in, and they made their way up the hallway with the rank odor of chemicals in the air. At the top of the stairs Benny hesitated, then opened his door. Opal took in the stark little room with its stained walls. Sniffing the air, she detected mildew. And something else. The scent filled the room the way the sweet and savory ones of breads and roasting chickens filled her own. It came as strong to her as hunger, and she had to have more.

She had never been with a man in a room that had a bed in it. Outside of the dance floors she'd hardly even been near a man. But here it was. The bed was narrow with a metal frame and it was made with clean sheets his mother had washed and ironed herself. Benny had put them on that evening before heading out. He could not bear to look at the stained mattress that carried the memory of other people's excesses and soon, he imagined, would carry his as well. Opal shook but not from her nerves. She was ready to be touched. She wanted to know what everything felt like—even the things she could not imagine, even if they brought pain.

At times it seemed to Opal that she had been raised under glass in some stale, protected shell, like moss in a terrarium. She was ready to taste every flavor and sniff every smell. She sat on the bed, bouncing on the springs. Despite the dingy room and the odors of solvents and sweat, the mattress was soft and the sheets clean and white. She could hardly imagine having a bed to herself, one that did not include her sisters. She lay back, spreading her arms and legs wide as a snow angel. She stretched out as she had never been able to before, her hair tumbling across the pillow.

Benny sat down beside her, stroking her hair, running his fingers through her tresses. "It's not so bad, is it?" Benny said, taking off his coat, his shoes. He saw a strange look in her eye. "What's wrong, Opal?" he asked. He confused her sadness with desire. He didn't know that the only thing she'd ever want was more.

"That billboard makes me sad."

Benny got up and pulled down the shade. "Better?" He sat down beside her again. He kissed her lips, her cheek. "We could decorate the room. Put up pictures."

Opal laughed, tickling his nose. "Pictures of what?"

Benny shrugged. "I don't know. Mountains. Paris."

"Paris," she said with a laugh. "I'd love to see Paris."

Benny held up his hands, shaping a frame. "How about right there?" Then he made a frame with his hands around her face, moving them until he found an angle he liked. "How about here?" Wrapping his hands around her cheeks, he kissed her. His tongue slid into her mouth. He caressed her face, slipping his hands down her neck, across her breasts. He was not in a hurry as he unbuttoned her blouse. He helped her with the snaps on her corset. He lifted her skirts.

In the light from the street he looked at her body, her milky-white skin, the rose of her nipples. Her pubic hair was the color of prairie wheat. She was thin as a wishbone; if he wasn't careful, he could break her. Benny probed, and her wetness surprised him. He fondled and kissed and licked her. He knew he should get up and walk away. She was still a child, though she was not acting like one.

But he wanted her. He rubbed against her side like a dog humping a leg. She trembled, moving beside him, whispering his name. She pressed against him as well, wrapping her legs around his thigh. He kissed and caressed her. Then Opal reached for him and he couldn't hold back. As he pressed into her, she cried out. He hurt her, but he couldn't help himself. There was something inside of him that he could not stop. She cried out again, but it was not in pain. As she stifled her scream with her fist, Benny bit into his lip. When he came, he tasted his own blood.

When he woke, Opal was asleep beside him. He lit a cigarette and lay back with it dangling from his lip. He looked at her in the light that came from the streetlamp. He listened to the clangs of the streetcars, the garbage trucks. He pulled up the shade. It was still night. The billboard of the skinny blond smoking a cigarette was illumined. Clouds of smoke came out of her mouth. Opal breathed heavily at his side, her hair matted to her brow. He tried to wake her, but she slept. She didn't care if she was out until dawn. She'd make her wish on the morning star.

Illicit love was everywhere. In the saloons and gambling halls. In alleyways. Above laundries. On the South Side two boys were having a lover's quarrel. They came from rich Jewish families and were expected to have brilliant careers. One spent his afternoons reading detective novels. The other was a self-taught ornithologist who shot and bagged birds.

Nathan Leopold spent his weekends trudging through Indiana swamps and woods, searching for nests of Kirtland's warbler. He wore a birding suit and glasses with a special hinge. Richard Loeb read mysteries and wanted to commit a crime. They kidnapped Bobby Franks, a child, chosen at random, and murdered him with a chisel. They drove to Indiana, stopping to eat hot dogs with the boy's body in the backseat. Leopold took Loeb to the culvert where he went birding. They poured acid on the body and left it there.

At "the trial of the century," Clarence Darrow pleaded for

mercy. In his twelve-hour summation, Darrow argued that the boys' youth, genetic inheritance, surging sexual impulses, their wealth, the fact that they were raised by governesses and not loving parents, led them to commit their crime. "We live in a deterministic universe," Darrow said. "Life is a series of infinite chances. Nature is strong and she is pitiless. She works in mysterious ways and we are her victims." Benny, too, had been dealt an unfair hand. It was his fate. He could not be blamed. Besides, he hadn't murdered anyone.

Twenty-Five

Napoleon was growing used to his scar. He liked to run his tongue over it before he played a set or said something that he believed was important. He wore it as a talisman—the way he wore his gris-gris bag. A badge of honor. As the Black Butterfly he believed he was invincible. And he was playing everywhere. He had so many bookings he didn't know what to do. Napoleon was renowned for what had happened to him, but once people heard him, they came back for the music. While Maddy warned him that this knife stroke was just the teaser, the warm-up act, he grew more defiant. "I dare them to touch me now," he swore.

Still, he'd heard the stories of those who'd defied the Chicago Outfit. Just last week a club owner, missing for weeks, was found, encased in cement. A piano player had his right hand crushed by a hammer. He claimed he'd been hanging shelves. Benny warned Napoleon, too, but the more he was warned, the less he was inclined to heed the warning. The more people knew about him the better. He was determined to do whatever he wanted. He knew that at any moment the ax could fall, but that just made him angrier. He played the Rendez-Vous and the Plantation Club, too. Bandleaders begged him to join them even for a night or two. The Black Butterfly was good for business. He was a free agent, a sideman. He went rogue.

Rumors about him flew. Musicians said he could hit notes higher than Armstrong's high C. The cut made it sound as if two horns were playing, not just one. Some women on Forty-Seventh Street whispered that his lips were capable of previously unknown pleasures. Some said that his tongue was also sliced in two like a lizard's and this drove them wild. Women who'd been faithful to their husbands for decades clung to his arm and dreamed of the Black Butterfly in their beds.

His kiss was said to bring good luck. He ended dry spells. People who'd lost jobs got new ones. The brokenhearted found love. Stubborn ulcers healed. Fans stuck money in his pockets in exchange for a quick pucker. Newspapers were filled with testimonials. Critics raved that his horn was even better than before. The cut amplified his sound. Some compared him to Armstrong, though most hesitated to go that far. Every night he'd show up at a different club. He was an amulet, a charm. The audiences came to see what the mob does to a man who defies it. But they stayed because they loved his sound. Most important, for the club owners, he packed the house wherever he went. Even if he wasn't booked, he was invited to sit in, and the musicians were more than happy to share the sizable pot.

He was playing a late set at the Owl Club—an all-white club on the North Side, run by the O'Banion Gang. Dion O'Banion was from Kilgubbin, that Irish neighborhood known as Little Hell. He had a tenor voice. When he was a boy, O'Banion sang Irish melodies in bars that made customers sob into their pints while his cronies picked their pockets in the cloakroom. O'Banion liked good music and he paid his bands well. Napoleon knew he had no business playing in a North Side club. He belonged to the South Side. He wondered how far he could take this. For now he was beating the odds.

The band was belting out a chorus when Napoleon caught a glimpse of two men from the corner of his eye. Outside of their heft, they were nondescript. They wore plain dark suits and overcoats. Not the same men he'd seen before, but he knew why they were here. They didn't have to grease anyone's palm to get a table near the front. The minute they walked in, room was made. One waved at the musicians, egging them on. The other took out a toothpick and began to clean his teeth.

Napoleon sucked in his breath and belted out the chorus louder and sharper than he ever had. He dug for notes he'd never reached before. His scar ached. He rubbed it with his tongue. Then played some more. In his solo he soared. He flew above the city, hovering on his dark wings. He brought out the saddest tune he'd ever found. It was the sound of empty beds and eating alone, children locked in a room and widows with nowhere to go. Somebody said that on the eighth day God created loneliness. So Napoleon must have been close to God because he was making it come out of his horn. Then just when it seemed everyone would start crying, he changed his tune. He left sadness behind, and the trickster took over. He made his song silly almost and light as if it had all been a joke and everybody needed to laugh.

When Napoleon passed the tune back to the band, there was huge applause. Most of it was coming from the thugs. They'd enjoyed his music, and now they were going to kill him. He gave them a grin, his hands trembling, as he finished his set. Napoleon stooped down to put his horn away, and when he looked up, prepared to meet his Maker, the men were gone. It made no difference. They'd be waiting for him somewhere. In the next alley. At the next club. The all-night diner. They were playing him the way you played a song.

It was a chilly November night, but Napoleon decided to walk. He buttoned his coat and tucked his hands in his pockets. He'd never gotten used to the cold, but tonight he didn't mind. He followed State Street, walking north. A light snow fell. Napoleon looked at his footprints. In a few weeks it would be Thanksgiving. Maddy had already talked about getting a turkey and making her candied yams. He could almost taste those potatoes, all buttery and coated in brown sugar. He wondered if he'd live that long. As he headed out into the morning, he sniffed the air. He wanted to devour strips of bacon and a bowl of grits, drink black coffee. Maybe he'd find that waitress on the after-hours shift and curl up in her thin, white arms. He wanted to get his fill of all the things he wouldn't be tasting again. Because

Napoleon had no doubt where his future lay, and he faced what was ahead with resignation. No one could tell him differently. He was a dead man.

Across the street he saw the lights of Holy Name Cathedral. The façade of Holy Name was riddled with bullet holes. Several gangsters had been shot down here as they left mass. For good luck, brides put their fingers in these holes and made wishes. Napoleon wanted to go inside where it was warm. He wanted to say a prayer which he hadn't said since he could remember. He paused in front of Schofield's florist. He liked the display. It was filled with red and yellow roses. He sniffed the air as if he could smell their sweetness. He pressed his face to the cold glass.

In a few hours, as Napoleon slept in Maddy's warm bed, Dion O'Banion would open up his shop. He'd slip his key into the slot and rub his cold hands together. He'd spend the morning putting the finishing touches on a funeral wreath. The wreath was an elaborate job of bachelor's buttons and yellow roses. By day O'Banion was a florist, and by night he was a gangster. He specialized in orchids and manslaughter. He sprayed mist on his orchids every morning. O'Banion was fond of cut flowers and was very good at arranging them. Soon he'd be filling in the wreath with white carnations, Queen Anne's lace, and baby's breath. He was partial to white. The order called for gardenias, but his shipment never arrived. He'd waste an hour, arguing with his supplier. The wreath had to be delivered across the street to Holy Name. It was for a funeral the next afternoon, though O'Banion had yet to receive the name of the deceased.

O'Banion was adjusting the carnations when two men walked in. O'Banion thought he recognized one of them. He had big broad shoulders and stood like a vault. They'd come to pay for the wreath. They wore dark overcoats and black bands of mourning on their sleeves. Under their dark coats they wore suits the color of Christmas ornaments. They paused to admire the wreath. One of the men sniffed the yellow roses. O'Banion offered his condolences. As he shook the man's hand, he inquired after the name of the deceased.

"Dion O'Banion," the man replied as the other pulled out a

tommy gun. O'Banion almost smiled. The year before he'd brought the first Thompson machine gun to Chicago. He purchased it on a vacation he'd taken with his wife to Colorado. Machine guns were readily available in Colorado, and O'Banion had been pleased to introduce them to Chicago. The wreath was delivered on time the next afternoon. The card read "To the O'Banion family. My sympathies. Al."

It was no use telling Opal to stay home. It wouldn't have done any good. She had no intention of listening to any of them, and she'd just as soon run away. In exchange her siblings ignored her. At night as she sat, combing her hair, dabbing rosewater behind her ears, Pearl acted as if Opal wasn't there. As Opal slipped into a dress of strawberry silk that she'd stolen from Klein's, swabbed on red lipstick, and pinned a cloche hat to her head, Pearl tried to convince herself that it didn't matter. But it did. Pearl could see that something had been unleashed inside of this child, and her time with Benny had only made her ache for more. If Anna were alive, she'd say that a dybbuk had set up residency in her soul. Pearl could not have guessed that being with Benny hadn't made Opal want him. He was just the appetizer, a sampling. He only made her hungry for more.

The conductors on trams didn't ask to see her ticket, and cabdrivers turned their meters off long before they reached her destination. They'd never transported an angel before. Opal may as well have had wings and a halo around her head. If it weren't for the red lipstick and the fishnet stockings, they would have believed it was so. Still these mere mortals rarely tried to ask her out—though they would long for her as they lay beside their wives who no longer resembled the women they'd married. In the morning the men went back to their trains and cars, sniffing for the scent of rosewater, a trace of blond hair, just to be sure she was real.

In the evenings Opal went from club to club, bribing a bouncer here, a bartender there, until one night she saw the crowd in front of the Dreamland and a sign announcing that THE BLACK BUTTERFLY would be playing there. The place was jammed, and patrons were spilling out into the street. It was mostly a black crowd, flashing their greenbacks, trying to bribe their way in. Dreamland was known for its thousands of electric bulbs and huge dance floor. Opal was pushed and shoved, but she wouldn't faint like Pearl.

As the crowd carried her forward, she could hear the sound. It was wild, leaping up and down, crazy jazz that went through her body and down to her toes. She had to get on that floor and dance. Opal shoved ahead and some of the crowd stepped back. One man excused himself because she was so thin and golden. A black man dark as pitch said to her, "I don't want to hurt your wings." She made her way past the bouncer and into the club, into a room packed with bodies and glitter and sweat. She followed the music, pushing and shoving, and almost feeling as if she couldn't breathe, but the throng ejected her onto the dance floor where a black man grabbed her by the arm and began to twirl her around.

And the sound grew louder and the music was running through her bones like fire to her fingertips, her toes, and back again. "Who's that playing?" she asked her partner because she couldn't see the stage, but she recognized the sound.

"Oh," he said, "you don't know? That's the Black Butterfly." He made a space in the crowd for her to see. She looked up and saw Napoleon, his face puffed, blowing away.

Opal began turning up wherever the Black Butterfly had a show. Every chance she got she stole money from the till, went into the candy store where she grabbed whatever flapper dress she was wearing at the time, and hopped the tram to the South Side. Pearl stopped asking her sister where she was going. In fact Pearl had stopped asking her much of anything. Opal wasn't a baby. She had a fire inside of her, and she let it burn. She didn't care what club she went to. She'd tip a bouncer fifty cents if she had to, which wasn't often. No one would turn Opal away. She stood out in this black crowd like a gold coin dropped on a dark street.

Napoleon couldn't miss her. Even though he had to squint for his eyes seemed to be narrowing into a tunnel of light, this bright beacon lit his way. He spotted her in the darkness.

When he glanced up, Opal was cutting up the floor in her indigo flapper dress. A young man with thin brownish hair whipped her out and pulled her back, but he could hardly keep up with her. Napoleon blew louder as if music could break a spell. He pierced the high notes he'd been able to reach with his scar. But he couldn't take his eyes off of Opal.

Rhythm streamed out of the piano, and the beat emerged from the bass, but it was lust that came from the trumpet. The mouth that closed around it, the tongue that worked its way in, the horn itself like that private part of a man, rising up for the high notes, burrowing into a woman, then coming back down. Napoleon was sweating from head to foot. His eyes had that dreamy bedtime look of a satisfied man. He gazed out into the audience, looking for his beacon of light. He looked for her the way he'd looked for fireflies on a summer's night.

When he spotted her, he ran his tongue across his scar. Opal danced with her hand wrapped around a whiskey sour. She'd lost count of how many she'd had. Napoleon was hoping she'd pull herself together and go home. He'd told Benny he'd meet him after hours for a little jam session. But it was past midnight, and Opal wasn't making any attempts at heading home. She was going to close the place.

When the set was over, Napoleon put his horn away. Without looking up, he slipped out the side door. He was heading down the alleyway when he saw that beacon of light coming toward him. He saw her before he heard her call his name. She caught up with him, clasping him by the arm. At first Napoleon resisted. He didn't really know her that well, but he doubted that she was even eighteen. He didn't know that she was as hungry for men as he was for pale women who wouldn't leave him on a delta porch. When he felt her mouth smash against his, he kissed her back.

He thrust his tongue into her mouth, and she bit into the ridge of his scar. Suddenly he was fumbling with her skirts, pressing up against her big and hard, so big she wondered if she could even take him in when, with his enormous hands, he lifted her into the air against the brick wall and sank her onto his pulsating member from which he exploded like a firecracker and, just when Opal assumed that this was done, he got down on his knees, raised her skirts, and proved to Opal that what she'd heard about his lips wasn't just a rumor. It was true.

Twenty-Six

The recording studio was in a run-down warehouse on a South Side street. Its windows were smashed or boarded up, and it looked abandoned as Napoleon made his way there. He stood on the dark, slick sidewalk, wondering what to do. He glimpsed one dim bulb, shining through some wooden slats. Otherwise the building was silent and dark. But Napoleon had told Benny and the rest of the band to meet him here. He checked the slip of paper where he'd written the address. This was the place.

Instead of going inside he stood in front of the door, unable to move. He'd woken that morning, knowing that he'd just made the second-worst decision of his life—the worst being defying the mob. The second was making love to his best friend's girl, and a white girl at that. In the South he'd be swinging from a chinaberry tree. In the North he just had to face his friend.

He had never been a good liar. He tended to drop his eyes to the ground. The one or two times he'd tried to lie to his grandmother, she pinched his cheeks and told him to look at her. She'd terrified him so much that he'd never mastered the art of telling a fib. Even with Maddy the few times he thought it would hurt her less if he didn't tell her the truth, she knew right away. So now he was preparing to lie to his friend. Liars like cowards look away, so Napoleon told himself that he'd better look Benny in the eye.

He knew that the first thing Benny would ask when he saw him was where he had been last night. They were supposed to rehearse for the record. Napoleon thought of how he'd answer. He forgot, which he never did. He was sick, which he probably wasn't. Something came up. He chuckled to himself. Yes, indeed. Something did come up. And now Napoleon cursed, wondering how he'd managed to get himself into these things. It was as if they came looking for him.

A few weeks before, Benny had shown up at a gig where Napoleon was playing and told him, "I want to form a band with you."

Napoleon was wiping the sweat from his face. "Oh, that's great, Moon. You tell that to my union. Who's going to pay my salary? You play good for an ofay, but I ain't playing with you."

"We could try it . . ."

"There aren't going to be any black-and-white bands earning a living," Napoleon replied. "Not in this city, or any other city, for a long time." He pointed at his lips. "And I'd still like to live to see tomorrow."

Still they jammed on off-nights. They played breakfast dances and rent parties. And on Monday nights when the Rooster was closed, they played the Jazz Palace. They never had to set it up. They just showed. And in fact they were expected. The week before during a break Napoleon, wiping his brow, turned to Benny. "So I got an offer to make a record with Gennett."

"I thought you weren't going to record."

"Well, this guy is willing to pay for the next Negro music and apparently that's what we're playing." Napoleon shined his trumpet with a cloth. "And I've seen the light. It's the only way I'll ever make a living."

"Well, you could hold down a day job like me."

"I've had a day job," Napoleon said, "and it didn't pay the bills. The recording session is tomorrow night. I want you on keyboard."

Benny looked at him, surprised. "What about the Judge? He does your keyboard."

Napoleon shook his head. "I can't count on the Judge anymore . . ."

"I don't know . . . Would they let me sit in?"

"Why wouldn't they? No one knows what color you are on a record. Besides"—Napoleon had paused—"I need you." And he'd given him the address.

Now Napoleon had to face his friend. He went inside to a large, cold room. It was illumined by a single overhead bulb. Thick curtains covered the windows and walls. They would keep the street noises out. In the middle of the room sat a large cone-shaped horn, and it was hooked up to a wax disk. His bass player and drummer were already there. Through the boarded-up windows and curtains, Napoleon hadn't been able to hear them from the street.

Only Benny was missing. This troubled Napoleon more than it should. Perhaps he'd forgotten. Perhaps he'd lost the address. He could be angry that Napoleon missed their rehearsal, or maybe somehow he knew. Napoleon decided he deserved this and more. Still he'd wait and see. He wouldn't bet money on it, but he believed that Benny would show.

In the cold evening Benny was walking toward the studio, hands thrust into the pockets of his trousers, but he was taking his time. He ignored the music that poured out of every door and the girls in blue fox coats who called. Something was bothering Benny. It had been bothering him all the way here like a seed caught in a tooth, something you can't quite reach. He couldn't name it, but it was there. He felt empty, let down, as if he needed something to eat, and maybe he did, but it wasn't just about food. Napoleon hadn't shown up the night before for their rehearsal. They were going to go over the new songs. Benny had waited for him until almost 2:00 a.m. Then he'd gone back to his room. It wasn't like Napoleon not to show. It wasn't like him at all. When it came to his music, he was all business.

Benny reached the recording studio. It was a dreary, abandoned-looking place, but it suited his mood. Hesitating on the steps, Benny heard laughter and the sound of a standing bass, tuning up. Inside, the other musicians were waiting for him. They were fiddling with their instruments, adjusting their strings, and they were restless as Benny walked in. "Hey, Moon, you're late," Napoleon said.

"I wasn't sure if this was the place."

"Well, it is, and you're late."

Benny shrugged. "Yeah, and where were you last night?"

Napoleon tried to look Benny in the eyes. "I got held up."

Benny shrugged. "Yeah, sure you did." He sat down at the rickety upright and ran a few scales. It was out of tune so he'd have to play above the band. "Anyone I know?"

Napoleon frowned, then looked away. "You need a few moments, Moon?" Napoleon asked.

"No, I'm ready . . ."

"Okay," Napoleon said, snapping his fingers together, " 'Night Owl Blues.' Let's take it from the top." And he counted out one-two-three-four. Then he blew a pig's squeal on the upper register and a horse's neighs, all the funny sounds that had amused Pearl when she was a girl. It slipped into a lullaby, and Benny carried the melody, soft and lilting, as the other musicians nodded as if they were going to drift off to sleep. Then Napoleon brought it back and the drummer picked up the tempo, and soon they were swinging. They went through a few choruses and everyone took a solo. They were laughing and sweating when they were done.

After "Night Owl Blues" and "Rags 'n' Bones," Napoleon looked over at Benny. "Moon, you pick one."

Benny thought for a moment. " 'Wild Boy Stomp'?"

"Naw." Napoleon shook his head. "Not some old standard everyone knows." He paused for effect. "Let's do one of yours."

"Are you sure?" Benny was stunned. "I thought this record was yours."

"I'm asking you, aren't I?" Napoleon nodded.

"Okay," Benny said. And he called out " 'Twilight Blue,' " which a few of them already knew. He roughed out the melody, gave the other musicians the chords. Benny started with an intro. It was slow as a Monday morning when you had to drag yourself out of bed to a job you didn't like. He thought about all those days at his father's caps factory. When he'd rather be playing ball or hanging out with his friends. That was where this tune began for him. But he had other places to be, other things to do.

Benny snapped his fingers, and let it roll over into his "State Street Shuffle" and the musicians followed. He was moving away on a train, heading south. Down to St. Louis, to New Orleans. He could almost see the cotton fields and dusty roads zipping past. He tucked his chin into his chest so that the spot where his hair was thinning showed, and hit the keys with everything he had. Laughing, Napoleon picked up his horn, and blew hard enough to blow his brains out, and the band did whatever they could to keep up.

When they finished, Napoleon told them to go ahead. He'd close up. His lips throbbed the way Maddy's knees throbbed when it was going to rain. Something was going to happen soon. He had a funny feeling in his gut. The boys were heading to one of the downtown clubs, and Napoleon said he'd catch up with them there. He stayed behind, trying to tease out a song from a stubborn tune. He was content with the session. It had gone well. Still, he was left with a sense of unease.

It was later than he'd expected when he was locking up. He shivered, but it wasn't because of the cold. Fear was rustling deep inside. Napoleon felt the men behind him before he heard them. He didn't even turn when they touched him on the elbow and invited him to take a ride that he assumed would be one-way. "Hello, gentlemen," Napoleon said. "I've been expecting you." His lips throbbed as if they had a pulse, and he ran his tongue along his scar.

The men looked at each other, perplexed, then back at him. They said nothing as they led him into the chilly winter's night. Pausing in the back alley, he took a deep breath that he assumed would be one of his last. But they weren't in a hurry. These men were going to take their time. His teeth chattered as he buttoned up his overcoat. He felt bad for Maddy and hoped she'd find someone to care for her. A black limo was waiting. Napoleon resisted the urge to laugh as a uniformed chauffeur opened the door.

The limo smelled of new leather, smoke, and booze. The men offered him a brandy that they poured from a cut-glass decanter. Napoleon sipped it slowly. He wanted to savor every moment, extend every final pleasure. If he were in prison, he'd order fried chicken and collards for his last meal. But given that this was Chicago and he was in a gangster's car, brandy would have to do. As he finished his drink, one of the men pulled something out of his pocket. Napoleon flinched. The man looked at him with eyes that displayed a hint of regret. "Sorry, buddy, but I've got to do this."

Napoleon nodded, but his heart was pounding so hard in his chest. "You gotta do what you gotta do." With that the man placed a hood over his head. It was scratchy, and at first he couldn't breathe. Sweat poured down his brow. He wondered if they planned to suffocate him first. It was no longer a matter of when they were going to kill him but how. He wanted it to be quick. He knew that begging was no use with these men. He'd defied them too many times.

They drove for a long time on what seemed to be a highway. Then they slowed down, turning right and left. They must have been on streets with traffic lights now because it was stop and go. No one spoke. Where were they taking him? A vacant lot? A frozen lake with a hole carved in the ice? A garbage dump where it would be easy to leave a body? He had no idea. He lost track of the time. It could be an hour. Three hours. He had no idea how far they'd gone or in what direction. His head was spinning. The silence in the car was deafening. For all he knew they'd been driving around in circles. He heard a train whistle and felt the car rumble as it drove over some tracks. A car backfired. Somewhere there was a siren. A dog barked. But nothing told him where he was going on his final journey.

Then they stopped. Car doors opened and slammed shut, and he sensed that he was alone in the car. Then the door beside him opened, and along with the cold air there was the scent of oil and rancid meat. Was this the stockyards? His hands were shaking. He shouldn't have been surprised that his defiant actions would lead him to this place. And yet he could do nothing to stop the fear that rose from his flesh and his bones. His body was not ready to die. He wanted to pray. He wanted to drop to his knees and beg for more time.

They ordered him out of the car and led him through a door. "Watch your step," one of them said politely. The door creaked.

They dragged him into a room where there was noise and light. He heard voices, laughter. Someone pulled the hood off his head. He blinked in the brightness. As his eyes came into focus, he saw streamers and a bar, filled with booze. Men were dressed in suits of shiny silk. Girls wore short skirts and flapper dresses. Everyone was smoking cigarettes. People milled around, laughing.

At a table off to the corner Al Capone was seated. A birthday cake with pink frosting sparkled before him. Napoleon looked at him with sweat still streaming down his face. Was he supposed to beg for his life? He had no idea, but he would not beg. He would not grovel. He was a proud black man. Capone threw his hands up in the air at the sight of Napoleon. "Happy birthday, boss," one of his men said. Napoleon was confused. Capone pulled back a chair and motioned for Napoleon to sit down. Slowly he came to understand that it was Al Capone's birthday, and he was the present.

Capone patted him on the back and asked what he wanted to drink. Napoleon shook his head. He wanted to be sober. He didn't want to forget what was happening to him on this night. And he wanted Maddy to believe him. "Ginger ale," he said.

Capone looked at his men impatiently. "Ginger ale, the man said." As the thugs scurried off like schoolboys in the face of a playground bully, Capone turned to his gift. "My boys," he said, "they're always trying to make me happy."

Napoleon nodded. A woman came by to offer him cigarettes, a flute of champagne. "Well, you deserve it, sir."

Capone smiled as the ginger ale arrived. "Why didn't you let someone know you had a problem?"

Napoleon trembled. "What do you mean?"

"You know, that you wanted other gigs. Not just the Rooster."

"I didn't know who to tell."

"I like musicians." Capone slapped Napoleon on the back, then reached his finger up to Napoleon's lips. He ran the finger over his own slashed cheek. "Hey look at us. We both got scars. Anyway it didn't have to be like this," Capone said it as if they were lovers, and he was trying to make amends. "We could've worked something out. But it's over now. You can play wherever you want except on the weekends. Friday and Saturday I want you at the Rooster." Capone held out his hand, and Napoleon shook it. "Okay, so it's a deal."

Napoleon nodded. He was going to cry. He wanted to collapse into this man's generous arms. Capone patted Napoleon on the back. "Just play a few for me, will you?" At the bandstand was a piano man and a drummer. They picked a few tunes that Capone loved. He swayed to "Moonbeam Melody." And he tapped his fingers to "Mama's Pajamas," a tune Napoleon wrote. Capone liked the beat and Napoleon kept it up until he thought his scar would split open.

Napoleon had no idea what time it was when Capone yawned. This was the cue to his men. They stood up, went to the doors. One helped him on with his coat. On his way out Capone patted Napoleon on the chest and stuffed some C-notes into his pockets. They put the bag over his head again and in the cool air of dawn drove him home.

Twenty-Seven

≡

In the late summer Hannah put up preserves. She had vats of sugary water boiling with peaches and cherries on the stove. She added vinegar to others filled with cucumbers and onions. Tomatoes for sauce. As she lined up her jars of pickled beets, sauerkraut, and green tomatoes, she wondered what was wrong with her eldest son.

He was altered. Different from whom he'd been. Hannah was the first to notice that something was wrong. She was a barometer for it. She'd always been this way. She sensed fevers before they came on. She could tell by the pallor of one of her boy's skin if a stomach virus was about to overtake him. Just before Ira came down with scarlet fever, Hannah had seen the lethargy in his bones. That day when Harold wandered off in the snow, the drifts were higher than he was, and he'd pleaded with his eyes not to go. Yet she had slipped the rope through their belt loops. She'd paused with each boy to make a sturdy knot. She relived that moment over in her mind.

Why couldn't she take it back? A mistake, an error of judgment. When the wind was strong across the prairie, for it was still a city filled with open spaces, or when the blizzards came down from the north across the lake, she had tied them so that they would stay together. But now she knew, as she had known since the day he had gone missing, that Harold should have been in the front, right behind Benny, and Ira should have been at the back.

It was logical. It made sense. He was the littlest boy, dangling out there alone. But she saw this only in retrospect. For the weeks until they found him Hannah was like a wild animal searching for her cub. She wandered the streets in just a shawl with a daguerreotype in hand, asking if anyone had seen this child. She flung herself onto snowdrifts and dug with her bare hands until they were frostbitten and raw.

Her vat of beets was boiling over. Juice bleeding onto the counter. It splattered against the walls. On her knees Hannah tried to scrub it out of the floor. The confusing smells of onions and strawberries, vinegar and beets, greeted Benny as he walked in the door with a flat parcel tucked under his arm. *Sweet and sour,* he said to himself, as he sniffed the air. He was searching for a phrase, a way to resolve his "Twilight Blue." If a tune had an odor, it would smell like this. An apartment in the late afternoon when his mother was boiling preserves. A silence, if silence, and loneliness, can have a smell.

Pausing in front of the mirror, Benny stared at his reflection. He examined his gray eyes set wide apart, his prominent nose, and thick lips. A Jew, but in the summers he was so dark he passed for black. He couldn't understand why he and Napoleon couldn't form their own band. Why couldn't they play together? It seemed only right. Straightening his tie, he adjusted his fedora.

He opened his parcel. Inside was a vinyl record. From the kitchen came the sound of dishes, water splashing in the sink. Benny wanted to surprise her. He put the record on the Victor talking machine, or Victrola, as it was called, and listened as "Night Owl Blues" filled the living room. He snapped his fingers and swayed to the beat.

Beneath the scratchy needle he heard his own playing come back at him. It was the first time he'd ever listened to himself. His sound was smooth and he could swing. Benny smiled, tapping out his own beat. Then Napoleon came in with his screeches and honks and Benny tapped until the end of the tune. Then he flipped the record and put the needle on his "State Street Shuffle." Benny stopped moving. This was his own music. He had written this tune, composed it himself as he walked along State Street. Once this had been a sound inside of his head. Now it came churning from inside a record machine.

He picked the needle up, drawing a deep breath. "Ma," he called. He waited. When she didn't come, he called again. "Hey, Ma. Come listen to this."

Still she didn't come. Snapping his fingers he went into the kitchen where he found his mother, scrubbing stains from the wall. He slipped up behind her and leaning over, gave her a kiss. Hannah jumped in the air. "Oh my God," she said, pressing her hand over her heart. "You startled me."

"You didn't know I was home?"

"I didn't hear you come in." She was breathing heavily.

"I didn't mean to scare you." She always used to hear him even before he'd reached the landing.

"Come here, I want you to listen to something."

"Benny, please, I've got work to do . . ."

"Come on." Despite her protests, Benny coaxed his mother into the living room. "Here," he said, "just sit." Looking at his mother, her hands thrust into her apron pockets, he longed to see her smile. It seemed like a long time since she'd smiled. He decided to go with "Night Owl Blues." He moved the needle to just the right place—at the start where Napoleon puts his trumpet to his lips and all these barnyard barks and squawks and oinks come rushing out, and for a moment he thought she would grin. Instead she leaped back. "What is that noise?"

"Ma, it's a record. Just listen. Here . . ." He took the record off and turned it over. "Try this." And he put the needle to "State Street Shuffle." She cocked her head as the piano began, quiet as a whisper. A lullaby took over, filling the room, and for a moment Benny could almost remember when he was a boy and she sang them to sleep with songs from the old country. Ancient melodies in Yiddish and Polish that her own mother had sung to her.

Benny could hear these same songs in his opening bars as his mother's eyes, so dark, brown-gray like mud puddles to splash in, welled up. Hannah looked at him as if she was remembering something, but it was so far away that it would take years to come back to her. Then his solo was over and the tune went away, and along with it that look on her face, and Napoleon came in, blaring and bleeping, and that quiet moment was lost to the drums and the horn and Benny was all over the keys.

Hannah paused, seeming to linger while Benny tried to read her face. Wiping her hands on her apron, she was as opaque as she was dark. "I've told you before. Don't bring that Negro music into this house," she said in a husky voice.

Benny laughed. "Negro music?" he said. "Ma, that's me."

Hannah glared at him with her beady eyes. "That's not you. And I don't want to hear it ever again. Now turn it off."

Benny did as he was told, and without a word Hannah went back into the kitchen. Benny stood alone in the living room. The scratchy sound of the Victrola died down. He stood in his hat and tie, ready to go out but not going anywhere, a young man, feeling old. Around him the furniture was tattered. A layer of dust coated the oak piano lid. In front of the mirror Benny straightened his tie once more, then went into the kitchen where he found Hannah at the sink.

She was back to rubbing the beet juice off the wall, and Benny took a cloth to help, but she pushed him away. "You're all dressed up," she said. "You'll get yourself dirty."

"Ma," he said, "I'm going out now." He wished she'd say something. That he looked nice. Or ask where he was going. Instead she kept at her scrubbing.

He bent forward to give his mother a kiss. "Is it going to come out?"

"I don't know." She looked at him with tired eyes. Then she went back to the stains that were red and stubborn as blood.

That night at the Jazz Palace Benny sat in for a set or two. Opal was waiting for him as he slipped out the door. She didn't resist as he led her into the alley. It was a blustery night as they walked down Ashland to the laundry above which he rented his room. In the entryway she kissed him, then laughed., and he kissed her back twice as hard. Laughing again, she wiped her mouth with her hand. "Are you trying to hurt me?" she said, egging him on. His grip was almost too tight as he led her up the stairs. This was what she brought out in him and in any man who came near her.

Opal enjoyed driving men wild with her yellow hair, her tinsel laughter, and unpredictable ways. She could have two. Or four. Each one could fill another part of the void, plug up the emptiness inside of her. The more men, she reasoned, the better the chance of being satisfied by one. But this wasn't the case. The more she had the more she needed. And the hungrier she grew. Sex was a curiosity like some shoplifted item—a comb or lipstick—that she wanted to fondle and steal but in the end would matter very little. As Benny pressed his lips hard against hers, she kissed him back. As he fumbled with her skirt and blouse, she fumbled with his buckles and zipper. He clasped her breasts and she moaned in his arms. She was good at pretending. It was one of her many secrets. Still, when he was finished, she asked for more.

The green-felt pool table at Local 10 was full of rips and tears, but it was good enough to pass the time until they got a gig. Benny and Moe had become members of the all-white American Federation of Musicians, and they began hanging out at the union office, shooting pool. They were playing pockets. "Hey, Benny," Moe said, "put a draw on that ball." Moe lined up a shot for him. "Drop the cue down." Benny hit it low and square, and the crack and crash of the ball as it went into the pocket was deeply satisfying.

Benny was also hanging out at Local 10 because he needed to stay away from his room above the laundry. Opal had begun showing up without warning, and it was making him nervous. At first he was enjoying himself, but then it didn't seem right. She'd arrive in the late afternoon or early morning when he was still asleep and he'd let her in. She'd show up after a set or before a gig and he didn't send her away. He knew he should, but he couldn't turn his back on her rosy nipples, and the longing he felt between her legs. She wanted something he couldn't give her and didn't even have, and that made him afraid to open his door.

"Hey, you guys," the union secretary said, "I've got a job for you." Benny hoped it was at a place like the Friar's Inn, even though the New Orleans Rhythm Kings had a longstanding gig there.

Maybe someone was sick. Maybe they had to fill in. Instead they were told to report to the Mirabeau for a vaudeville act. Still, it was work and they were happy to have it. When they arrived, the theater was packed, and the manager told them that they were to perform in blackface in a little revue entitled *Plantation Blues,* and they had to be on in fifteen minutes. They were rushed into a dressing room where they smeared on a concoction of burnt cork and water that made their skin feel tight and drawn and were rushed onto a stage set of cotton bushels with blackface singers sitting on them in overalls and calico, pitchforks in hand.

For the first five minutes they played the arrangements that were in front of them. Then Benny looked at Moe, his face coated black. "I can't do this," Benny said.

"Neither can I," Moe replied.

"Let's jazz it up," Benny said. They improvised on the chords, taking off in whatever direction they pleased. The singers stared at them perplexed, then not knowing what else to do, clapped along. The audience joined in. Everyone loved it, except the manager who fired them at intermission. They washed the blackface from their skin and headed back to the union office. They were playing pool when the secretary told them that Freddie Giltman was looking for musicians who were willing to travel in an old jalopy around the Midwest. Benny shook his head. "I'm going to start a combo of my own."

He put the word out, and before long he had assembled the Benny Lehrman Quartet, which consisted of himself and a drummer who could barely grow a mustache and a string bass player who lugged his battered bass everywhere he went and Moe on the slide trombone. Benny pulled together musicians who liked to improvise and solo, nothing fancy, just good, reliable players. It wasn't elaborate, but they got work in smoky basements, in the back rooms of speakeasies and in private dining rooms. Benny wanted to add a trumpet but couldn't find anyone he liked, and Napoleon's union wouldn't let him play with them. On weekends the quartet played the Cumberland Dance Hall and the Western Gardens, coming up with their own renditions of "Ain't We Got Fun" and "Ma, He's Makin' Eyes at Me." By the time they were winding down with "Meet Me Tonight in Dreamland," they had girls hanging from the bandstand.

He was thinking that with his combo he'd branch out. Maybe they'd tour. Maybe at last he'd get out of town. Benny started out fast, banging all the rags he could think of and a few tunes he'd borrowed from Armstrong. He played "Struttin' with Some Barbecue" and "Wild Turkey Stomp." He reached up and grabbed some numbers he'd written with Napoleon. Then improvised on his "State Street Shuffle" and for the laughs he dipped into "The Night Owl Blues." Once their blood was churning, he switched moods. He struck the opening chords of his "Twilight Blue." He riffed on the phrase, but he couldn't get very far. There was a tension in the piece that he still couldn't resolve. And just as the room got sleepy and started yawning, he pushed up tempo to "Satan's Mile."

In the evenings when he didn't have a gig Benny headed to the Stroll. He needed to stay away from the North Side. He wandered into the Deluxe and the Apex Club. One night he stopped at the Red-Headed Girl, but he wasn't that into the beat that rose from the piano, the easy bang on the drums. Restless, he pushed on to the Lucky Lady, then poked his head in Charlie's Place. Nothing grabbed him the way he hoped it would. He ended his evening at the Rosario Sisters Club.

The elder of the Rosario Sisters, Evelyn, had taken Benny under her wing. She was touched by the piano-playing Jew with the big hands and the sad eyes, gray as fog. She had a soft spot for men whom she suspected of nursing a broken heart. Despite her sister's protests and the fact that no man was ever admitted back into the Rosario Club without spending fifty dollars the night before, Evelyn Rosario invited Benny in as long as he played. He played for them until Evelyn decided his tunes were too mournful for their clientele and the men were coming out of bedrooms, their eyes filled with longing and tears, just to listen to the music.

"If you want to keep coming around here," she warned him, "you'd better jazz it up."

Amid the grimier brothels of the city, the Rosario Sisters shone with their mansion of many rooms and their white carriage drawn by four black horses that took them around the city. On Thursday evenings some of the finest poets in the Midwest read their poems there. Benny was dazzled when Evelyn let him try a different room and a different girl every night.

She led him into the Gold Room with its gold-rimmed fishbowls and gold spittoons, the miniature gold piano where he played the blues, the girls in gold lamé who sat on either side. She lured him into the Chinese room where he could set off firecrackers, and the Rose Room with its rose-shaped bed, festooned with rose petals and a bathtub filled with a blend of rosewater and gin. In the late evening Benny pounded with the huge door knocker and dined on fresh oysters, rare roast beef and champagne, aphrodisiacs intended to get his blood boiling. He ate and drank as much as he pleased and found himself enjoying the taste of real liquor more and more. He banged out tunes and played a few hands of poker, which he often won, then lost himself in the arms of a sad midwestern girl whom a gangster had loved and left behind.

Twenty-Eight

≡

Opal wasn't feeling well. She floated through the house, drifting off to sleep if she just sat down. Once seated, she could barely lift herself out of a chair. Ruby thought it was the warm weather, but Pearl looked at her pale skin that seemed even whiter than before and declared that Opal was anemic. Pearl bought slabs of liver that she sautéed with onions on the stove and that Opal refused to eat so their brothers did instead. She cooked steaks that Opal was too tired to chew.

Whatever chores Opal did were done in slow motion. She couldn't describe what was wrong. Except to say that she felt as if she was moving through a dream. In her slowness she'd put on weight. Once Pearl woke in the middle of the night and found Opal in the kitchen, scrambling eggs in a frying pan. For years she'd been an orphan waif, lithe as a Popsicle stick, but now a thickness sprouted around her waist. She was ripe for the picking, Moss said.

When her dresses didn't button, when her corset didn't pull as tightly as it should, she pouted. Lately she'd taken to sucking on her thumb. Still, no matter what she did by day Opal managed to muster the strength to head out in the evening. If it was a warm night or a cold rainy night, nothing deterred her. She became feral as the alley cats that cried in the night.

Everyone acted as if this was normal. Laundry still hung out on the lines to dry. The saloon was opened at four every afternoon like clockwork and closed when the last drunk staggered home. At the breakfast table Pearl sipped her coffee, waiting for Opal to come and join them. Ruby had laid out plates of toast and butter and boiled eggs, but Pearl hadn't touched her food. She just sipped her coffee, black. When she heard the footsteps, she bristled. It was midmorning as Opal dragged herself out of bed. When Pearl asked her what was wrong, Opal just shrugged. She was tired, she told Pearl, down to her bones.

How could Opal tell her sister that she wanted to be free of the smells of dirty socks and sour breath of drunken men, the smell of boiling chicken and fatty soups? She could escape this world and she knew, just from looking at herself in the mirror, that no one would ever mistake her for a Jew. She'd make her way as a taxi dancer, a chorus girl. If she dabbed rosewater behind her ears, it was to rid her of the world of rank odors, one she couldn't abide. She couldn't sit around the table, eating brisket and potatoes while unmarried sisters and brothers slurped their soup and wondered about the next shipment of gin. *I want to be free,* Opal shouted to herself. *Free of you and this house. I'm going to go and you can't stop me.*

A storm was brewing—the kind of weather that comes down from the far north, making landfall on Chicago's shores. And as the winds blew from Canada and across the Great Lakes, ships were lost in the turbulent seas, beaches were devoured, debris sailed through the air, and small children and old men clung to lampposts in the gusts. Bundling up in a wool coat and shawl, Pearl headed to market. Things were needed at home. She checked the pantry and she saw that there was a shortage of bread and lettuce and beans. When she was gone and Ruby had left for her drawing class, Opal went into the bathroom.

She stood before the mirror, touching her yellow hair. Then she picked up a scissors and began to cut it off. She cut one clump, then another. She didn't care how it looked. She hacked away, making it shorter and shorter until she looked like a haystack. On the ground her hair lay like spun gold. When Pearl got home, soaked from the rain, she found Opal with her hair shorn like a sheep. "Oh, my God, what have you done?"

"What I've wanted to do," Opal replied. And Pearl raised her hand and brought it down across Opal's face.

Opal shook her head. "I hate you." She said it slowly and simply in such a way that Pearl knew it was true. Then Opal ran to the steps. She raced out the door, into the wind-swept streets, leaving her sister to pick up her fallen tresses. She rushed through an alleyway, the rain stinging her face, but no more than Pearl's slap had done. The storm pummeled her as she ran, dressed in only a dark skirt and a thin cotton blouse that clung to her breasts. She should have taken a coat or a shawl, but she didn't. She dashed along Lawrence to Ashland until she reached Benny's doorway and rang the bell. When he didn't answer, she huddled in the rain.

Opal had no idea when he'd return, but she'd wait. She could be as stubborn as anyone, and certainly as stubborn as Pearl. She shivered as the wind swept in from the stormy lake. She shivered against the door as the afternoon dragged on and the day grew colder. She was never going home again. She kept thinking she saw him, but it was always some other man. When Mr. Walenski passed, he looked at her, and Opal huddled even smaller, but Mr. Walenski didn't recognize the girl with chopped-off hair.

The skies darkened as hail, the size of golf balls, hit the pavement. Opal pressed her back against the door. Her teeth were chattering as she saw him coming. He looked away, pretending not to see her. "Benny," Opal cried, "it's me." Her yellow hair, cropped and matted, clung to her head, and her rosebud nipples shone through her blouse.

He had taken her for a homeless waif. He touched her face, her neck. "What have you done to yourself?"

She shied at his touch. "I've run away."

He ran his fingers along her scalp. "You've cut off your hair." Benny shook his head, taking her by the arm. "You're shivering," he said. "Let's get you inside." And he led her up the stairs.

In his musty room he helped her off with her wet things. She was soaked through her underclothes, and blue veins ran up her neck and arms. Even her breasts were eggshell blue. Benny gave her a blanket to wrap around herself. He made her a cup of strong black tea and hung her clothes on the radiator to dry. "Now drink this," he said. "What were you doing in the rain?"

"I'm not going back," she told him. "I'm never going back there again."

"Of course you are . . ."

"No, I hate Pearl and I'm not."

"Opal, you have to. She's your sister. It's your family . . ." Benny hesitated, thinking for a moment about his own family. Hannah, miserable in her rooms, dreaming of a daughter she never had and a son lost in the snow. His father, despondent over baseball logos. Benny had his own thoughts about running away.

"I want you to come with me," she said. "We can get married. I have money. Not a lot, but enough to go somewhere. I don't care what Pearl says. I want to live with you." Opal kissed his hands, his lips. She told him that more than anything she wanted that. "We could go to New York. Or California. No one would know us there. I'll dance. You'll play music." She laughed that crystalline laugh.

He put his hand on her wet brow and touched her bones that were thin as a bird's. "You're burning up," he said.

Opal grabbed his hand. "Keep it there," she said. "It feels good." His hands were dry and warm. Her blue lips quivered as Benny swaddled her in the blanket. He didn't want to run off, and he wasn't sure he wanted to get married. Not now. Maybe never. And probably not to her. "Opal, you're a dreamer."

"You're a dreamer, too. Why can't we?"

She ruffled his hair, then sighed, shaking her head. She lay back on the bed, wrapping her naked arms around him. He was such a silly boy. Such a poor, silly boy. She pulled him to her, drew him down, then kissed him. Even as he bit her throat, the soft skin on her arms, and rolled on top of her, he knew that no woman would ever have the part of him that she had.

"Maybe when you are older . . ." Even as he said this, his words had a hollow ring. He was lying to the girl, but he hoped by the time she grew up, she would forget about him. He would lay low. Keep his distance. He had wanted her, it's true, but he didn't love her. He didn't love anything, really, beyond his music and himself. "But we aren't going to be together at all if you don't make up with Pearl."

When her clothes were dry, Benny walked her home. He'd already made a decision that he hadn't told a soul. He was leaving Chicago. He was going to New York. Maybe Moe would come with him, and maybe he wouldn't, but either way he was going. He couldn't make anything happen here. He couldn't breathe. He blamed it on the city and on his own solitude. For it was solitude that shaped him. It was solitude that made him who he was.

The rain stopped, but there was still a chill in the air.

Benny left her at the door of the candy shop. "Aren't you coming in?" she pleaded.

"I don't want to get my head bitten off." He kissed her on the nose. "Go inside. Be a good girl. And I'll see you tomorrow."

But he had no intention of seeing her tomorrow. Or the next day. She was a crazy girl, and she had lopped off her golden hair. Benny knew trouble when he saw it, and he would stay away for now. He didn't want to run away with her, and he didn't want to have to marry her. Already the heat in his loins had cooled.

The rain had stopped and the wind died down. Benny thought he might head downtown, hit a few of the clubs. He strolled, taking in the air. Cars drove by. Somewhere in the city gunfire punctuated the night. He was a young man, twenty-seven years old, the same age as the century. And he wasn't about to settle down.

Everything seemed possible. He could still go to New York and start his life anew. That same year Charles Lindbergh had flown across the Atlantic and Gertrude Ederle swam the English Channel, humming "Let Me Call You Sweetheart" all the way. In Soldier Field Jack Dempsey lost the heavyweight championship to Gene Tunney. The crowd was livid. A radio announcer had a heart attack. And Al Capone conducted "Rhapsody in Blue."

Twenty-Nine

≡

Pearl needed dark water, the lake grass between her legs, tiny perch that darted before her eyes. The water calmed some part of her that could not otherwise be calmed. Trudging across the sand, she dropped her towel and bag on the shore. Except for one man walking a dog, the beach was empty. She went into the lake slowly, letting the frigid waters seep around her ankles, her toes, up her thighs, her belly, her breasts. She dove as if she were looking for something. Perhaps she'd been a fish in another life.

As she swam in the water that was numbingly cold, she thought about Benny. She heard his laughter. She saw his big hands and long arms, the way he dropped his head when he played. He made her want to dance. She did not want to let go of him even for Opal, but she could not bear the silence anymore. She could not love her sister and have this wall between them.

Pearl swam in long strokes back and forth along the shore. Though her hands and feet were numb, she pulled harder as if she were trying to swim away. When she had exhausted herself, she floated on her back. The sun beat down on her, warming her face. *Opal can have him,* Pearl said to herself. Her decision was made. It was what the swimming had taught her. She belonged to the great sea, a universe much larger than herself. She'd let him go. He wasn't hers anyway to give. Pearl would find the way. Perhaps it was jealousy that had driven her. Perhaps Opal was right. She dove, twisting her body, swimming in slow, sinuous movements. She swam until a policeman blew his whistle and told her it was time to go home.

When Pearl returned, refreshed, her skin glistening, her mind clear, she found her sister wrapped in a blanket near the stove. She wanted to tell her. "Opal, I have something to say . . . ," but that was as far as she got. The cold of the last few days was followed by a breath of spring, but Opal, her delicate bones chattering, was trying to stay warm. "What is it?" Pearl asked her, the color draining from her face. "What's the matter with you?"

"It's nothing," Opal said with a wave of her hand, "I'm just not feeling that well." Pearl brought her hand to Opal's forehead. Her skin was clammy and she was trembling. "I ache," she said. Pearl made a bath of hot water and salts, and as Opal soaked, Pearl rubbed her sister's neck and arms, and she did a trick that her mother had once done for her. She tugged on the lobes of Opal's ears. Opal cooed like a mourning dove, and, for the first time in many months, nestled into her sister's arms.

But that night Opal was still sick and the pain was spreading down her back, her legs. She ached when touched. She begged Pearl to let her sleep alone. Pearl agreed. Perhaps, she reasoned, Opal might rest better by herself. Pearl got clean sheets and a pillowcase and made a path into the spare room, removing the hatboxes and suitcases that stood in her way. It was the room of the boys who'd drowned. Almost no one ever went into that room except to store winter clothes in summer and summer clothes in winter. Now Pearl dusted and made up the bed. Then for the first time in their lives, she tucked her sister into a room by herself. She sat at the edge of the mattress, stroking Opal's moist brow until she fell asleep.

In bed with Ruby, Pearl struggled to stay awake. She wanted to listen if Opal needed her in the night. But she was so tired from her swim and from her concerns that she drifted off. In the middle of the night Pearl woke to the sound of moaning and Opal calling her name as she had in her bad dreams as a child. Rushing into the spare room, she found her sister, pale as a ghost, curled into a ball, groaning in pain. Opal gazed up at her with her milky eyes and mumbled an apology that Pearl could scarcely hear. Around Opal a pool of blood blossomed as it spread. In her arms she cradled the perfectly formed fetus of a boy in its caul, the way she had been born, but this child was stillborn and black as a lump of coal.

Pearl stifled a scream and ran to wake Jonah. While he raced for the doctor to staunch the bleeding, Pearl raised Opal's legs and stuffed pillows beneath them. Squeezing her hand, Pearl placed a cool cloth on Opal's brow. Gently she lifted the infant from her sister's arms. His body was slippery and still warm. Pearl was surprised by the peaceful look on his face, as if he would wake up into the world at any moment and wail. She'd never held anything so small. His fingers and toes were perfectly formed. His hands and feet were miniatures. A tiny penis dangled like a little ornament between his legs. He seemed too perfect to be dead. She touched each dark finger and each dark toe. Then she swaddled the child in a clean white towel.

Pearl clasped her sister's hand. She remembered when she had first taken Opal in her arms—a perfect porcelain doll. How she had cared for her sister all of her life. Opal lay as pale as her gown against the sheets, sucking her thumb. Already she looked like an angel. Before Dr. Rosen could be aroused from his bed and brought to the house, Pearl felt her breath slip away. She died in the morning along with the child who, no matter what, probably wouldn't have lived. The name of the baby's father never left Opal's lips.

When Dr. Rosen arrived, shaking his head, for he had helped bring Opal into this world, Pearl pleaded with him. No child was mentioned on the certificate of death. Pearl called her siblings together and told them, "She died of influenza." And despite their sadness they agreed.

In the room where their drowned brothers once slept, Pearl and Ruby stretched out Opal on the bed. They cleared away all the boxes and swept around the bed. They lifted her body as they removed the bloody sheet and put on clean ones. Upon it Opal lay in a white linen gown, awaiting the women of the burial society that would bathe and prepare her for her burial the next day. The family tore their sleeves and covered the mirrors for the youngest girl, born in a rim of blue moonlight inside her caul.

As they prepared to sit shivah, each went about their task in silence. Jonah tied a black ribbon across the door and closed the Jazz Palace. While Moss wiped down the mahogany bar and polished the mirror, Pearl swept. She swept under all the tables and stools. Tears streamed down her cheeks as she dug her broom into places that hadn't been reached in years. She cleaned every crevice and knocked cobwebs off the chandeliers. She swept the pile of dirt into the candy shop and out the door. Then she began wiping down and dusting off the candy jars and bins.

Inside one of the bins she came upon a satchel, tucked far into the back. In the bag Pearl found the yellow silk dress and shoes that Opal had worn when she danced with Al Capone. In an envelope was the money Opal had taken from the till that she'd been saving for her escape. It was hundreds of dollars in single bills and coins. Without a word Pearl returned it to the cash drawer. When the burial society women arrived, she handed them the gold dress and matching shoes. "She'll wear this," Pearl said.

Just before the burial Pearl asked to be alone with her. Opal lay washed and dressed in her coffin in her yellow dress, as beautiful as she'd ever been except for her cropped-off hair. Pearl sat with a bundle in her lap for a few moments, holding Opal's cold and stiffening hand. Then Pearl opened her bundle. She lay the corpse of the baby between his mother's legs. This was the custom when mother and child both died at birth. Once a coffin like this was exhumed, and it was rumored that the baby had made its way to its mother's breast.

The regulars who came to hear the music and have a drink now arrived with their arms weighed down with baskets of fruit and flowers, casseroles of noodles and sliced beef. Some came inside to offer their condolences and drop off their offerings, but many just left them at the door of the candy shop. They scribbled notes and slipped them through the speakeasy slot. Soon the petals of roses littered the front of the saloon, and rodents nibbled at the fruit. The notes were dropped into a basket and never read.

As the tedium of mourning took over her life once more, Pearl sat despondent at the bar, staring at the mural of the family Ruby had painted so long ago. It was coated in grime and had lost its sheen. When Pearl tried to clean it, paint came off in chips. She stared at the corner where the gem sisters were shown on their bed. Ruby had painted herself with her blaze of red hair turned away and Opal with her big eyes gazing up toward the sky. Only Pearl was staring, her face dark and expressionless, straight ahead.

After shivah they tried to reopen the saloon, but none of the children had the heart for it. Glasses gathered dust and deliveries of bootlegged liquor piled up inside the candy shop door. Mice darted between the barstools. Just when it seemed as if the Jazz Palace would not open its doors again, and even the regulars had begun to search for other bars, Napoleon appeared. He'd been gone for days, and Pearl never asked why, but when he came by now, he saw the black ribbon above the door. Pearl looked up as he walked in, his hat in his hand. He glanced around the saloon and, within moments, he knew. The laughter and spun gold were gone. Then he saw Pearl's crestfallen face.

Pearl couldn't bring herself to look at him. For days she'd been thinking the obvious. The fetus that killed her sister was Napoleon's child. But now that he stood in his gray flannel suit in front of her, she wasn't sure. The child she'd placed between her sister's legs was dark as ink and Napoleon favored the high yellow of the mother he barely knew. Still Pearl could not bring herself to greet him. As he bent down to embrace her, and Pearl pulled away, he assumed it was because of her sorrow and not her rage. "It was the flu," Pearl told him. "She was never strong."

That night Napoleon went looking for Benny. He searched for him in the clubs because he didn't know where Benny lived. But he knew where he'd eventually find him. He looked for him the next night and the night after that and finally found him playing at the White Peacock. Napoleon waited out the set, and when he was finished, he went up to Benny. "Come outside while I grab a smoke."

Benny followed him into the street. Napoleon lit his cigarette. Then he told him. "She died, Benny," he said. "The angel left us."

"Who?" The color went out of his face, and Benny shook all over.

"Opal." Shaking his head, Napoleon flicked the ash. "She's gone."

Benny looked as if he was going to keel over. "It's not possible . . ."

"You should go and see them." As Napoleon wiped his own tears away, thinking of the girl whose skirts he'd raised in an alleyway, Benny staggered back inside to finish his set. Afterward he cruised from bar to bar, getting himself drunk. He stayed holed up in his rented room, coming out only to prowl the clubs. He didn't stop by the Jazz Palace, certain that Pearl and her siblings would never speak to him again. He stayed away until Napoleon found him again at the White Peacock. Benny was so drunk he'd stumbled past, and Napoleon had to grab him by the lapel. "You need to go home and clean up and pay your respects."

"It's my fault," Benny told him.

Napoleon wanted to share his own fears. This was his fault, too. "I have something to tell you, Benny," Napoleon said, gripping his collar hard. He almost told him. He almost said what he didn't dare say. But in the end he couldn't. The secret would die with her. "And it may come as a surprise, but not everything is your fault. If you looked at her, you could see how frail she was. That girl was sickly. She'd always been . . ."

"She waited for me in the rain."

"I could wait outside all day in a blizzard and not catch a sniffle. It's sad, Moon, but it's not your fault, and you need to go and see that family and pay your respects."

"I should've married her."

"What you should have done was leave her alone, but you didn't kill her." Even as he said it, Napoleon knew he was speaking for himself as well. He should have stayed away, too, but he didn't blame himself for her death. Anything or anyone could have brought her down.

"People die around me."

"That's not the same thing as killing them." Napoleon took him to a nearby diner where he ordered a pot of strong coffee. Then they went back to his room above the laundry and waited as he showered and shaved. A few hours later they were knocking on the door of the darkened speakeasy, banging until Moss let them in. The Jazz Palace was dark and ghostly still, but Benny and Napoleon had come to play. The place looked as if it had been closed for years, not weeks. Cobwebs were in the corners; the countertops and tables were coated in dust.

With a cloth Benny wiped the piano and the bench. It was odd to be in the Jazz Palace with no one there as they began a dirge-like lullaby for the girl who looked like an angel. They began with the opening phrase of Benny's "Twilight Blue." Napoleon's playing was mournful. Some notes were ghost notes, barely audible, floating behind the tune. Some were fluffs—those missed notes on a trumpet that came from a quivering lip. When they reached the first chorus, Jonah came downstairs. He stood beside the bar, listening to their sad tune. He walked through the candy store and removed the black ribbon from the lintel, dumped the baskets of fruit and dead flowers into the trash. "I'm tired of mourning," Jonah said. And he opened the door.

The old customers in the neighborhood, hearing the music, flowed into the Jazz Palace as Benny and Napoleon lightened the mood. Opal, they both understood, would have wanted it that way. Lev Walenski and Mrs. Baum's dead husband made their requests and dropped coins into the musicians' cup on the piano lid. But upstairs in the kitchen, Pearl didn't budge. Even though she heard the music and knew that Benny and Napoleon were playing down-stairs, she sat at the table. She wore a black dress that fell below her knees, and her hair cut short into a bob that Fern trimmed for her every few months had grown longer. In her dark mourning she fondled the note that Ruby had left on their pillow two days before.

It was only a few lines long, but Pearl had read it over and over. It began "Dearest Pearl . . ." Pearl couldn't read on, but then she did. "I don't know if I'll ever be able to explain this to you or make you see, but I needed to go away." She was going to New York to be an artist. "I will write when I've found a place to stay." A chill ran through Pearl. It was not the shiver like being in the lake in the spring when the water was quiet and cold. This was more like death itself walking by. Pearl understood that for the first time she was alone.

She forced herself to rise. She walked down the stairs to the landing where she saw Benny hunched over the keys. From this vantage point she almost laughed. He was losing his hair. It amused her that somehow they had grown old. He was playing a light, easy tune, nothing too demanding for the late hour. When he looked up, their eyes locked. Pearl had a million things she wanted to say to him, but her silence was stuck in her throat. She wanted to tell Benny that she missed Opal. That Ruby was gone, and she would have to learn how to sleep in an empty bed. And even though Pearl knew that Opal's death was not his doing, it seemed as if he was to blame.

She smoothed her hair and went behind the bar. Without a word they played on into the evening when Napoleon had to go to his gig downtown. After Napoleon had left, Benny just sat fiddling at the keys. Soon the neighbors went home. Her siblings went back upstairs. When it was only the two of them, Benny rose. He closed the piano and sat on a stool across from her. "I haven't seen you in a while," she said.

"I'm sorry . . . I should have come by sooner." He shook his head back and forth. His eyes were sunken as if he hadn't eaten in days. "How are you?" he asked.

"I've been better." She fingered the letter that she kept in her pocket.

"I'm sure you have," he said. "Pearl, I want to tell you . . . about Opal."

But Pearl held up her hand. "There's nothing you have to tell me," she said. "And honestly even if there was, I don't want to know."

"Would you like me to stay for a while?"

After a pause Pearl rose, shaking her head. "No, actually I wouldn't. It's late and I'm tired. I think it would be better if you leave." He had never heard such coldness in her voice as her dark eyes stared into his own. He nodded, slipping on his cap.

"I'll go now." But Pearl was already walking up the stairs.

Benny watched her leave, and he felt as if he would fall down and weep. Instead he walked out into the warm night and began wandering the streets. He walked with no purpose or direction. He felt as if he had a hollow place inside of him and something had slipped through it and was lost to him forever. This was what his "Twilight Blue" tune was really about. In its sad refrain he could hear that now.

It was the middle of the night as Benny made his way to his room above the laundry and sat on the bed. The musty smell seemed stronger than before. He touched the folded sheets and then lay back, staring out the window into the gray skies. The girl in the billboard was smoking her Lucky. Benny's hands were shaking. It was as if they belonged to someone else, and they were pale and trembling as an old man's.

Thirty

On a November morning Al Capone wanted to go duck hunting. He hadn't had a vacation in years, but he wanted one now. He thought that shooting birds out of the sky would do him some good. He walked into Marshall Field's and paid three thousand dollars on gear for himself and his entourage. He bought a dozen pair of waders and dark flannel shirts. He bought green hats and Bowie knives, shotguns and rain ponchos. He bought hunting rifles and silver flasks, hand-painted duck decoys and fur-lined jackets. For a week he and his men clomped around in rubber boots and waterproof jackets. They were good marksmen and they killed many ducks. As he trudged through dense forests and across mucky streams, Capone had time to think.

After all he'd done for Chicago the city still didn't appreciate him. He'd tried to make people happy. He provided entertainment and booze. "Public service is my motto" is what Capone said, but still they blamed him for everything. This made him sad. It made his stomach sour and his bowels flare. He had never killed anyone except in self-defense. He had never intentionally hurt anyone. He had brought money to many public officials and police officers and saloon keepers. He had a good heart. His family knew this. Musicians knew this. Still he was misunderstood.

There in the northern woods Al Capone decided to leave Chicago. He was going to go to Florida, but he learned that he'd be unwelcome there as well. He was twenty-nine years old and no one wanted him. He'd never been west, so he decided to go to Los Angeles. That far coast. It was a good place to get a fresh start. Capone traveled with his bodyguards in a special car. It was designed only for him with velvet curtains, real whiskey, and bulletproof glass. This was his first adventure. He'd never been anywhere except Brooklyn, Chicago, and East Lansing. He was surprised by the vastness of the country. He didn't know that the sky could be so blue and the land stretch so far. He was humbled before so much space. He thought of his older brother, Two-Gun Hart, who packed a gun in each holster, was a lawman somewhere in Kansas. He put people like his own brother in jail every day. Richard was his real name. He'd turned his back on his family long ago, breaking his mother's heart.

Everything on this sojourn surprised him. The people were blond, with pale skin and vapid blue eyes. They were thin and tall. They grew corn and wheat and their vast world was yellow. They lived in small towns. He had no idea how people lived in these towns or what they did in them. How did they pass the many hours of the day? These states were dry. There were no saloons or bars, not even any speakeasies to console them. What was it like for them at night? He rode through Colorado and came to the mountains. He had never seen mountains. He'd never seen deserts. It all frightened him. There was nothing here.

When he arrived in Los Angeles he was greeted by the messenger from the chief of police and told that he had twelve hours to get out of town. Instead Capone checked into the Biltmore. He took a tour of the houses of the stars in a bulletproof limo. He paused to admire Pickfair, the great mansion where Mary Pickford lived. He toured a movie studio where he watched Union soldiers fighting the Battle of Gettysburg and saw an actor named Buster Keaton slip on a banana peel and fall into a woman's arms. He called filmmaking a great racket.

His journey ended abruptly when Detective "Roughhouse" Brown arrived to escort Capone out of town. "Why does everybody pick on me?" he lamented to reporters at the Los Angeles rail terminal as he was getting ready to leave. He boarded the *Santa Fe Chief.*

It took him east, back to where he'd come from. This time the journey made him tired. He had no stamina for travel. If he could help it, he'd never go anywhere again. On his way to Chicago the train stopped at Joliet. When Capone descended from the train to stretch his legs, he was met by six policemen. They had their guns pointed at them. To make matters easier Capone handed over his .45-caliber pistol and all his ammunition. They arrested him for carrying a concealed weapon. He spent eight hours in a Joliet jail. Then he posted bail. He got back on the train and returned to Chicago. He was officially Public Enemy Number 1.

As Capone's train pulled into Union Station, Benny was thinking about how soon he could be boarding one to leave. He had his own dreams of departure, each ending years later with a triumphant return. He'd come back with his own orchestra and a longstanding gig. He'd have record contracts and fans clambering to hear him. He still had his red suitcase, packed, and his tunes, tucked in the zipper pouch. As the days passed after work or in the evenings he went for long walks. It seemed as if only by moving he could make any sense at all of things. He was drawn to the activity of the streets—the vendors and peddlers, the smells of roasting meats and baking bread, the pace of the inhabitants. Each morning he walked through a different neighborhood. The Polish and the Slavs of Pilsen, the Chinese, the Irish. He wandered through Greektown and along Maxwell Street. Everywhere he passed strangers. No one knew his face, and he knew no one. It would be so easy to join this crowd, to melt in where no one would recognize him.

Benny wondered what it was that made people disappear. Bad debts, failed love, petty crimes. Maybe he should disappear. He didn't have to stay here. He could leave, head off to New York and work for Paul Whiteman's band, or to Paris where he'd play in the clubs of Montparnasse or the burlesque houses of Pigalle. He'd start in New York. He'd heard that the music was different there. The bands were bigger, and they called the music swing. In Chicago people danced the Bunny Hug or the Black Bottom. In New York people still danced, but in most places they sipped martinis and applauded when a solo was done.

He'd saunter into the hotels, through lobbies of crystal chandeliers and wall tapestries. Doormen would tip their hats. He'd write letters home on sheets of creamy stationery with raised lettering, telling his parents about the gigs he'd landed and the recordings he was making. He'd tell them that he was living in a spacious room with a view of the park, but it would be best if they write to him in care of the general post office as he might be heading out on tour soon. He'd always include a check. His mother would write back to say how proud she was. And his father would be proud of him, too.

He'd rent a tuxedo and go to the Cotton Club. The Cotton Club, he'd heard, was built like a Southern mansion with large white columns and a backdrop painted with weeping willows and slave quarters. The orchestra performed in front of the double doors of the mansion. All the musicians were black and all the dancers light skinned. All the patrons were white. The musicians performed on a platform, and the dance floor was below. It was shiny as an ice rink. The dancers wore feather headdresses and pretended to be Indians. The murals on the walls depicted jungle scenes. Waiters in red suits carried trays of cocktails and shrimp.

Joe Oliver had been in line to play there, but he held out for more money. While he was waiting, Duke Ellington took the job. Now Joe Oliver was in Savannah, working as a janitor in a school. Duke played fast and furious. He was an affable man and he smiled, but his mind was always on his music. There were rumors that he was queer. His eleven-piece orchestra swung. Benny had heard a couple of recordings. The music was moving to New York. The recording studios were there. He could pick up sessions work. Maybe it wouldn't be enough to send home to his family. Maybe he'd just be living in another dingy room with another view of a billboard of a smoking girl, but his brothers were running the factory now so his parents would be taken care of, and Benny could earn enough to keep himself alive.

He rarely went to see his parents. Mostly he went to his job in the pit and stayed in his room. He got gigs when he could find them. He was trying to save up his money so that he'd have enough to leave. On a cold February night he sat, eating bananas and sipping warm gin. He stared down at the street. Below couples strolled in the chilly evening. Women clutched red roses in their hands and clung to the arms of men they adored. It was Valentine's Day, and he longed to have someone beside him. He listened to the sirens in the night. Everywhere there were emergencies and crimes and deaths.

Outside the billboard girl seemed to be watching him, and he found himself wanting even this woman who eluded him. He'd been without a companion for so long. He thought of all the women he'd spent a night with or more. The sad whores at the Rosario Sisters and Opal who had once aroused him and now was gone. His mind wandered back to the Polish girl with the thick braid who'd been in his history class. The girl with whom he'd imagined dancing when he was a boy, standing on the Clark Street Bridge. He hadn't thought of her in years, but now he did. What had become of her? She was probably fat and sold pierogis on the West Side of Chicago with a bevy of kids and a husband who drank.

None of these women stayed with him. They were as ephemeral as smoke. But as the night wore on, his thoughts brought him to Pearl. He was surprised to find himself thinking of her, but there she was. Once Napoleon had told him to look at her from a different angle and now he did. He saw her from afar. She was like a painting that didn't make sense up close. He had to step away. He saw her as a memory. Her skin, tawny in summer, her rich, dark hair. Her lean swimmer's body. He felt a longing that surprised him, but it wasn't to make love to her. He wanted to talk to her. He decided that if she didn't want to see him he would write her a letter. He would explain why he was leaving. Whatever he told her, it would be the truth.

In the small desk in his room he had paper and envelopes—not the creamy beige he'd envisioned for himself, just plain white paper and a pen. He tried to start the letter a dozen times. He'd addressed the envelope, but that was as far as he got. The words wouldn't come. He wanted to tell Pearl that all he knew were mistakes. Everything that once mattered to him was gone. He needed to get back inside his music again. It was as if he was standing on the outside of his own life, gazing in. But he couldn't put his sadness on the page. He only knew how to say those things with his fingers on a keyboard, not on paper with a pen.

The sky was lightening, the city waking up, when he folded the blank sheet of paper, put it into the envelope and stuffed it back into his drawer. He'd finish it another night. He slept for an hour or two, and then went out to get coffee. On a windy corner a boy was hawking the morning papers, and the headline caught Benny's eye. "Seven Gangsters Slain." He bought the paper and read it as his coffee grew cold. A squad of men posing as police officers had walked into a garage on Chicago's North Side. They'd lined the members of the Moran gang against the wall. They made them spread their legs and raise their hands high. The Moran gang joked among themselves. These raids happened all the time. You greased a palm or two, and then it was done. They were about to start laughing when the machine guns opened fire. Within moments they were dead. When neighbors saw cops leaving the garage, they assumed a bust had been made. Then they came upon the grisly scene.

Newspaper photographers rushed to the garage to snap pictures as they had when the *Eastland* sank. Images of bloodied bodies were splattered on all the front pages. No one had ever seen such a crime. Chicago became known as the city where boys murder boys for no reason, and grown men are gunned down. Capone was in Miami at the time, staying at his villa on Palm Island. He spent the day betting on horses. In the afternoon he went to the dog track. He was shocked by the news. Two days later he threw a party at his villa. More than a hundred guests arrived.

Thirty-One

Napoleon's world was shrinking. Darkness was descending upon him like a shroud. He didn't need a doctor to tell him that something wasn't right. He had been slipping into a tunnel for some time. Streets were narrowing; rooms were getting small. Soon he feared that all that would be left for him were pinpricks of light. He was memorizing the world around him so that at least for now nobody would know. He counted the steps to the tram, going to the Rooster, and the steps coming home. He learned the bumps of the road, the grade of the curb. He was nocturnal anyway so this would only make it a bit darker than it had always been.

Perhaps this was God's way of punishing him. After all he'd hardly been a good man, though he had been kind to Maddy. He'd never been her lover, but he had been faithful in his heart. Now he was losing his sight, and all he could think was that it was for his sins. And there were too many to count. But then if God really wanted to punish him, wouldn't he take away his hearing instead?

For now he'd just have to listen harder for the clang of the street-car, for the chimes of a clock. But how bad could it be for a musician to start really listening again? Listening not just to the notes but also to what was happening between them. What was in the pauses when there was no sound? Maybe all of music happened in those pauses anyway. Maybe all of life did. So he listened more carefully. It wasn't that he'd ever really stopped. It's just that before he could see things, too.

He didn't want anyone to know. Anyway he wasn't blind yet, and he could still see enough to see that something wasn't right. You didn't have to be a genius to figure that out, and you'd have to be really blind—blinder than Napoleon hoped he'd ever be—to miss it. It came to him the minute he laid eyes on Benny. Or rather the minute he heard the flatness in his sound. He'd sensed it the last time he'd seen Benny as well, but he hadn't been able to put his finger on it. It was as if Benny's problem had to do with him. And as his hand went to his throat, he knew.

Napoleon touched his gris-gris bag and held it up to his nose. He sniffed it and cradled it in his palm. Long ago he'd intended to give Benny the gris-gris bag that contained John the Conqueror, the trickster, the one with the sense of humor that would set him free. Instead he'd given him the mandrake root and the skin of the turtle to make women love him. The one his mother had given to him.

Napoleon had had his own share of problems with love. White women who kept his mind racing in the late hours. It was white women he'd risk life and limb for. He was glad he'd left the South. He'd have been lynched for the thought alone. Napoleon had loved the wrong women, too, so why should Benny be any different? Women wanted him. They followed him with their lavender perfume, their powdered skin. They followed him in their silk stockings and dresses that now rose almost to the knee. When he walked down the street, when he walked into a bar, Napoleon could see that they did. Too many loved him and most were the wrong kind. Napoleon had brought the wrong magic into Benny's life. And perhaps he'd brought some of it into his own.

That morning Maddy asked Napoleon as kindly as she'd ask him to take out the trash or pick up a loaf of bread if he would leave. She'd met someone, she told him. He knew he had no right to beg her to change her mind, though he was surprised at how crushed he felt. The darkness seemed to be sweeping down on him even faster than before, but this he would never tell her. Especially not now. Pity was the last thing he wanted. "I'll have to find a new place," he told her.

And Maddy patted his hand. "Take your time."

Thirty-Two

In October the market crashed. Lines of people waiting for food or jobs cropped up all over the city. Half of Chicago was unemployed. A former banker wore a sign around his neck, offering to do day labor. A woman who'd never ironed a blouse in her life posted a notice that she was taking in wash. In Union Station children slept on beds of cardboard. Tents sprang up all around Lincoln Park. Benny lost his job at the pit. Gigs were scarce, and his money was dwindling. He started going home for meals. His mother, whose eyes were dark and sunken and who had begun to smell of old age, claimed she didn't think she'd make it to Passover. His father's hands trembled as he ate his soup. Despite the fact that Benny was almost thirty years old, he gave up his place above the laundry and moved back into his child-hood bedroom.

There was nothing wrong with Hannah that having her son move home wouldn't cure. It wasn't that she hadn't been unwell. She had been weak and sickly, barely eating. Nerves, her doctor said. But one morning she woke up early and began cleaning the house. She put fresh sheets on his bed, and then she went shopping. She was roasting chicken, making broth. "What is it with you?" Leo asked her when he saw her up and about, but she just shook her head.

"Sonny's coming home," she said. Later that afternoon when Benny knocked on the door, carting all he owned in his red suitcase, he found his mother, robust, puttering around in the living room, arranging a plate of cookies, looking better than she had in years. He gave his parents a hug and then went into his room where he opened his drawers and put his starched shirts and silk ties away. He emptied the red suitcase, except for the zipper pouch where he kept all the tunes he'd written down. Then he shoved it back under the bed.

At dinner Benny didn't seem so restless anymore. Except for cutting his chicken and moving the fork to his mouth, his big hands were still. *My boy is back,* Hannah thought as she pressed her own hands to her chest. She didn't mean simply that he had moved back home, but rather that whatever it was that had possessed him was gone. The demonic light she'd seen in his eyes had dimmed, and in its place were two dull stones. It didn't occur to Hannah that the life had left her son.

The house depressed him, and he had no idea where he'd find work. There were the old odors of schmaltz and musty air and none of the lilac perfume and cigarettes he had grown used to. Both of his brothers had married and moved into apartments of their own. But he couldn't even afford his rented room. In the room next to his he listened to the steady thrum of his mother's sewing machine, a sound that only served to remind him of his defeat.

After dinner he put on his coat and said he was going for a walk. Hannah didn't argue with him. She knew it would do no good. He headed out into the cool Chicago night. He didn't know where he was going; he just let his feet take him. He walked until he was chilly, then hopped a streetcar and got off at the river where he kept going, hugging the banks.

He came to the Clark Street Bridge. It had been a long time since he'd stood here. If he paused, he could still hear the screams in his head, and he didn't want to listen. He kept going on to the "el," heading south. He thought of going to the Jazz Palace but decided to stay away. He brought disaster with him wherever he roamed. Children drowned, a girl he loved and a brother he adored had died. He could not inflict himself on anyone who mattered to him anymore. Perhaps if he'd actually written that letter to Pearl, this is what he'd say. Night after night he wandered the city until the cold made him turn back.

Meanwhile Arthur and Ira had begun to make a success of the factory. At Ira's insistence they'd diversified. "Too many eggs in one basket," Ira said. It wasn't just caps now. They'd branched out into baseball memorabilia. Key chains and coasters. Now Ira was looking into T-shirts and ashtrays. Arthur, who was the bookkeeper, tried to keep Ira's excessive ideas in check. He balked when Ira suggested that they mail out little catalogs with all their products. "Trust me," Ira said, "in a few years people are going to be shopping without going to the store."

When Benny showed up at the factory, he tried not to watch his brothers gloat. But Ira, the entrepreneur who'd grown round and redder and had married a woman with a bronze helmet of hair, saw that Benny could be an asset. No one knew the South Side of Chicago the way his older brother did. Any white person, that is, and he offered Benny what he knew he wouldn't refuse. He gave him all the accounts south of Union Station. Near Comiskey Park small retail concessions were sprouting up, and Ira saw a need. Benny carried a leather satchel that contained samples of the coasters, caps, T-shirts, and ashtrays. He went through the motions of heading down to the South Side where he opened his sample kit and display coasters with images of the White Sox and Cubs, ashtrays where you could flick your ashes onto the face of Dutch Henry or Garland Braxton.

During the days he found himself pounding the pavements, trying to sell his souvenirs.

In the evenings he returned home where he stayed in his room, listening to music, or he snuck down to the bars after dinner to drink. Except for his evening meal he never saw his family. He avoided the Stroll and the Jazz Palace and all his old haunts. Soon he'd have to be making his decision if he was going or staying. No matter what, he couldn't keep working for his brothers. He had to find another job.

Then one afternoon the phone rang. Benny didn't budge until his mother stepped into his room. "It's for you," she said.

Reluctantly Benny moved into the living room and put the

receiver to his ear. "So, Moon, I heard you moved back home," Napoleon said.

"Who told you?"

"I ran into that friend of yours. That trombone player. Moe."

"Yeah, I moved home," Benny replied. There was a silence between them that had never been there before.

"Well, I've got some sessions work," Napoleon said at last. "Not much money in it, but it's work and I could sure use you . . ."

"I'm busy," Benny said. "I've got a job." Benny made his excuses.

"Come on, Moon," Napoleon said, "I need you."

It was the same studio off Forty-Seventh Street where they'd recorded before. Benny took the "el," then walked along the dark streets of padlocked clubs that would soon be torn down, making room for the projects. The feds had been running raids on the clubs of the North and South sides. They went in and took down the name of every patron. After a raid people tended not to come back again. On these streets where midnight had once been lit up like daylight it was pitch black, and Benny could barely find his way.

The streets known as the Dahomey Stroll were shuttered and silent. No more bluesy notes, no more high Cs were blasting down South State. The maids and delivery boys who put on their fancy duds and strutted out any night of the week were gone. In their place were hungry men, sleeping on the street. Eliot Ness, who would spend his later years drinking himself to death in bars as he recounted his exploits, was on a mission to get Al Capone by enforcing the Volstead Act. Ness and his "Untouchables" decimated the Stroll. The market crashing killed it. Capone would be charged with five thousand violations of the Volstead Act, but he would go to jail for tax evasion instead.

In Chicago the full orchestras that played in the movie theaters were being disbanded. Sound systems for talking pictures were being installed instead. A few musicians formed small combos and roamed the Midwest in crammed cars to play in roadhouses. The tavern where Benny had once stood, listening to Honey Boy, was closed, and all that was left of the Rooster was the red sign that glowed in the headlights of passing cars.

Benny walked in late, and the musicians were grumbling. It was cold inside, and they were trying to keep warm with their coats and gloves on. Benny didn't know the drummer or the bass player, who didn't even look up. But Moe was there with his slide trombone, and he gave a little wave. "Sorry. I got lost," Benny said. His breath formed a cloud in front of him.

Napoleon shook his head. "You never used to lie to me, Moon." Benny shrugged and noodled with the keys, trying to warm up his fingers. Even the keys seemed stiff because of the cold. "You need some time?" Napoleon asked but Benny shook his head.

He'd barely run a scale when Napoleon was snapping out the beat, and they dove into "Flash in the Pan." It was one of Napoleon's older songs, and Benny knew it well. He'd transcribed it himself a few years back. This was a fast, up-tempo tune, but his heart wasn't in it. He was only going through the motions. It was how things had been with him for a while. That was a song he needed to write. One called "Going Through the Motions." For now he was just playing to keep time.

His mind drifted to the dark, windblown streets and padlocked doors. Tired people, lining up or wandering the city, looking for jobs. Black eyes staring at him from these streets. He thought of Marta and her little girl and wondered what had become of them. That girl would be how old if she'd lived? She would be almost Opal's age. He envisioned Opal stretched out on his bed with her golden hair. An angel he'd turned his back on, and now she was gone. And Pearl was gone, too. She'd turned her back on him. He was lost in a voice that looped through his mind, and in the final chorus of "Going Through the Motions," he came in late. There was no mistaking it; he missed his entrance, then rushed to catch up, fumbling on the keys.

The other musicians glanced his way, but Napoleon waved his hand to calm them down. After the take, the drummer wanted to do it over, but Napoleon said they'd keep it. "It's good enough," Napoleon told them.

"It's a flub," Benny said. "Anyone can hear it."

"You'd have to be listening for it," Napoleon said.

"Well, I hear it." He lit a cigarette, and walked out of the studio. He stood on the steps, smoking slowly, then walked down the alleyway. He walked to the street. Inside the studio the musicians waited.

Napoleon emptied his spit, then drummed on his valves. "We'll do it without him," Napoleon said. "He won't be back."

Thirty-Three

≡

For weeks Pearl had been moving like a sleepwalker. She rose in the morning. She cooked and cleaned. She prepared the Jazz Palace for the evening by washing down the counters and making the glasses sparkle. These were the gestures she'd been doing for years, but now they were only that. Without her sisters Pearl didn't know how to sleep in the bed. She flailed from one side to the other as if being tossed at sea. Her dark hair grew matted from all the twists and turns. Her eyes had the circles and her skin had the pallor of the restless and the ill. Often Jonah found her outside of the covers, talking in her sleep. Once he came upon her sitting at the edge of the bed, but when he touched her, she was startled. "Why did you wake me?" she asked.

She hardly went to the lake, and when she did, often it wasn't to swim. Sometimes she just she sat on the shore, drawing random patterns in the sand. When she went into the water, it seemed so cold and chilled her in a way that had hardly mattered before. Pearl didn't hear a word from Benny. The rest of the spring and all summer he never appeared. She expected that he would have already stopped by, but then the last time she saw him she'd sent him away.

She thought he'd come to see her, too, but he hadn't. Perhaps he still blamed himself for Opal's death. She wanted to tell him the truth, and maybe one day she would. She found herself waiting for his knock, hoping that the door would open and he'd walk in, sit down, and play the piano as if he'd never left. But he didn't. Though she tried not to wait, she did.

Over the past year she let her hair grow longer and wore it tied up in a bun. She wore shorter skirts and, as she walked along Michigan Boulevard on her way to work, men admired her trim and shapely legs, her smooth muscular arms. In the winter she began swimming in an indoor pool. She found she could not go long without putting herself underwater, without that steady rhythm of breathing in and breathing out. Still, the pool wasn't the same as the lake. The lake had no boundaries. She was drawn to its limitlessness, the sense of possibilities. The lake gave her hope.

She couldn't help herself. At night she dressed for him. She put on lipstick. Pearl didn't like to wait. She thought about trying to phone him, but she resisted. In the end she decided that he would not return. If he had planned to see her, he would have by now. Slowly her longing transformed itself into rage. He didn't have to come, and she didn't want him to. Pearl resigned herself that she would live out her days with her brothers who had remained unmarried, as she knew she would, above the saloon.

In the fall a salesman walked through the candy store and knocked on the Jazz Palace door. He had no trouble finding his way. He had been to dozens of speaks all over Chicago. He brought with him a booklet that described a new machine, illumined with colored lights, that played tunes, one after the other. It had an arm that reached for the wax recordings and, for a nickel, placed them on the turntable.

Moss and Pearl read the booklet from cover to cover. Moss was as taken with the machine as was Pearl, and they purchased one for the saloon. It arrived on a truck a few weeks later and took three Teamsters to unload it. The salesman came back to help them install it and put in the records they wanted to hear.

Pearl dropped the first coin in, then watched amazed as the lights flickered red and yellow and the arm dropped, scooping up a record into the slot. Now they could have all the music they wanted. But on Monday night when Napoleon showed up, he took a shot of whiskey and gazed at the illuminated box sitting in the corner. "What's that doing here?" he asked.

Beaming with pride, Moss put a nickel in, and the machine lit up. Yellow and red lights flashed. A hand dropped down, picking up a record, and "St. Louis Blues" came on. Napoleon's eyes opened wider. Then he got up and walked across the room. Moss handed him a nickel and "Wild Man Blues" followed. Napoleon stared at the blinking display of red, yellow, and green, standing there in the middle of the saloon like a fiery beast, spewing Dixieland music and jazz.

Despite his failing eyesight Napoleon could see what this machine with its bright lights and blasting sounds meant to live music. "That's it," Napoleon said. "We're through." And he began calculating if he had enough money saved for a steerage ticket to Paris. He knew that with the invention of the jukebox, and Eliot Ness closing the cabarets, live music was doomed. His future would happen elsewhere.

That night he called Benny and had him meet him at a downtown bar, where Napoleon pleaded his case. "Come with me to Paris," he said. "We can make something happen there." There wasn't much holding Napoleon here. Maddy's children were grown and she'd found a man who shared her bed during the hours she was in it. She was all right to see him go, and Napoleon was ready to leave.

Benny sat fiddling with the piano, shaking his head. "You'll be back in no time," he told him. "And I'll be right here."

Napoleon looked Benny straight in the eye. "Nobody would have heard that flub. It was a simple mistake."

"It was my mistake." Benny shook his head, staring at his hands. "And I heard it."

Napoleon understood that Benny was referring to many things. He shrugged. "Who cares?"

"Nice title," Benny chuckled. "Anyway, that's not the reason."

"Music is dead here, man. Or it's dying soon." Then added, "Why? Why won't you come?"

"I don't want to."

"I don't believe you."

Benny lowered his eyes. "I have responsibilities."

"That's true, Moon." Napoleon nodded. "You always did."

Benny winced, then glared at his longtime friend. "It's more than I can say for some people." He waited for a reply, but none was forthcoming.

Already Napoleon was walking out the door. "I'll see you in Paris," he said.

Late that night after a day of selling coasters, Benny headed home. It was a cold night, but he didn't bother buttoning his coat. His parents were asleep when he got in, and the living room was dark. He was shivering as he sat down at the piano. Its keys shone in the dark like teeth. He played a scale or two, fiddled with the phrase from his "Twilight Blue." Then he sat with his head down like a scolded child.

It was as if someone had pulled a plug in him, and water drained out. The music had left him as easily as it had come. He had no idea how long he sat, his hands barely resting on the keys. Then he went to the window. He was grateful for the silence of the apartment, glad his parents were asleep. A light snow fell. It was the first snowfall of the season, and he stood, staring. It wouldn't stick. With his eyes he followed one flake, then another. He watched them go. Down to the ground. One flake at a time, joining the millions of other snowflakes. One after the other landing on the sidewalk, melting there.

For a long time he didn't move. Then he put on his coat, his rubber boots, and his cap. As he tiptoed toward the door, his father rolled in his troubled sleep while Hannah, who lay awake, clasped a hand to her heart. Something was different in the way Benny closed the door and left the house. At the bottom of the stairs he braced for the cold. A raw wind shrieked down from the north. Wrapping his scarf tight around his neck, Benny walked along Ashland. In the snow the streets were almost deserted. The occasional car sped past him. A taxi stopped to see if he wanted a lift, but Benny waved him away. He wanted to walk. He was cold and shivering, but he didn't think about where he was going and why. He let his feet take him to wherever it was he was going. It was as if he were on a horse that knew the way home, even if he didn't.

His footsteps had a rhythm. A beat of their own. They made a little shuffling sound. He slipped and had to catch himself against a wall. A light powder covered the sidewalks and his footprints disappeared almost as quickly as he put his foot down. No one could follow him. Not that anyone would. He turned east. A dog in an upstairs flat started barking at him and Benny shushed the dog and told it to quiet down. A drunk lay in an alleyway. Benny paused, slapping the man in the face until he woke. "You better get up," Benny told the man. "You'll freeze to death here." The drunk slurred something, then struggled to his feet. Benny helped steady him until the drunk lurched down the street.

Benny kept heading east. He walked under the "el" tracks where for a moment the snow paused until he came out on the other side. He walked farther until the streets grew familiar. He recognized certain houses and shops. The kosher butcher with its Hebrew lettering. The dry-goods stores. Then he knew where he was going. He chuckled when he figured it out. He could turn around and head back but what was the point? He'd been going here all along.

Pearl was sitting up at the bar, her head resting in her hands, unsure of what to do with herself. For the first time since she could remember, all the tasks that had occupied her for so long were finished. There'd always been someone to care for, some chore to perform. And now there was none. She longed for a room that needed straightening. Something she had to fix. Perhaps the bar should offer olives and cheese on crackers. Perhaps she should clear out the candy shop and serve lemon ices again. But it all seemed like busywork. None of it was the task for which she was intended—though she had no idea what that task might be. It occurred to Pearl that this must be what it felt like to grow old.

A draft brushed past her, causing her to shiver. She rubbed her hands on her arms and tightened the shawl she'd thrown over her shoulders. Looking up, she saw Benny, standing in the doorway. He was covered in a light coating of snow. His eyelashes were glazed with tears. She wondered what had taken him so long. "Benny, come in." Pearl rose, gesturing his way. "You'll catch your death." He nodded and, as he took Pearl into his arms, she brushed the snow away.

His hands were freezing as she rubbed them with her own. He trembled, but it wasn't from the outside. It came from his bones. He clasped her for a moment as he tried to get warm, then pressed his face into her hair. He had a million things he wanted to say, but it only came in a whisper she barely heard. "Thank you," he said. She had him sit down while she made a pimento-and-cheese sandwich and a hot tea with brandy and honey that he drank in great gulps, though it scalded his mouth. She brought the heat back into his body as best she could. She knew he had come for something. And it was not just for her. He had lost his way.

The piano sat, cold and abandoned as Pearl had been in a corner of the room, and Benny looked it over as if he saw a stranger he thought he recognized. His fingers were still as he wrapped them around the hot mug. "I shouldn't be here," he managed to say, and Pearl ran her fingers across his brow. "You shouldn't be anywhere else," she replied.

All the rest of that winter Benny came to the Jazz Palace, but he rarely played. Once in a while he fiddled, but mostly he sat at the bar. His hands and feet slowed, then came to a halt. His tapping fingers had ceased. Since the first time he appeared with Napoleon at the saloon door, Pearl had only seen him in motion. Now in his stillness she could see how lonely he'd been. As the weeks went on, she let him be. Perhaps in time he'd figure something out. Meanwhile she had other concerns. Customers were dwindling and money was scarce. No one had disposable cash. Even Balaban and Katz rarely stopped by. People could barely eat, let alone pay for music and beer.

Clubs all over Chicago were closing their doors, and in the late spring Jonah and Moss decided to shut the Jazz Palace down. At first Pearl resisted, but when she saw the tallies in the accounting books, she agreed. They sold all the fixtures. The crystal chandelier and glasses went to the Edgewater Beach Hotel. They sold the mahogany bar to a prominent men's club and the bistro tables and chairs to a nearby synagogue. A restaurant that specialized in hamburgers bought the jukebox. But Pearl wouldn't let them sell the piano. No matter who came in or how much they offered, Pearl was firm. It was not for sale. She had her brothers cover it and move it into a corner of the candy store. Then they rented out the ground floor to a dentist who professed to have a silent drill and a painless way of straightening crooked teeth with a metal wire. He hung a sign of a tooth above what had once been the entrance to the bar.

Pearl took a job at Saks in the lingerie department, where she helped women stuff themselves into corsets and bras. In the evenings if Benny came by, they went to see a show or have dinner. Afterward if the weather was fine they went for walks. Some nights he held her hand. If Benny had the car, they might go and catch a set at the Three Deuces, then drive over to Buckingham Fountain to watch the light show. One evening Benny asked Pearl if she'd like a ride in the mornings to work. "I drive with my father," he said. "It's not out of our way to pick you up."

On Monday morning when Benny picked up Pearl, she saw that his father was in the front seat. Leo didn't get out to let her sit in front and merely nodded when Benny introduced them. In the evening he picked her up and his father was still there, staring straight ahead. For weeks it went on like this with Benny picking Pearl up in the morning and driving her home at night and his father sitting in the front seat, staring straight ahead. Some evenings Benny dropped his father off, and he and Pearl went out for dinner and afterward they often took a walk that stretched into the wee hours because neither of them had given up their lifelong habit of being night owls.

One night as they strolled in Lincoln Park, they crossed over to the lake. It was a warm, breezy night as the grip of cold had left the city. Summer was ahead, and Pearl was thinking about taking her first lake swim of the season. As they meandered along the shore, she told Benny how, since she was a girl, she'd been coming down to the lake. She told him that once her mother had tried to drown her and Opal in the steely-blue waters. It was so long ago, like a distant dream, but she'd been coming to the lake to swim ever since.

The air was fresh and clean as they walked and the moon so bright that it made Pearl wish she could dive into the waters. Benny slipped his hand in hers. His hand was warm, his fingers strong. Though they had promised so many years ago when they'd first met never to talk about this, now she did. It was on her birthday, she told him, July 24, the same day as when her brothers drowned. Benny kept Pearl's hand in his, and she felt him shiver. He grew very quiet and for a long time nothing was said. Around them everything, even the lake, grew still. All they could hear were the waves lapping the shore. He paused and looked at her the way Napoleon told him to. Sideways, not straight on. "I was on the bridge that day," he told her, "when the ship went down."

A thin smile crossed Pearl's lips. "You were the boy whose hands couldn't stop moving. You dropped your package into the water."

Benny stopped and stared into Pearl's eyes. "You knew?"

"Yes." Pearl nodded. "I've known for a long time."

Before he left that night, Benny invited Pearl to come to dinner on Friday. "My mother would like to meet you," he said.

Hannah had no idea what to do. Her son had never brought a woman home for dinner before. Years ago she gave up believing he'd ever settle down. As soon as Benny told her that he was bringing Pearl home, she began cleaning the house. She scrubbed more than she ever had before. She washed all the curtains and dusted all the fixtures. She got on her knees and washed the bathroom floor. Twice she asked Benny what she should make for dinner and twice he told her, "Anything." There would be noodle soup and salmon mousse. She debated between a lamb stew and chicken with prunes. In the end she decided on the chicken.

When Pearl arrived, Hannah clasped her hands. It occurred to Pearl that Hannah didn't care if she had green skin and antennae for ears she was so pleased that Benny had, at last, brought a woman home. At the table they talked about their jobs. Pearl asked polite questions about Benny's brothers, and they asked Pearl what it was like to have lived above a saloon. "Oh, I didn't only live above it. I ran it," is what Pearl said.

On Monday morning when Benny picked Pearl up, Leo got out of the car. He held the door for her and waited until she was comfortable in the front seat. Without a word he got into the back. That weekend Benny and Pearl strolled near Lincoln Park. A chorus of cicadas filled the humid air. They held hands as Benny led her off the trail into a grove of trees where he kissed her. His tongue, his hands surprised her. She had never been kissed before, and yet it seemed as if she had a memory of this kiss.

That year Prohibition was repealed and public drinking resumed. Bartenders noted that more ladies than ever were showing up at the bars. A black man named Teddy Wilson started rehearsing with the Benny Goodman Trio. Al Capone was in jail, and Germany elected an obscure Austrian politician as chancellor. Mayor Cermak of Chicago took a bullet meant for FDR, and a Nash street rod was rattling along a road north. The car rattled so much that Benny wondered if they'd make it to Charlevoix at all, let alone by dark.

It was a hot afternoon. His fingers gripped the wheel as Pearl fanned herself with the sports page of the *Tribune*. Beads of sweat coated her brow, and she kept wiping it with her handkerchief. They had just driven past Union Pier. They would have stopped here, but Jews weren't welcome at these resorts. Pearl didn't mind the long drive. She had never been so far from home. She had never seen this side of the lake.

"It's so blue," she said.

"Just as blue on the other side," Benny replied. He was sweating in his shirtsleeves.

"But it seems bluer here." She wished she could go for a swim.

She longed to dip her feet into the cool water, let the waves lap at her toes. Instead they sipped warm root beer. In the afternoon they stopped in a park near the beach for a picnic. Oaks and elms loomed above them. Pearl lay a blanket on the ground. She took some sandwiches and hard-boiled eggs she'd made from a basket. They ate lazily as the lake churned below and a breeze blew through the canopy of trees.

After lunch Benny got up to stretch his legs. He walked back and forth, then paused beneath some trees. For a long moment, with his head cocked, he stood ever so still. Then his fingers began moving. To anyone else they'd be imperceptible, but Pearl noticed right away. They'd been quiet for so long. They were tapping against his thigh, and, as soon as she saw them, Pearl knew that he was listening again. He was listening to the birds.

They'd been married that morning in a simple ceremony. When the judge pronounced them man and wife, a shock rippled through Pearl. Benny had proposed three weeks before. The Century of Progress had just opened in Grant Park, and Benny invited Pearl to go. Together they'd strolled along the Great Wall of China, past the golden-roofed Lama Temple from Jehol and a teahouse from Japan where kneeling women in silk robes, their faces painted white, served tea the color of grass.

At the nunnery of Uxmal, Benny had asked Pearl if she'd marry him. She was gazing at the ancient Mayan calendar where time went in a circle, not a straight line. Pearl said nothing as they moved on to the bathysphere. It had taken William Beebe twenty-two hundred feet beneath the sea. Benny slipped his hand into hers as they marveled at the aluminum globe in which Auguste Piccard soared fifty-four thousand feet into the stratosphere. They roamed a diamond mine with its million-dollar display of glittering stones and stood before a robot that gave lectures on diet as it explained the workings of its own insides. They gazed at Tom Thumb, the huge engine that pulled. As Sally Rand danced naked behind a pair of ostrich feather fans, Pearl said yes.

The fair was illumined by the rays of a distant star. Arcturus was chosen because its 240 trillion miles to earth most closely corresponded to forty light-years. The light had left Arcturus in 1893 during the Columbian Exposition. Now it had reached earth. It was harnessed to set aglow miles of incandescent bulbs and colored tubing. As the city sparkled in neon lights, the fate of Chicago was linked to the universe.

ACKNOWLEDGMENTS

Almost two decades ago I asked Stuart Dybek to read a twenty-page memoir piece. Afterward his only comment was that I was writing a saga, not a story, and I should just sit down and write it. So my first thanks go to Stuart. I want to thank my many friends who have been readers and believers including Russell Banks, Jane Bernstein, Barbara Grossman, Rodger Kamenetz, Marc Kaufman, Michael Kimmel, Carina Kolodny, Valerie Martin, Varley O'Connor, Peter Orner, Jodi Picoult, Dani Shapiro, and Susan Shreve. Also Christina Baker Kline, who shared many of her insights with me. Thanks to Jane Supino, who was always there when I needed her and whose presence I always feel beside me. And Carmen Corcostegui and Josef Badies, whose generosity provided the perfect writer's retreat in Barcelona in which I was able to complete the final revisions of this novel.

Thanks to my jazz experts, Krin Gabbard and Jamie Katz, who lent me books, spent endless hours answering my questions and pounding out rhythms on restaurant tables; jazz pianist Roberta Piket, who taught me how to play "Blue Monk"; Kevin Kendrick, who imagined some of the tunes; Tim Samuelson, historian with the city of Chicago, Department of Cultural Affairs; and the late Henry Grady Johnson, who shared with me his music and his stories of Chicago and Forty-Seventh Street. And to my cousin Mike Bell, my

Chicago geography and logistics expert, who showed me where the trams and trolleys didn't go, and who drove me all over the city like a location scout.

Thanks to the Chicago Historical Society, now the Chicago History Museum, for the use of its library and archives, especially its photo collection, and to Sarah Lawrence College, which provided me with assistance from the Ellen Schloss Flamm faculty development fund. My deepest gratitude to the Romare Bearden Foundation for allowing us to use *J Mood* on the jacket of this book and Emily Mahon for her beautiful design. And if one can thank a city, I want to thank my hometown of Chicago for its richness of history, stories, and its wild cast of characters.

While this is a work of the imagination, many books inspired and helped inform this novel. My mother perhaps started me on this journey with her favorite book, *Fabulous Chicago,* by Emmett Dedmon. I am also grateful to William Howland Kenney's *Chicago Jazz* and Laurence Bergreen's excellent biographies of Louis Armstrong and Al Capone. Also Krin Gabbard's outstanding *Hotter than That,* a history of the trumpet. And two brilliant books of Chicago history, *Black Metropolis,* by St. Clair Drake and Horace R. Cayton, and *City of the Century,* by Donald Miller. I am also grateful to the writings of Ben Hecht and Studs Terkel. Mezz Mezzrow's *Really the Blues* helped me sink into the language of the era, and Geoff Dyer's magnificent *But Beautiful* helped me get into the head of jazz musicians.

I don't even know how to begin to thank my wonderful agent and friend, Ellen Levine, who always believed in this book. I know that *The Jazz Palace* would never have seen the light of day if it hadn't been for her loyalty and perseverance. And Nan Talese, who likewise stuck with this novel and whose brilliant edits have made this book so much better.

My late parents Rosalie and Sol Morris, both of whom lived a hundred years, made this era come alive for me with their stories and their music and their colorful expressions whose meaning only became clear to me in the years I spent reading and researching this book. It has been a great pleasure to dip into their world, and I will miss it as I miss them. To my daughter, Kate, whose insights and aerial vision helped me see the way to making changes I was reluctant to make and who truly shaped the final version of this book. Last, there are no words to express my gratitude to my husband, Larry, who has lived with this book almost as long as he has lived with me. He never told me to give up, and he never stopped listening.